THE MAMMOTH AWAKENS

MAEGWEN SALLEY-MASSIE

An imprint of Green Ferns Publishing House

Copyright © 2023 Maegwen Salley-Massie
Cover copyright © 2023 Miblart. Cover designed by Miblart.

Library of Congress Cataloging-in-Publication Data
Salley-Massie, Maegwen
The Mammoth Awakens/ Maegwen Salley-Massie
456 pages.

Summary: "The young queen, Sealyn, and her allies must break Len Nove's curse before their enemy claims Len Nove's powers. Stepping in for her sister, interim queen, Siany, faces battles from the darkness. Can the two sisters win against time and evil?" –Provided by publisher.

979-8-9870525-3-2 ISBN (paperback), 979-8-9870525-4-9 ISBN (hardback), Subjects: High Fantasy—Fiction. Love—Fiction. Adventure—Fiction.

Printed in the United States of America

To those who struggle to maintain focus.

May you find the answers to your success

in this book.

TABLE OF CONTENTS

CHARACTER PRONUNCIATIONS

Adalina (ad-ah-Leen-ah)
Adma (Ad-ma)
Adomin (a-Doe-Min)
Aellizzabelle (Ale-Lizz-a-Bell) aka Lizz
Aerrick (Air-Rick)
Ajorn (Ae-Jorn)
Anadelvia (an-ah-del-vee- ah)
Ashur (A-sh-ur)
Atticos (a-t-e-coe-ss)
Audayia (Aw-Day-ee-ah)
Barm (B-arm)
Basalt (Ba-salt)
Bip (b-ip)
Brandle (Bran-Dill)
Brehan (Bree-Hon)
Brenna (Bren-nah)
Caelimont (Cae-li-mon-t)
Char (Ch-Ar)
Cian (See-an)
Corentine (Coer-en-teen)
Dag (Da-g)
Doebromir (Doe-broe- meer)
Drifa (Dri-fa)
Drystan (Drih-stan)
Ebbalee (Eb-bah-Lee)
Edvard (Ed-var-d)
Egil (Ee-gil)
Elmond (el-mon-d)
Ezen (Ee-Zen)
Favien (Fae-Vee-in)
Finn (Fin)
Pyry (Peer-Ree)
Quinley (Quin-Lee)
Raquel (Rah-Kell)
Rav (R-av)

Fraeya (Frae-Ya)
Graegory (Grae-gor-ree)
Graelynd (GRAY-Lind)
Grant (Gr-ant)
Haedon (Hay-don)
Hueweyn (Hui-When)
Jace (Jay-ss)
Jadelyn (Jae-d-lyn)
Jaequel (Jay-Kell)
Jashun (Ja-Shoo-n)
Jdru (Droo)
Jem (Gem)
Karis (Care-Ris)
Kipnor (Kip-nor)
Kolt (Colt)
Lezlin (Lez-Lin)
Lulana (Loo-La-nah)
Obeesi (O-Bee-s-eye)
Madilina (Ma-di-lee-nah)
Maekel (May-Kel)
Malum (Mal-um)
Marin (Mar-Rin)
Matticus (Mat-ti-cus)
Max (Max)
Menry (Men-Ree)
Mimby (Mim-bee)
Miola (My-O-La)
Nanceline (Nan-see-leen)
Nawrooshall (Naw-Roo-Sholl)
Nijeel (Nie-Jeel)
Norella (Nor-ell-lah)
Novaly (Noe-va-lee)
Pinx (Pin-X)

Revalyn (Re-va-lyn)
Rielen (Ry-Len)
Rivers (Ri-ver-s)
Royce (Roy-SS)
Runihura (Ru-ni-hur-a)
Ryker (r-EYE-ker)
Ryland (rEYE-Land)
Saemelina (Sae-me-lee-na)
Saemeon (Say-Me-on)
Sakul (Sa-Kool)
Saven (Say-Vin)
Saven (Sae-vin)
Sealyn (SEE-LIN)
Shaenna (Shae-na)
Siany (SEE-On-EE)
Sorcha (Sore-Shah)
Stawyer (Staw-yer)
Stev (St-ev)
Sune (Soon)
Temm (Tem)
Tilmond (Til-mond)
Tintallina (Tin-Ta-lee-na)
Toven (TOE-Vin)
Trit (Tr-it)
Tybalt (Ti-Balt)
Verraetor (Ver-ae-tor)
Zephnon (Ze-f-non)
Zuri (Zur-ee)

A note to the reader…

While reading, you will see an * appear in front of the name of a creature when it's first mentioned.

This * lets you know that more details about this creature are available in the Library of Creatures, found at the back of the book.

I did not want to interrupt your reading of the story with too many descriptions, so if you want to know about the creatures you meet, flip to the back as you come across an *.

Enjoy.

The Cursed Seven Kingdoms
The Ge
Glatar
Sacharo Lagoon
Oichinos Channel
Hava's
Dragon Cove
Melting Water Seas
St

Seas
Len Noye
Golden Lake
Shunal
Golden Lake
Elysium
Pax Island
The Sna
Hostile Channel
Emerald Lagoon
Ira Channel
Korpam
The Margyger
The Southlantian Seas

The Ge...
Zykoan Port
The Snaer ...
Zelkath Port
Len Nove
Pantorian
Tholgerton
Golden Lake
Ciderton
Fort Kippen
Avondelle
Sallen
Elysium
Calenburg
Port-Rowlin
Hostile Channel
Emerald Lagoon
The Margyger

PROLOGUE

Journal Entry 21,

Today is a good day. It has been a solid three weeks of me recovering in the rose room. I will have to agree with Lady Pinx. This is the best room in the palace to recover. Fresh roses are filled in the eight vases daily, and they smell heavenly.

I can say words in a whisper now, which is a huge improvement. Normally, a person would die from my wound, but from what I've gathered, the giant green phoenix held me in his wings for seven days, and those magical wings saved my life. In my professional opinion, I have assessed that the healing properties of the wings must equate to at least six months of recovery; otherwise, I would still be in a critical state.

I'm looking forward to solid foods, but I'm not quite there yet. I'm predicting that I should be able to manage small bites within the next week, but for now, I am still enjoying the palace's famous broth. Yes, broth. The spices and herbs the palace Nichts add to it make it delightful.

Sakul continues to read to me each day. Two days ago, we finished the first book in the adventure-romance series called *The*

Orphan's Enchantment, and yesterday, we started book two, called *The Princess's Magic*. Book one was about the orphan raised by wild phoenixes, who then meets and falls in love with the crown prince of Elysium. It was wonderful. Sakul didn't appreciate it because of all the romance, but he liked the adventure part. I'm looking forward to book two.

We would have gotten further in book two yesterday, but I had a surprise visitor. Lady Adalina, the beautiful, black-haired "knows everything about everyone's business" friend. She wore such a fantastic dress, pale green with tiny pink roses all over. The dress matched her almond-shaped green eyes. She's always so stylish. With her came all the latest gossip.

She told me about Queen Sealyn banishing Lady Pyry, Drystan's wife, and her family to their house in Port Rowin. According to Adalina, she and Brenna think Pyry had something to do with Drystan's betrayal. I believe her exact words were, "There's no way she could be married to a man and not know his every movement, or at least, that's how it will be when I'm married." I don't know if I agree with her, but our queen did have to do something. Adalina also told me that Queen Sealyn gave Lady Pyry's large estate to Lord Favien and Lady Pinx as a future wedding present. It is written in the contract that if your spouse or family member betrays Elysium, then you forfeit your lands, so I agree with Sealyn. She made a wise decision.

Adalina overheard Pinx and Norella talking, but first, she had to describe their outfits. "I heard Lady Pinx and Lady Norella in line at *Nijeel's Choice* talking about Lord Favien. Pinx was, of course, wearing her usual green corset top with a pink flowy skirt. You know that's her signature outfit. I need to find my signature outfit, too. Norella had a flowy mint green dress with sheer sleeves. I just know Princess Annadelvia, Sealyn's cousin, styled her. Oh well, back to Favien. He's going to stay at the new estate to get a feel for it, and Pinx will stay at the new chateaus Queen Sealyn has built near the palace. I can't wait to get mine."

It's unfortunate that I don't have a voice to tell Adalina to stop talking, but I shouldn't complain. It's nice to have company. I was just happy to know Favien survived his bad concussion. For the first few weeks, he had trouble with his memory and slurring words, but Lord Prince Brandle, Sealyn's cousin, worked tirelessly on exercises to help him recover. Brandle is such an amazing doctor. I hope I can be half as good as him one day.

Lady Adalina said she went on a carriage ride with one of the archers, who happened to inform her that Lord Stawyer miraculously made a full recovery yesterday. Apparently, Lady Zuri had help from some magical potions from someone in the village, but she didn't know who. I've always wanted to learn more about magical potions, purely for medicinal purposes, of course, but they intrigue me. However, my father is very against me learning about those.

Adalina is great, especially for the village chatter, but who I really want to hear from is Sealyn. I know she keeps coming by, but she always stops by when I'm asleep. She leaves notes and treats for me to let me know she was here, but I would still like to know how she's doing.

I wish people would talk to me about what happened so that I can have closure. All I can gather is that the palace held a huge funeral service, so someone very close to the royal family died, and I can only think of one person. It's the same person I see each night when I close my eyes.

My nightmares always start with the dark old war room. I can still smell the damp, musky smell. The level of fear sends tingling sensations to my toes. It's hard to breathe. We guard the children in a circle as we watch Favien get struck in the head with a chair. I hold on tight to Pinx, not wanting her to be caught in the battle. I watch as Sakul's eyes change to panic, and he's punched in the face, then someone grabs me from behind. I scream, but I stop when I feel the cold blade against my neck. I hear yelling, but it's muffled because I can't concentrate. Nausea starts to creep over me. I can't control my breathing. I see Sakul crawling towards me, and I feel warm tears stream down my ebony cheeks. My mind keeps saying I don't want to die, but words never come out. Doebromir circles my captor, but my eyes stay on Sakul. If I am to die, I want his eyes to be the last green eyes I see. Then I feel the soldier tense, and as he moves, my gaze shifts to Char leaping in the air, and I witness the Stoltlander stab him in the belly. I open my mouth to scream, but a different tingling sensation happens at my neck, which immediately feels like it's on fire. I try to breathe, but my lungs won't fill. I'm choking. I want to scream in pain and fear, but I can't, and then everything fades to black.

This is why I believe Sealyn doesn't come by when I'm awake. It's my fault. Because of me, her best friend, Lord Char, is dead. Till tomorrow,

Sorcha

Commander Malum,

I write with urgency. You are immediately to take your full force of troops to Len Nove. This will be the first kingdom Elysium will seek an alliance with. Elysium embarrassed our kingdom, your royals. I expect the plans that we discussed earlier to be carried out with vengeance. You will be my voice and ears while occupying Len Nove.

Take as many of the disgusting Fire Nichts with you to help melt the ice. We must find its source.

Failure does not exist in your vocabulary, Commander. Once you find the source, or if there is any sign of Elysians contacting the throne, send word to me. My dragons will do the rest.

Magnanimously,
Queen Corentine
Forever Stoltland's & Queen of the Seven

CHAPTER 1
WHAT'S A LUXEN?

Sunlight warmed King Ryker's green cloak as he stared out his bedroom window, watching the two *exiguums playing. The two fuzzy, miniature elephants rolled over one another, and he chuckled slightly. Ryker's brown hair had thinned some, but his sweet face remained. He wished the exiguums' happiness could take away his thoughts. With visions capturing his mind, he kept replaying the bloody scene. The horrible sight of his commander dying in his arms. Commander Elmond was like a brother to him and gave the ultimate sacrifice—his life. Ryker saw the Stoltland sword plunging through Elmond's heart a hundred times a day. Was there anything he could have done differently to save his friend? Each scenario he played in his head led to blood splattering the walls and flowing down the stone floor.

Ultimately, he knew he could not have saved him, but somehow admitting that felt like a betrayal, and he did not want to betray his comrade's memory, so he held on, forcing the nightmare to repeat itself. "Stoltland," Ryker growled. "Always, Stoltland."

Queen Mother Graelynd leaned against the open doorway, watching her husband torture himself. She hated watching him do this each day. "Planning on destroying Stoltland this early, my darling?"

Ryker smiled a half smile, "I was hoping to finish them by lunch."

"Proactive. I like it, but perhaps we should have breakfast first?" She saw her husband hesitate. "Care to share your burdens, my love?"

Ryker let out an exasperated sigh. "Death leaves behind a rotten stench of regret and guilt."

"Go on."

"That wretched metallic sting of blood stays in the air for days, but something strange happens, something tormented. You want to know what that is?" Graelynd shook her head. "The same blood that poured from loved friends and family, that blood enriches the soil and blooms glorious plants. Us survivors then have the anguished pleasure of strolling beside blossoms nourished by our comrades' slaughter. How does one face the beauty staring back after a loss so great?"

Graelynd paused. She knew Avondelle felt this to its core, yet it seemed as though nature decided to kiss the face of Elysium and grant their kingdom an endless supply of intoxicating landscapes. Thick, lush greens cascaded everywhere. Even nature's sounds were more like a grand orchestra of birds, waterfalls, and wind. "I believe our loved ones would want us to still enjoy the beauty they sacrificed themselves for. Without this, we cannot hope for a better future. Look for your friend's face in the trees and hear his laugh in the wind. He gave you his blessing to continue living when he gave his life, but what is living without enjoyment?"

"How did you get to be so wise?"

"Motherhood," Graelynd giggled her intoxicating laugh.

"Speaking of breakfast, full stomachs always make better decisions." Ryker offered his elbow for his wise wife to take, then escorted her down the stone hallways. He breathed in the eucalyptus aromas, hoping the scent would calm his grief.

"Ryker, Commander Elmond's death weighs on me too, but we cannot change the past nor live there."

Ryker nodded slightly, "I know, love. I just feel like I lost part of myself, but I'm hoping to gain that back—one day. I sometimes don't feel like I should be the one standing here. Should it be Elmond and not me? I know I cannot forever torture myself, so let's hold onto one day."

Graelynd echoed the words "one day" in her head. "One day" seemed like an eternity away. "One day" seemed impossible. Avondelle still felt the wounds and losses of the Battle of Betrayals. So many died in that battle, then the doubts about loyalties came soon after. Whom could they trust?

They stopped at the large window that faced the back gardens. The palace pools sparkled with sunshine, which beamed across Avondelle. Yellow butterflies danced to their own tunes while tiny *lenettes glowed among the dancing butterflies. It was strange to see lenettes. These small double-winged creatures had not been seen for thousands of years, but now the whimsical insects were back. Each one had the body of a golden baby caterpillar with two sets of wings: pink outer wings and orange inner wings. During the day, they soaked in the sun's rays, then illuminated the darkness at night.

These were not the only creatures who returned from the old days. Once Queen Sealyn unknowingly broke Elysium's curse, she unleashed the ancient magic that had been waiting dormant. The magic brought creatures of the light back, but it also brought monsters of the dark that haunted people's dreams. The kingdoms were now wild—life was untamed. Doorways, cabinets, tunnels, and scrolls appeared that were never seen before. It was like a veil had fallen to reveal an unseen world.

This was a great change, and everyone felt it.

A long day of planning sat before Queen Sealyn and King Father Ryker. The war room was carefully stocked with large pitchers of Madam Bip's PurFizz drink, fresh Puffin Pies, and even Chocolate Jabbles. In the corner, the large Green Phoenix sat quietly, eyeing each person in the room carefully. Sealyn needed a name for him, so because he felt like her fortress, she called him Dun, from the old language.

Seated at the round stone table were the commanders and leaders of Elysium's military divisions, along with the War Council and King Jace, husband to Sealyn. Jace smiled at his gorgeous wife. Sealyn's olive skin and long dark brown hair made him dizzy. He was obsessed with how brave and brilliant she was. He spent half his days in shock at what his life had become. He was now the king of Elysium, formerly the gray-eyed outcast of Stoltland—loved by no one, now loved by the most powerful woman in all the lands. By Elysian law, Sealyn did not have to crown him king, but she chose to make him her equal. However, he still felt guilty and distant from the people of Elysium after what his family orchestrated with the Battle of the Betrayals.

His mind trailed to the memory of sending his family away after they were released from prison. He watched as they were escorted in chains onto their ship. He felt as if a part of him was in chains, being carried away with them. How could he feel like this when they had caused the death of so many? Anger boiled inside him, and a flash of orange flickered in the grey storm of his eyes.

He could still feel the tight grip of his mother's hands holding onto his as the soldiers ripped her away at the port. Her vibrant red hair whipped around with the coastal winds, and the words, "You know me, my son. Remember that. I will always be your mother," echoed in his ears. Her tears and screams haunted his dreams. Was he now the traitor? Could their relationship be salvaged? Jace remembered the Elysian military's faces scowling at him. He felt their judgment and understood it.

He wanted his pain to sail away with his family, but it lingered and festered. Where was he supposed to go from here? How would the Elysian people ever trust him? In his moment of feeling isolated as he watched his family sail away, he felt the caress of Sealyn's fingers interlocking with his, then the tender touch of a large wing fell over his back. He looked up, seeing the Green Phoenix towering many feet over him, watching the ship. Did the phoenix sense his pain? Did this legendary creature actually notice him? Why? He was nothing, just a no one standing next to a someone.

One by one, the Elysian people knelt before all three of them. Sealyn's words inspired forgiveness from her people. "Today was a day of great pain and mercy. My heart is broken just like yours, but let us remember that the faults of a parent do not belong on the shoulders of the child. In this case, the son has chosen his own path. A path that leads him away from the curse and into the loving arms of Elysium. I know you may see a Stoltlander, but allow me to tell you the truth. I was a whole person but only half a queen before. But with *King* Jace, I am now the emerald queen Elysium needs. Now, we heal. Now, we rebuild, for tomorrow is decided from what we do today."

Jace brought his mind back to the present, to everyone conversing around the table. He was unsure how they would overtake Len Nove, but Sealyn set a deadline for the quest to begin in one week, so they had to be ready.

Doebromir's bald head turned red with anger, and he slammed his goblet. "How are we supposed to prepare our wagons for snow and ice?"

"Easy, Doebromir," Favien calmed. "We can trade wagons for sleds at Fort Kippen. They even have trained dog sled teams to lead our convoy. Trust the palace guard, too. They are trained well for all seasons." Favien wore his green military leather without the silver armor. His clothes were still sweaty from practice.

Prince Adomin, uncle to Queen Sealyn, twirled his quill. "I'm more concerned about Len Nove. Lord Finn and Lady Zuri have barely given us details on how to overtake their former kingdom."

Finn, who sat beside Jace, lowered his blue eyes. "I apologize. I wish I had more answers. My brain clouds when thinking about Len Nove. My current concern is for the new creatures that the old magic has awakened. We only have knowledge of the recent past and childhood stories of the old. I don't know what's real and what's a myth."

"For now, Finn and Zuri, it's best to tell us myths and truths. Better to be prepared," Sealyn nodded.

Zuri tucked a lock of her long brown hair behind her ear, exposing more of her perfectly smooth ivory skin. She sighed. "We just must stay moving. Len Nove seems to make time stand still."

"Stand still?" questioned Tilmond. "What does that mean?" Tilmond, cousin to Sealyn, took Commander Elmond's place.

All Elysian green eyes looked at the fierce blue-eyed Zuri, waiting for her explanation. She shifted in her chair and smoothed her pale blue fitted dress. "We know the curse of Len Nove. We can expect its agenda to push for us to do nothing. When I did get a chance to speak to a Partial, she told me of a cave with people literally frozen in time. They became one with the ice."

"Are they alive?" squawked Max. Max was always the first with questions.

"As far as I know, yes. Yes, they are living in blocks of ice." Zuri hoped she was giving information that was helpful and true. She could not bear to lead Elysium into a massacre.

Favien shook his head and scratched his dark brown beard aggressively. "Partial? Did I miss something? What is a Partial?"

Zuri blinked in astonishment. Did Favien live under a rock? "A Partial is half cursed. I was once a Partial, and I guess still considered one, but the pull of the curse is not as great here as it is in Len Nove. It's like walking waist-deep in icy water, or, Elysians, it's like walking in quicksand. Your mind is also fighting battles." Her voice cracked. "A blue fog seems to block forward-thinking, but Partials are fighting their way out of accepting the curse, refusing the last strands of their heart." She paused and felt the sting of tears forming in her eyes. She needed a minute to gather herself.

Tilmond saw the opportunity to talk strategy rather than make Zuri relive past traumas. "I think it would be wise to have three teams moving toward the capital city on foot." Tilmond stood and started moving pieces on the map to show his plan. "If we have just one force, that's one large target. Three branches will give us the best advantage. We will also be able to encircle the capital once all three have arrived at their appointed checkpoints." He slid the three small Phoenix pieces to their checkpoints on the outskirts of the city walls. "We will train with the Ice *Nichts daily to prepare for snow and icy terrain."

Sealyn nodded, "Excellent idea. I approve." Dun snapped his beak loudly. "Oh, yes. Well, I guess we need to discuss the…" She paused. "The old magic."

Everyone shifted in their chairs. How would they fight against the old magic? Day and night, the scholars studied the remnants from the martyr's coffin, which Queen Sealyn and her cousins dug up during the hunt for clues to the Heart of Elysium. Scrolls of border spells, shield spells, healing incantations, and so much more overwhelmed the scholars. This was foreign. This was dangerous. This was life and death. If Elysium had old magic, then so did its enemies.

Prince Adomin's dark black hair glowed slightly from the candlelight. He looked nervously at King Father Ryker, "One of my biggest concerns was the mention of Luxens, but," he pushed his spectacles up his nose, "moreso, the Umbrals."

Max's head was spinning. He was tired of hearing words he could barely pronounce and had no clue about their meaning. It was time for someone to explain. "Would someone please enlighten me on exactly what those two things are, and why I should apparently be scared?"

Once Sealyn nodded to him, Ryker spoke, "From what we've read, Luxens are those who can wield the magic of the light. This Luxen magic works differently with each individual according to his or her strengths and weaknesses. The Umbrals are those who have given themselves fully to the dark. They allow the darkness to flow through them, doing the bidding of the dark mist."

Several green eyes shot a glare toward Jace. Jace's mother, Corentine, had been seen conjuring this dark mist in the Battle of the Betrayals. This meant that the queen of Stoltland was an Umbral.

Ryker continued, "Before the Second Chance, great wars were fought between Luxens and Umbrals. The devastation from these wars would take hundreds of years to repair, which is why we must act fast, learning the border spells to protect us further. We have no idea how many Umbrals have figured out their powers, nor do we know if any of our own people are lost to this." Dun snapped his beak again and shook his head.

Tilmond started putting the puzzle together. "Queen Sealyn, have you witnessed anyone exhibiting any symptoms of being a Luxen?"

Sealyn's face went hot. Her hands started to sweat and burn. She did not want them to know everything. She did not want her people to fear her because she feared herself. She did not want them to see the real reason she wore gloves. Her glowing green palms made her uneasy. She had burned through a dozen different types of gloves since the release of the magic. The only gloves that seemed to resist her palms were made from dragon scales, so immediately she ordered every style of glove made from dragon scales from Shunal. All had to look inconspicuous. Sealyn shrugged toward her cousin. "It's too soon to tell. We are forming a new task unit to help spread the news of the changes our people may experience. Anyone witnessing or exhibiting these changes is to report to the *Caelidon training grounds."

Max sat a little taller at the mention of the Caelidon training grounds; after all, it was his wife who was the first ever to ride this breed of winged horses.

Tilmond understood his cousin's dismissal of his question, so he changed the subject for her. "Has anyone confirmed what or who actually broke the veil of this old magic?"

Ryker beamed at his daughter. "That would be your queen's doings. We found a diary entry from King Perdon that stated,

> *'Only the light can dissipate the darkness of the old. Three.*
>
> *The curse must be washed three generations over. This is the antidote.'*

Our great King Saven was the first, then my Queen Mother Graelynd was the second, and Queen Sealyn is the third. She was tested and chose the light when her people needed her the most." Dun squawked happily and seemed to smile at Sealyn.

Max scrunched his face yet still remained attractive. "Sure, that broke the curse, but how did that unlock the old magic?"

The giant phoenix stood, having to lower his head not to hit the top of the room; then he spread his enormous green wings and smacked one of his golden feet on the stone floor. Instantly, green flames surrounded him. Gasps were heard around the table.

Doebromir shook his head. He remembered a conversation he had with his friends about the legend of the green phoenix: pure of heart and standing in ash and flames. "So I guess the tale is more prophecy than fiction. Sealyn was pure of heart and happened to be standing in ashes and flames and chose to fight for the light. She broke the curse and awoke the old magic at the same time." Ryker nodded.

Sealyn blinked and saw the goblets of her people lifted. She closed her eyes to steady herself and saw her arrow pointed at Corentine's heart, while the Stoltland soldier held a knife to Jace's throat. She saw the blood drip from his neck again. She opened her eyes to clinking glasses and smiles. Her heart started panicking. She felt the heat of the burning library. She smelled the burning books and fabrics. Darkness crept over her vision, seeing Corentine's black spear cutting through the air straight for her, then there was warmth. She felt an arm around her shoulder and tilted her head up. The darkness disappeared. She saw her peace—Jace's grey stormy eyes. Her lighthouse, her pulse.

CHAPTER 2
SECRET LETTERS

Lady Zuri dipped her fingers into the blue waters of the palace's pool that matched her long gown. The swans glided by, uninterested. She picked a white water lily and braided it into her long brown hair. Her flawless porcelain skin was filled with sadness. She tried to forget the quest that was nearing. Her people had suffered so much and wanted the curse broken, but the dangers that lay ahead would inevitably cost lives.

Sealyn cleared her throat, "I hope I'm not disturbing you, Lady Zuri."

"Of course not."

Sealyn sat on the edge of the pool and brushed her light green gown. She motioned for Zuri to sit. "I wanted to make sure you were feeling well. I know my uncle came across harshly." Zuri shook her head, "He's only wanting to protect his people. No one can blame him for trying to make it sound like I haven't been honest."

"And have you been… honest, Zuri?" It pained Sealyn to question her friend, but she could not afford to be ill-prepared for this quest. "I'm not accusing you of lying, but I'm curious if you've told me everything. You've only spoken about the people. What about the creatures living there?"

Zuri stiffened her back, "What of them?"

"Easy, Zuri. I just want to know what creatures we need to prepare ourselves to either fight or flee from." Sealyn raised her eyebrows slightly and tilted her head, trying to ease her into sharing at least one more detail, but what she received was not what she expected.

Zuri sighed, "Mammoths."

"Mammoths?" questioned Sealyn. "What about mammoths?"

Zuri's blue eyes filled with tears, "It's very painful to talk about.

Our people can feel them. I told you about my people being frozen—alive. Well, our mammoths are also frozen and alive."

Sealyn's mouth gaped. "Yes, I know it's strange. At Len Nove's beginning, our High Lord Atticos, who quickly became our first king, signed a treaty with the mammoths. The treaty was of the old magic. Mammoths could speak to us through our minds and hearts. What affected one affected the other. We worked and lived in partnership with the land. We never hunted mammoths, nor did they harm us. We protected each other. At the end of each season, we would bring a portion of our harvest to the mammoth tribes as homage, and, in return, the mammoths would shed their coats and tusks for my people to use as shelters, clothes, blankets, tools, and weapons. It was perfect harmony until the final battle before the Second Chance." Zuri dropped her head and shook it sadly.

Sealyn placed her hand on Zuri's, "You're safe here, Zuri. You're doing great. Keep going."

Zuri wiped her nose with a handkerchief, "You know the Second Chance was thousands of years after the beginning, so our king at the time of the last battle was not nearly as strong-hearted as King Atticos." Zuri paused, "Betrayal!" She cried out in sobs, "He betrayed the mammoths! King Zephnon and his spineless queen commissioned a deal with Stoltland." Sealyn gripped the sides of the pool at the mention of Stoltland. "Our lands were fighting Havas and Glatania. Elysium soldiers were battling on their lands against Shunal, so we couldn't receive food supplies. As you know, Stoltland separated into two forces. One joined Havas, Glatania, and Shunal, and the other joined Elysium, Korpam, and Len Nove. Obviously, we all know it was a coup staged with Korpam, but regardless, our forces were starving—an intention of this coup. They wanted to break Elysium's strongest ally. Stoltland convinced King Zephnon to kill the mammoths for food instead of waiting for the seasonal exchange. Everyone felt the killing of such innocence. They watched as our people slaughtered each other. It became a civil war along with the global war. Our rivers ran red with blood for weeks, and then the Second Chance happened in a flash. King Zephnon received the curse's warnings, but we had an extra punishment linked with the curse. Our mammoths, the source of life for us, would be trapped alive in ice for 100 years—only 100 so long as we did not bow to the curse. Here we are thousands of years later, and my people, along with the mammoths, are still trapped in ice."

Sealyn stood and paced, trying to sort through everything she had just heard. Mammoths, betrayal, Stoltland—always Stoltland, and curses. Len Nove needed to be free. It had to gain its strength to once again be Elysium's strongest ally and finally live in freedom.

"Zuri, I'm so grateful you shared this with me. Our history books had nothing about your mammoths. It's understandable now why the mammoth is Len Nove's animal symbol. I vow to do everything in my power to free all of your people and the mammoths," Sealyn placed her hand on Zuri's shoulder. "This was a lot for you. Why don't we go have some coffee at Nijeel's and share a Jam Pie? I'm sure the hustle and bustle of the market will help distract your mind."

Zuri hugged her tightly, "Thank you, Sealyn. Thank you for the sacrifices I know will be made for my people."

Lord Jashun re-read the crumpled note again. Since receiving it, he had read it at least a hundred times. His heart leaped each time. What did that mean? Why did he feel such a pull at this note? He stood in the musky military trunk room and stared blankly at his aumbry. The military aumbries were carved several feet into the stone wall. On top of the stone bench sat a trunk dedicated to the high-ranking soldier, and above the trunk were hooks for the soldiers to hang garments, helmets, or weapons. Jashun kicked his dirty boots under the bench in frustration.

He heard voices coming closer, so he quickly stuffed the note deep in his trunk. He brushed his raven black hair and tied the brown strings of his green tunic. Doebromir and Favien entered the trunk room, lost in their own chatter. Jashun tried to remain calm and not attract any unwanted attention. He needed to be his usual friendly self. "Doebromir, how's the leg handling against the Ice Nichts?" Jashun asked innocently.

Doebromir smacked his leg twice. "Managing quite nicely. Thank you for asking, Jashun. I saw your sword skill is improving. Have you been taking extra lessons from someone? I may have to steal you from Favien's Groundlers!"

Favien shoved Doebromir. "Just go ahead and try! We can scrap right here!"

"No need to fight over me, ladies." Jashun grabbed his belly and jiggled it. "There's plenty to go around." They burst into hard laughter.

"What did we just miss?" Finn asked as he and Jace entered the trunk room.

They bowed to King Jace. Doebromir rubbed his shiny bald head. "Oh, just how Jashun is plenty of man for the both of us." He took off his armor and laid it in his trunk.

Jace laughed. "One of those days, huh?" Jace hung his bow and arrows on his hooks and then slid his thumb over the gold plate of the trunk with the engraving that read, "The King of Elysium." His heart fluttered still at the sight of it.

Finn and Jashun exchanged glances. Finn bulged his eyes and nodded at Jashun, trying to convince him to be the one to say something. Finally, Jashun reluctantly gave in. "Uh, Jace. I mean, King Jace," Jashun stuttered through the words.

"Call me Jace here, please."

Jashun nodded. "Jace, why haven't you practiced any sword fighting? We've only seen you perfecting the bow and arrow."

Jace looked around the large rectangular room as it fell silent. He felt like the stone walls were closing in. Even though the room only smelled of sweat and old leather from trunks and military uniforms, Jace thought he smelled burning books. He had to keep telling himself that the mist he saw was only from the shower room down the hallway. Steam came from the hot springs, which the military enclosed for them to use after training. Jace closed his eyes to help focus on the question, but when he did, he saw the flames. He saw the burning library. He saw the dark mist. He saw his sword plunge into Drystan. He saw the blood.

Jace shook his head. "I —I can't pick up a sword since that day."

"Since you killed Drystan?" Favien asked softly. Jace nodded.

Doebromir placed his hand on Jace's shoulder. "We all understand. I get squeamish every time I think about Feydom or running in general. Sometimes I wake up in a pool of sweat because I was dreaming about jumping in that trap Drystan made. I hear the snap over and over, but with time, my king, you will recover. We all will recover."

Tears formed in Jace's eyes along with the others.

"It's the same with me," Favien added. "I don't like to talk about it, but after that head injury," Favien paused and shook his head. "Let's just say I didn't think I was ever going to be me again, so I sometimes flinch when something gets close to my head." Jace patted Favien's shoulder.

Doebromir wrapped his muscular, long arms around Jace and Favien, and then the rest followed suit. They formed a tight circle, and with a lump in his throat, Jace said, "This is the best brotherhood a man could ask for."

Finn's blue eyes sparkled. "Well, now I need a drink. Everyone good with a few ales at *Liquid Courage*?" Nodding and high-fiving, they all packed away their armor in their assigned trunks and hung their helmets, then they were off to their favorite tavern of the capitol. Yet, even in the empty trunk room, a silent whisper could be heard coming from the depths of only one trunk.

Sitting in the afternoon sunlight at one of the outside café tables, Lady Pinx sipped her hibiscus tea, which inadvertently matched her pink summer dress. She felt relief pour over her after each sip. The wind slightly blew her long, black waves of hair, which then made her catch the small scroll of notes on the table. Lady Norella, who was sitting opposite her, gasped.

"Pinx! Why did you bring that with you?" Norella sharply whispered.

Pinx's green almond-shaped eyes glared. "Because, Norella, I didn't think just anyone should find this type of news. What if someone else had read it?"

Norella twirled her long blonde hair with her finger. "If I agree with you, then what? This information falls sorely on our shoulders. Us! You and me, Pinx! We were the ones charged with reading the scrolls from the Martyr's coffin." Norella pointed her finger for emphasis.

Pinx's face scrunched like it always did when she was frustrated. "I understand that!"

"So, you understand that we're withholding valuable information from the Queen of Elysium? And to make matters worse, you stole the documents from the palace!"

"But Sealyn is our friend, our sister. She should hear these words from those who have no agenda to hold over her. She's going to be devastated by this."

"Ugh. Fine! But you need to hide that scroll and keep it safely secure."

Nijeel walked up to the table and placed Norella's Blue Lily of the Valley tea in front of her. Nijeel scratched his scruffy reddish beard. "Why don't you taste it first to make sure this is to your liking?"

Norella sipped it and smiled. "This is delightful, Nijeel. Well done."

"Why thank you, Lady Norella."

"We've enjoyed your efforts this summer. Adding new teas to boost Avondelle's spirits has certainly helped."

"I certainly hope so. Seeing such sadness just sparked something inside me to try to do small gestures to help make daily life a little better." Nijeel adjusted his small spectacles. He was a tall man with a balding head and shoulders that had a small slouch, but he had the best sense of humor and a golden heart.

"I believe this may be my favorite one," Pinx announced.

"Well, make that two, please, Nijeel," said a voice from behind Norella.

They all stood quickly to bow to Queen Sealyn, who was walking with Zuri and Sorcha.

"Your majesty. I'm ever so happy to have you join us on such a beautiful day. Allow me to fetch you whatever you require." Nijeel quickly grabbed extra chairs for them.

"Excellent. Zuri and I will try the hibiscus tea, and Sorcha, weren't you just saying you wanted to try the peppermint and aloe tea?"

Sorcha cleared her throat gently. "Yes, majesty. I think that will help nicely with my throat."

Sealyn winced at the word "throat." She stared behind Pinx and saw a Stoltland soldier holding a knife to Jace's throat. She froze. She feared making any sudden movements. The blood slowly dripped down Jace's neck—that muscular neck she had nuzzled so many times.

"Queen Sealyn, did you hear me?" asked Zuri.

Sealyn blinked, and the Stoltland soldier and Jace were gone. Jace was safe. She was safe. It was all in her head. "My apologies. I was thinking about the meeting I have later today. What was the question?"

Zuri's blue eyes narrowed. "I asked if you wanted anything from the bakery. I was going to get us a Jam Pie if you want."

Sealyn started to speak but noticed a tiny hand waving out of the corner of her eye. She glanced up, and there, seated on top of *Nijeel's Choice*, was Maekel with two other Nichts. Sealyn chuckled. She knew what that wave meant. "The Jam Pie will be great, and can you also get a box of Chocolate Jabbles while you're there?" She saw Maekel and her friends' wings flutter with excitement. She handed Zuri several gold coins and sipped the fresh tea.

"How are the preparations for the journey coming along?" asked Norella

Sealyn was about to answer when Lady Adalina, Lady Brenna, and Lady Lulana hurried over to join them.

Catching her breath, Adalina wheezed, "Queen Sealyn, we heard you were here, so we rushed over. We were being styled by your cousin, Lady Princess Anadelvia. It's all the talk of the market that she's here—well, that, and now your arrival."

"Yes, everyone's lining up at the doors of *Look Twice*. The twins seem overwhelmed but happy about all the new business. I'm shocked you let Anadelvia come, Sealyn," remarked Brenna.

Sealyn tilted her head. "And why's that?"

"I only meant that she's the royal stylist, not a commoner designer."

"Have I not said that I intend on being the queen of the people and for the people?" Brenna nodded hesitantly. "Then why would I keep new fashions only for myself? If the people want new styles of clothes, then I'm happy for Anadelvia to lead the fashion quest." The girls chuckled, except for Brenna. She looked more like she had just tasted something bitter.

Zuri was walking back to the tables with the Jam Pie in one hand and the box of Chocolate Jabbles in the other when Maekel and her friends dove for the box. They startled Zuri so much that they easily took the box of Jabbles and flew back to their perch. "You wicked little wasps!" shouted Zuri. She lifted her arms in frustration at Sealyn.

Chuckling, Sealyn responded, "Don't worry, Zuri. The Chocolate Jabbles were always meant for them."

"Sealyn, you were just about to tell us the latest news on—" Lulana suddenly cut off Pinx.

"Speaking of news, here come some of the boys." She nudged Brenna, who was looking intensely at Jashun.

Sealyn turned to see Jace smiling. He looked so happy. He looked like he was finally fitting in, like he was home. Sealyn had worried how the people would react to him after the Battle of Betrayals, but they understood forgiveness. They lived and breathed it. She felt his gaze. She felt hot all over—tingles zipped through her fingers down to her toes. She had to compose herself. Jace smirked. He knew what she was feeling because he was feeling the electricity too. A loud scream came echoing across the market. Everyone paused for only a second before they heard more screams. They were coming closer to them. The royal guard sprang from their hiding places and surrounded the king and queen. Favien, Doebromir, Jashun, and Finn drew their swords with the royal guard. Sorcha began to panic. Her breathing was so rapid she could barely draw breath. Sealyn wrapped her arms around Sorcha, trying to help keep her calm.

They could hear growling along with the screams.

"We must get the king and queen to safety."

"Form the perimeter! Nichts send for backup!"

"Bring the horses now! Get the king and queen mounted on the horses. Don't stop until they are in the war room."

A ferocious growl rippled through the crowds of people running. The royal guards, who were stationed right outside the market entrance, swiftly arrived to take Sealyn and Jace to the palace. Once they were mounted on their horses, Sealyn saw the beast turn the corner in front of the bakery. Her heart stopped. She had never seen such a creature. Blistering screams bellowed from her friends. Her horse bucked and whinnied in fear.

She tried to steady him, but how could she when the entire beast stood facing the crowd in front of Nijeel's? It had the face and body of a wolf but was as tall as a bear, with red eyes and black scales on its back but fur under its belly. Its tail had sharp spikes ready to strike, but the biggest danger was the size of its razor-sharp claws and teeth. It was black as night. Stoltland. Stoltland had released this creature.

Sealyn felt anger boiling inside. She felt her palms heat. Her men stood ready to fight. The ladies had finally regained their composure enough to make their way out of the market. Several military carriages had arrived to escort them to the palace. It seemed like hours, but really only minutes had passed. Sealyn was proud of how fast her military had aided the people of the market. She wanted to help fight, but her guards urged her to leave.

Jace tried to calm his horse next to his bride. "Sealyn, we must leave now while we have a chance." But something pushed her to stay. She had no weapon, so what good would she be to face this creature?

The beast growled and then lunged at the guards. Two guards flanked to the left, only to be met with a crushing blow of the spiked tail. Loud sounds of cracked bones echoed. Two other guards dashed to the right, swords colliding with the impenetrable black scales. Favien lunged at the creature's jaw but broke his sword on its teeth. Pinx screamed for Favien, who ducked and rolled away from the snapping jaws. He glanced only for a second at Pinx. Sealyn knew Favien was compromised as long as Pinx was still near. She yelled for Favien.

"Favien, take the last carriage of ladies back to the palace. Guard them with your life."

"My queen, no. Please. Let me stay and fight."

"My own blood is in those carriages. Lady Princess Anadelvia. Get them to safety now. That is an order, soldier!" Favien ran to the remaining carriages and understood why Sealyn did what she did once he was next to Pinx.

More men joined the fight, trying to stab the beast, but more men's lives were lost. Lord Max and Lord Prince Tilmond arrived with the archers and horsemen. The animal let out a large growl at the sight of more men. Archers fired arrow after arrow, but each one bounced off the scales like dust. Tilmond led a charge of his fierce horses, but the beast smacked the horses with its claws, puncturing them with deadly holes. Tilmond was flung off his horse into one of the many shattered market tents. Broken pieces of wood cut his cheek and arms.

The creature began grabbing guards with its claws and squeezing them to death. In the rubble, Tilmond screamed as he watched a new recruit turn blue, then fall limp in the animal's black claws. Yesterday, Tilmond had just given that recruit a tour of the barracks. He was so young. The beast grabbed another man and bit his head off, spitting it back at the Elysian soldiers. Blood splattered everywhere. Max's mouth dropped open. He felt sick. He had never seen such monstrous violence. When the victim's head stopped rolling, Max barely made out that it was old Scrim, the captain who had retired seven times but always came back days later, bored. Max's eyes stung with tears and the stench of his comrades' blood. He fired three arrows as fast as he could, but not one penetrated the scales.

Sealyn stared at the animal's bloody mouth. That was blood from her men! Her Elysium. She had to do something before they all died right in front of her. She felt her palms grow hot again. Was this nerves or something else? She looked around and saw only soldiers and Jace. The creature's jaws snapped at Doebromir, taunting him.

Tilmond scrambled to his feet and managed to find his horse, who was unharmed, and rode back to Sealyn. "How do we fight this darkness?"

Sealyn looked down at her palms, which were now starting to make her gloves pool with sweat. "I believe you fight darkness with light, Commander."

"Sealyn, if you're a Luxen, now is the time to use that power."

Sealyn took off one glove, exposing the green glowing light from her palm. Tilmond's eyes opened wide at the sight of it. The beast stopped and sniffed—it was like it could smell the power. She took off the other glove, and it growled. She had no idea what to do. She rubbed her palms together, then felt the wind of wings. Dun landed behind her, startling Tilmond and Jace's horses. The animal crouched low, ready to pounce. Dun lowered his head, and instinctively, Sealyn leaped from her horse to Dun. Jace's mouth dropped open, stunned to watch his wife in action. Dun rose in the air above the creature.

Sealyn remembered how Corentine had formed weapons with the mist, so she tried the same with her powers. She imagined a big bow with sharp arrows that would grow larger as they sailed toward her target. When she opened her eyes, she was holding a giant bow that looked like it was made of green flames. The arrow was ready to fire. Dun headed toward the beast, who lept in the air, but Dun dodged, and Sealyn launched her arrow. The arrow hit one of the giant scales, ripping it off.

The animal howled in agony. Blood oozed from the open wound. Dun made another pass, and Sealyn fired a second arrow, and again, another scale ripped away. Max's archers took advantage of the open wounds and began firing their arrows.

Sealyn shot several more arrows, ripping more and more scales from the creature's body. Hundreds of arrows plunged into its exposed skin.

Dun landed in front of the dark animal. It had saliva and blood dripping from its mouth. Sealyn slid down from Dun and stood in between the two creatures. Jace leaped from his horse, trying to make his way to Sealyn. Sealyn dissipated her bow, hoping this would ease the creature into surrender. It inhaled one final breath for one final attack. Jace saw the beast tense its body. "Sealyn! Run!" Jace screamed.

The wounded beast flung its massive body at Sealyn. Dun let out a loud screech that made the creature's momentum slow. Sealyn threw her hands up, and, feeling all the anger she had from the loss of her soldiers, Commander Elmond's death, and Stoltland, she screamed as loud as she could—or at least, that's what she thought would happen, but instead of screams, green flames shot from her hands. An enormous green fire swallowed the beast until all that was left was a giant mound of ash.

Sealyn stood in shock, breathing heavily with tears running down her cheeks. She heard nothing. It was like silence had been silenced. Jace ran in front of Sealyn, grabbing her shoulders. He was panicked along with the rest of the army. They had just witnessed their queen incinerate an animal with her bare hands. What did this mean? Jace begged Sealyn to answer if she was all right. She could see he was trying to say something, but she could barely hear anything; his words were muffled.

Jace shook Sealyn, trying to get her to answer if she was hurt. She stared blankly like she was in a trance. She felt like she was gliding underwater but not drowning—just floating peacefully. For a second, she didn't want to return to reality. Floating sounded much better. Dun walked close and nudged her gently with his beak. Sealyn still did not respond. Jace's heart pounded, so he did the only thing a man in love would do. He grabbed her face and kissed her. He finally felt her relax and then felt her arms embrace him.

Bleeding from his head and leg, Doebromir limped over to Sealyn and Jace. "Easy, King Jace. With a kiss like that, you're liable to make an heir right here!"

They chuckled, but it was a painful chuckle. Sealyn scanned the remains of her fallen soldiers and the destruction of the market. She felt faint and looked at the ashes. "Collect the ashes and bring them to the war room. Gather the dead and take the wounded to the Old Crystal Fort hospital." She needed to lie down and didn't want to appear weak in front of her army.

Whatever magic just happened, it was draining her. She dabbed at her nose and noticed red smears. She must get back to her chambers immediately.

Sealyn turned to head back to the palace, but Jace caught her arm. "Wait, Sealyn. Do you have nothing to say?"

"Say? Say about what?" She tried to hurry him.

"About the green arrows. About the green flames that just shot out of your hands. About you blowing up a giant wolf that came from nowhere. What was that?"

"I am a Luxen, and I have no idea what that means."

Queen Corentine,

The first phase of the mission is complete. We took the palace with little resistance. Our main problems have been the ice creatures. It's difficult to defend in the snow and frozen conditions. I've never seen such beasts.

This will slow our search for the source, but have no doubts, majesty. We will find it.

Respectfully,
Commander Malum

CHAPTER 3
SOUNDS LIKE JEALOUSY

Tybalt paced the trunk room. He hated hearing the screams of the wounded. He cursed himself for not being there for his comrades. Then, an eerie silence fell over the trunk room. He could hear slight trickles of water from the shower rooms and the creaking of the old stone walls. He almost wished the screams would come back, but he didn't want to hear his comrades' pain anymore. Then a small hissing sound blew around the room. What was that?

He followed the hissing sound until he was standing in front of Jashun's trunk. "I swear if Jashun has a snake in his trunk, I'm going to kill him," he

said out loud to no one. He slowly lifted the trunk. A light haze floated out of the opening. Where is that coming from? Tybalt was confused and shaken. He moved around Jashun's armor and gear, and then he felt it: a letter. Tybalt hoped it was a juicy letter from one of the ladies.

He opened the letter and dropped it, cursing at the sight of what he saw. Stoltland's seal. Why in all creation would Jashun have a secret letter from Stoltland? He picked the letter up and read the words.

"My Dearest Jashun,

My family and I are fairing nicely, but as I'm sure you now know, the world has changed. New dangers are here. You would do well, my friend, to accept our help. We can provide the financial backing to make all your dreams come true. She will never look at another man again after what richness we can give you. Send a blank letter back, and that will be your 'yes.'

Magnanimously,

Queen Corentine of Stoltland, the Highest"

Tybalt read the letter three more times, trying to make sense of what he was reading. Jashun was loyal, was he not? He would not betray them, right? What did Corentine mean by richness? How much was Corentine willing to give Jashun, and at what cost? He had to talk to Jashun. He crumbled up the paper and walked to the infirmary.

Jashun's arm was already bandaged and was walking toward Tybalt. "What a stroke of luck," Tybalt thought.

"Jashun, I need to speak with you urgently and privately," Tybalt said in a low tone.

Jashun's head jerked slightly back. "What's this about, Tybalt? And can this hurry? I need to go check on Bre—I mean, the ladies. They were scared pretty bad."

Tybalt revealed the crumpled paper and threw it at Jashun's chest. Jashun barely caught the letter, then his eyes bulged, realizing what it was. "Jashun, I'm going to give you one chance to explain yourself, and if you lie, I'm turning you in right now!" Tybalt said, almost growling.

"Hush! Keep your voice down, Tybalt!"

"Are you a spy?"

"Tybalt, come on. You know me. I would never."

"I don't know anything, Jashun, except that you have a letter proposing treachery from our enemy."

"Just listen. Corentine sent that letter weeks after they had returned. I haven't responded. I swear!"

Tybalt crossed his arms. "Then why keep the note if you do not plan on responding? Why hide it? Why not turn it over to Sealyn?"

Jashun sighed. "Because I felt bad. I said too much to Corentine when I escorted her and the king to the dungeons. This letter is the repercussion of that."

Tybalt cursed. "What did you say?"

"Nothing like what you're thinking. It was personal, private information that only lives in the back of my mind, but somehow that witch weaseled it out of me."

Tybalt smacked Jashun's arm. "You better tell me right now!"

Jashun raised his arms in defense. "Calm down! Fine. Here's the embarrassing truth, Tybalt. I want to be with Brenna." Tybalt grinned wide. "I know, go ahead and poke fun, but for me to be a good prospect for her, I need to have a sizable fortune."

"Why sizable? I've seen the way she looks at you. I don't think it would take that much."

"She has a child, Tybalt. I need to have a way to provide for all three of us."

"And betraying your kingdom is the way to do that?"

Jashun folded his arms. "Tybalt, she's offering 60,000 gold coins, and all she wants is just to know how Jace is doing."

"Wait, what? 60,000 gold coins just to tell the witch that her wimpy son is obviously living the golden life of sharing a bed with our queen and living in our palace, drinking our Elysian wine, and eating our Elysian rich foods?" Tybalt brushed back his short brown hair and started pacing.

"I mean, that didn't sound bitter at all," he said sarcastically. "Relax, Tybalt. I'm not going to do it, though. What if she uses what I tell her against Jace?"

Tybalt scratched his chin. "What about me?"

"What about you?"

"What if I took the deal?"

"Tybalt, no! You can't! That would be treason! Do you want to end up like Drystan?"

"Hand me the letter, Jashun."

Jashun hid the letter behind his back. "What? No."

"I won't ask again. Hand it over."

Jashun braced himself, and Tybalt launched forward, grabbing Jashun's neck and pinning his arm against the wall. Jashun squirmed to free his arm, but he couldn't, so he thrust his knee into Tybalt's groin. Tybalt collapsed to his knees quickly, yelping in pain. Jashun gasped for air and coughed.

"Seriously, Tybalt? You would fight your own comrade for money?" Jashun spit at the moaning Tybalt.

Tybalt flipped to his back, still in a cradled position. "You're not the only one who wants to impress a lady. Mine comes from money, so how am I supposed to compete against everyone else who's much better qualified?"

Jashun wiped his nose. "Sounds like jealousy to me."

Tybalt froze and locked his green eyes on Jashun's stern face. "No! It's rational thinking." Tybalt staggered and rose, standing inches away from Jashun. He was taller than Jashun by at least four inches. He saw bits of dirt and blood still in Jashun's crow black hair, and he knew he only had one choice if he wanted that gold. "Jashun, I'm going to turn you in if you don't hand over that letter right now. Your name is on that letter. Yours! Not mine. The palace is itching for blood, so whom do you think they will believe? You, whose name is written all over that letter, or me, whose name is nowhere to be seen?"

Jashun dropped his head. He felt cornered. If Tybalt wanted to betray Sealyn and Jace, then he could easily let him, but he could come out as the hero of this endeavor as well. It would take putting his trust in several others, but he knew the girls were always up for some mischief. Jashun cleared his throat. "Fine, Tybalt. I won't fight you over this, but my name is still on that letter, so I want some assurances. I want to be informed and help so we don't get caught."

"Really? What do you have in mind?"

Jashun folded his arms. "Well, first, you need to tell me when you will write the reply. You can't just send the blank letter because then she'll send me the gold. Who are you going to use to send the message? You know you can't use your Nicht. He'll tell on you immediately."

Tybalt shifted uncomfortably. "I'll use military dispatch ravens. I'll travel to Calenburg at mid-day, so when I arrive, it will be dark. No one will be able to detect the ravens or me."

Jashun did not want to inform Tybalt of all the possibilities that could go wrong with that plan, nor that Sealyn uses *Nightsweeps at all her border hubs. Nightsweeps look similar to eagles, but their wings are similar to a bat's. Razor-sharp claws with black beaks and bodies. The eyes have perfect night vision. Only ravens that have the queen's seal marked on their necks can cross the borders. Tybalt would not be able to obtain one of those, so without the shiny seal. The raven will become the Nightsweeps' dinner (or breakfast, as they sleep during the day).

"That sounds like a solid plan, Tybalt. I'll make sure to cover for you when you're gone. So you'll write the letter tonight, then? Ensure to send your Nicht out for the evening so he doesn't happen upon it." Tybalt nodded. Jashun extended the crumpled letter to him. "Here, and may the Creator help you get everything you deserve."

Tybalt snatched the letter and ran towards his home. He knew there was a tinge of anger in Jashun's "blessing," but he did not care. He was running toward a rich, new life. One he and Norella could share without financial care.

Jashun watched Tybalt for only a few seconds before he darted in the direction of the Palace Chateaus. Queen Sealyn had these living accommodations for all the Vinurs of the Court and palace officials commissioned the day after she was crowned queen. They were positioned behind the gardens, which allowed plenty of privacy but were close enough to the palace for events and daily duties. Jashun enjoyed the closeness to his friends these provided, but most especially because he was able to eat breakfast and dinner with Brenna. Speaking of Brenna, he would need to enlist her and her friends in a scandalous plan to save himself.

CHAPTER 4
POOL OF BLOOD

The stables smelled of sweet hay and manure. They were quiet. Too quiet. Avondelle had lost too many horses today. The ones who survived were being tended to, and the others seemed to be in mourning. Siany brushed her horse, Little Lady, and leaned her head against Lady's neck. Tears flowed down her freckled cheeks. She was tired of death. Tired of the loss that lingered for months and years. Siany quickly turned when she heard footsteps.

Madilina curtseyed. "I'm sorry, Princess Siany. I didn't know anyone would be in here. I came to give the horses some honeyed watermelon. It helps calm them during hard times."

Siany dabbed her eyes and wiped her nose with her handkerchief. "That's very kind of you, Madilina. How are the Caelidons?"

"Oh, they're doing remarkably well. They're exceeding the ice training expectations." Madilina fed one of the candied watermelon pieces to a white horse, who enjoyed the delicious treat immensely.

"Excellent to hear. I'm sure they will be crucial for the expedition." Siany began to feel embarrassed. "Well, I really must be going. It was a pleasure speaking with you."

"Princess Siany?" Madilina said with a questioning tone.

Siany turned back to face her. "Yes?"

"You know that horses can feel everything you feel. They are very connected to us. They can sense your fears and weaknesses, but they can also be a comfort to the broken-hearted. Why don't you stay and let Little Lady mend yours?" She scratched the nose of a beautiful paint horse who had one blue eye and one green eye.

Siany faced Little Lady, rested her forehead on her forehead, and let out an exasperated sigh. "I'm just done with loss. Can't we have a moment of peace? I lost my sparring partner today. He was an excellent swordsman and friend, and that beast just snapped him in half like he was a doll. I should have been there. I should have helped with the fight. I should be going on the Len Nove quest, but I have to stay here! I'm always hidden away, not able to do anything for my people!" Siany blinked in shock at her honest confession to a girl she barely knew.

Madilina saw the shock in Siany's eyes. "Princess, you're allowed to feel frustrated, but never feel like you're not a valued member of the royal family. They need you. You know Queen Sealyn will charge headfirst into a battle without considering her wellbeing, so you must be kept safe to carry on your family's line. You are educating our people, which gives us all hope for a better tomorrow. Sealyn will secure peace, but you will secure prosperity. Why else do you think Sealyn put you in charge of educating the entire realm? She's depending on you to modernize us."

Siany's mouth gaped. "I hadn't thought of it like that before. Thank you, Madilina."

Madilina smiled and handed a candied watermelon slice to Siany. "Watch and see how Little Lady's eyes light up."

Siany fed the treat to her horse and saw the smile in her eyes. She beamed at Madilina. "Madilina, are you and Max moving into one of the larger Palace Chateaus soon? I heard those will be completed this week."

"I believe we will. Max says it will be better since he has more to do with planning for Len Nove, and he doesn't want me to be alone when the caravan leaves."

"Wait, I thought you were going? Isn't that the whole point of you training the Caelidons for ice weather?" Little Lady nudged Siany for more treats.

Madilina shrugged. "I think Max is too concerned for my safety. He said since I've never been in a real battle, I'm probably not ready."

"Well, if you never start, then you never will be." Siany folded her arms and walked cautiously toward Madilina. "If you would like me to speak with Sealyn, I will."

"Nothing has been finalized yet, so I will trust that our queen will make the right decisions."

The ladies of the Vinurs of the Court to Queen Sealyn sat around a pink stone table with glass on top. They were each on their second glass of deep red wine, trying to drown the events of the day into a distant memory. At first, they didn't speak, but it only took one sip before each lady began retelling her traumatic story of the day. Lady Adalina walked out of her new chateau, carrying a large wooden tray with fruits, cheeses, dates, olives, and pieces of bread.

"Look what just arrived. The palace just sent this to each chateau, along with a message saying that they will not be hosting dinner at the palace tonight. The main courses will follow soon."

Brenna reached for a cheese slice. "Sealyn must be shaken for her not to host dinner. Maybe some space will be good for them."

"I agree," nodded Lulana. "Why don't we give them a few days of space? We can each host dinner for us at our new homes." She tucked a few loose strands of her blonde hair behind her ear.

"Excellent idea, Lulana," cooed Brenna. "I can host tomorrow."

"How about a toast to the fallen heroes of today?" Adalina raised her goblet to her two guests with tears in her eyes. They raised and clinked their goblets.

The girls almost spilled their drinks when Jashun popped around the corner. "Good evening, ladies."

"Oh, Jashun," gasped Brenna. "You scared us. You're hurt! Are you all right?"

Jashun rubbed the bandage. "Nothing Lady Zuri couldn't handle. I came to check on you all. I know today was pretty terrifying." Adalina sniffed.

Lulana put her hand on Adalina's shoulder, and Brenna took another sip of wine. "Adalina is the most shaken of us all," said Brenna.

Adalina gasped. "Don't, Brenna!"

"What? It's only Jashun. He won't tell." Brenna turned her gaze to Jashun and leaned in. "Adalina and Landen were together."

Jashun's eyes bulged. "Landen? Really? He was such a good warrior. I know Princess Siany was extremely upset about his passing, too. You know they were sparring partners, right?"

"I know," huffed Adalina. "But he loved me. They were only friends. I don't know if I'll ever find a love like that again!"

Adalina broke out into another fit of crying and ran back into her chateau.

Lulana rolled her eyes. Her pale skin almost turned green, thinking about Landen and Adalina. "He didn't love her. He tolerated her. Adalina thinks every boy who says hello to her wants her. It's embarrassing and annoying." Brenna saluted Lulana with her goblet.

"Listen, ladies," Jashun started. "I also came here for another reason. I need to enlist you for a plan, but I need to know I can trust you without judgment."

Brenna placed her hand gently on Jashun's bandage. "You can trust us, Jashun, but I wouldn't include Adalina. She's quite the little gossip." The ladies pushed their chairs closer to Jashun to hear his plan.

Jashun told them about the conversation he had with Corentine in the dungeon, then about her letter. He told Brenna about his feelings for her and his reasons for the 60,000 gold coins. He hoped that would smooth over any treasonous viewpoints. Finally, he told them about Tybalt finding the letter and his threats, then revealed his plan to become Avondelle's hero.

Brenna sat stunned. "Jashun, I'm in shock." She clasped her hand in his to let him know the feelings were mutual.

"If what you say is true, then Tybalt is writing that letter now. We must act fast," squeaked Lulana. She stood from the table.

Jashun nodded. "I sent word to Ashur to meet us at the palace stables in the next five minutes. He's the new recruit from Port Rowlin. We can trust him."

Lulana's heart skipped a beat. She knew who Ashur was. She remembered the first time she saw him. Lulana had accompanied Lady Pyry to her father's Port Rowlin house. She helped her settle in for a week. Lord Ashur was stationed at the docks right across from the house. Each morning, she found herself staring out the window at him. When the sunlight bounced off his chocolate skin, she thought he looked like the most beautiful man she had ever seen. He was tall with perfect muscles. His face was young and handsome. He had raven black hair, shaved on each side, with a wide nose. She found herself bringing him coffee the last three mornings of her stay. Eventually, he surprised her by asking if she could find out if Avondelle would take new recruits. Lulana immediately wrote a letter begging Sealyn to allow Ashur to escort her home and to be a part of the capital's military.

She wanted him—bad! She tried to shake off the tingling sensations, so she grabbed Brenna's arm. "Hurry. We can't let a traitor get away with his sly plan."

"What about Adalina?" asked Jashun.

"Oh, who cares? We'll fill her in later once you're honored as Elysium's hero!" Brenna said excitedly.

Jashun and Ashur crouched low behind Tybalt's garden. Brenna and Lulana walked in front, or rather, hobbled. Trying to walk straight was difficult, thanks to the wine. The soldiers made their way quietly through the stalks of corn and rows of other plants. They peered through the window and saw Tybalt writing a letter on his kitchen table. Piles of crumpled parchment were scattered around the floor. He was obviously having difficulty writing the letter.

"His house is a complete mess," whispered Ashur. "How can he live like this?"

Jashun sighed quietly. "It's one of the reasons he didn't pass to become part of the Vinurs of the Court."

"Seriously? Being clean and tidy is one of the requirements?"

Jashun shrugged. "Grand Queen Karis added that requirement. Her viewpoint was that if you kept your private chambers messy, then that showed how you would be with your relationships. If you didn't care enough about yourself, then you wouldn't care enough about your friends and family. Oddly enough, she is right about Tybalt"

"How so?"

"Tybalt never invested in his friendships. He only considered you a friend if you participated in what he liked. He would sit silently at gatherings and never opened up. He had some anger issues, too. I'm guessing that's why that chair in the corner is broken into pieces."

Jashun put his finger to his lips. "I think I hear the girls."

Tybalt froze while signing his name to his fourteenth version of the letter to Corentine. He heard what sounded like giggling women; that could not be right, but then he heard it again.

"Tybalt! Come out here!" giggled Lulana. "We have some enchanting news for you."

Tybalt recognized the voice. It was Lulana. What was she doing at his house so late? Was she drunk? She sounded drunk.

He rose and walked cautiously to the door. He looked out the small window and saw Brenna with Lulana. They were twirling. Twirling! What was wrong with these women?

Ashur started to rise, but Jashun shook his head. He mouthed, "Not yet."

Tybalt opened the door. "Lady Brenna. Lady Lulana. Good evening. What are you ladies doing out here this late?"

Lulana grabbed Brenna's hands and danced around in circles. "We have some interesting news about Norella."

Tybalt took a step forward. "Norella? What news?"

Brenna stopped spinning and motioned her index finger back and forth. "No, no, no," she flirted. "You must come outside this gate for us to tell you her personal message. We can't be caught inside your gate at these hours."

Tybalt hesitated. Twenty-five feet stood between him and hearing a personal message from Norella. He could trust the girls. He would hear the message, then hurry back inside and pack up the letter. He would send his Nicht with a morning reply with a flower and hope that would be enough. Tybalt speedily closed the door and met the ladies outside his gate.

Jashun whispered. "That's our signal. Go."

Ashur picked Tybalt's backdoor lock with ease. They entered quietly and picked up all the crumpled papers. Jashun read Tybalt's reply letter. He cursed. "He used my name! Now I'll have to keep the original letter instead of burning it." Jashun grumbled to himself. They could hear the ladies chattering on like insistent hens. Jashun gave the letter to Ashur to hold. They both drew their swords.

Tybalt's eyes were beaming. Norella wanted to meet him at the old willow tree by Dovinus Lake. He knew what that meant. He was too excited, so instead of waiting for tomorrow with a reply, he told the ladies to tell her he would meet her there in one night. He could make it back in plenty of time. He saw something out of the corner of his eye. Who was that? He was running.

Brenna looked to see what Tybalt was seeing, and, to her fear, there was someone running toward them. She saw a shiny bald head and a large smile through a thick beard. Of course, Doebromir would be taking a late-night run.

Doebromir stopped beside the group, panting. "Good evening, everyone." They nodded, looking impatient. "What are you all doing out here?"

Lulana propped her hands on her hips. "We know why we're here, but the question is, why are you here?"

"Easy, Lu. To sleep, I need to run for a bit; otherwise, my leg will keep me up. It's weird, but it works." They nodded. "Now, is one of you going to tell me why you're gathered here and hopefully without any attitude?"

Lulana huffed. "We don't have to tell you anything."

Doebromir shrugged. "All right. Attitude it is. Tell me what's going on before I have to report something suspicious. I wouldn't want anyone to be labeled as a traitor like Drystan."

Tybalt caught a glare from Brenna. Why was she glaring when Doebromir said "traitor?" Did she know something? He felt like his heart dropped to his stomach. Jashun! Jashun must have told Brenna, which meant this was all a trick! Before he could run back to his hovel, Tybalt heard the yells from inside.

"Tybalt! Tybalt! Get inside right now! You must explain yourself!" yelled Jashun.

Doebromir cocked his head. "Well, now, this just got interesting. By all means, Tybalt, lead on." Doebromir motioned for him to go to the door, but Tybalt hesitated and looked at Doebromir's sword. Doebromir saw what his eyes were looking at, so he drew his sword halfway. "Today is not the day to test me, Tybalt. Move!"

Tybalt slowly walked to the house. His mind was spinning. How did this happen? Jashun betrayed him. He wanted the money for himself! Tybalt knew he had to act fast, but what was he to do? He never acted wisely when pinned in a corner, and he felt like he was in the smallest corner, fighting for his life.

Jashun's mouth gaped when he saw Doebromir enter with Tybalt and the ladies. He cleared his throat. "Uh uh. Tybalt, we found these letters. You were writing to Queen Corentine! Enemy to our queen, to our kingdom!"

"Why are you here, Jashun?" snarled Tybalt. "You were the one making deals with Corentine. Her letter is addressed to you! You're the traitor. Let's kill him, Doebromir, just like our King Jace did to Drystan!" Tybalt made a move toward Jashun, but Ashur blocked his path with his sword. Wild tingling sensations went down Lulana's body, and she gasped. Brenna looked at Lulana and nudged her.

"We have the proof that you were intending to accept Corentine's offer of money to spy on our new king. It's right here in your letter with your signature!" Ashur slammed the parchment down on the table. Lulana made another odd sound and looked up, taking deep breaths.

Doebromir stepped forward and read the letter. "Tybalt, what's the meaning of this? Surely, you're not accepting 60,000 gold coins to spy on our king?" He drew his sword and held it beside him.

Tybalt could see he was losing the argument. "Of course not. Jashun is lying. He's the one who is jealous of other people's wealth! He's infected with the curse!"

Everyone froze. To mention someone was infected was the highest level of accusation, and it was not meant to be taken lightly. Tybalt lunged and grabbed his sword that was leaning against the wall. He pointed it at Jashun.

"Easy, men. Easy. We're brothers. We've fought battles together. Today has already seen too much bloodshed. Let's calmly talk this through," Doebromir coaxed.

"No more talking!" shouted Tybalt, and he swung his sword at Jashun, but it collided with Ashur's sword with a loud clang. Lulana squeaked an "Oh my!" Ashur threw Tybalt back with the force of his sword, knocking Tybalt into a wall. Tybalt pushed off the wall, stabbing at Ashur. Ashur blocked the jabs with precision. Jashun lunged toward Tybalt, cutting his shoulder. Doebromir stood in front of the ladies, trying to provide protection.

The cut enraged Tybalt. He threw his chair and hit Jashun in the face, sending him to the ground. Tybalt sprung in the air, lifting his sword high above his head to make his final swing at Jashun. Brenna cried out, "No!" Ashur swung his sword upward with all his might, knocking Tybalt's sword out of his hand. The sword crashed through the window. Lulana felt all the sensations she needed to be hooked on Ashur forever.

Lulana watched intensely as Ashur circled the weaponless Tybalt. Ashur's chest was heaving. She watched sweat drip from his neck and seep into his green shirt. The sweat beads darkened perfectly around his sculpted chest. She could barely breathe. His words threatened Tybalt, but the sounds of his voice vibrated through her. Lulana could not help it, and she let out a loud moan and ran out of the house, breathing rapidly.

Lulana's yelp and fleeing were enough to distract everyone. Tybalt grabbed a knife from the floor and yanked Brenna in front of him. He held the knife against her neck, taunting Jashun to continue.

"I'll kill her, Jashun! Don't test me!" Tybalt yelled.

"Tybalt! Stop!" Jashun pushed the broken pieces of wood off and wiped the blood from his face.

Doebromir pointed his sword at Tybalt. "Drop the knife, Tybalt. If you're willing to kill for Corentine, then you're infected. You only have two choices tonight: come willingly with me, and the queen will most likely send you to Reformation Rock; or refuse and die." Jashun, Ashur, and Doebromir surrounded Tybalt and held their swords at him.

Tybalt threw Brenna at Doebromir, hoping his sword would collide with Brenna's stomach. Tybalt lunged at Jashun, who was watching Brenna fall into Doebromir's arms. With instinct, Doebromir dropped his sword to catch her. Ashur did not hesitate. He forced his sword through Tybalt's side, slicing straight through. Tybalt fell lifeless. Blood pooled around him. The metallic tang of blood filled their nostrils, along with the stench of old food. Brenna ran outside and vomited. Lulana rushed to her side, screaming.

Doebromir stood over Tybalt. "Jashun, you have some explaining to do."

Stoltland Battle Plan Entries

Task 17: Secure unsuspected Elysian citizen for mass distribution of poisoning.
Status: Complete

Military representative in charge of mission: Lord Haedon, Prince of Stoltland

Approved by: Queen Corentine, Queen of Stoltland and the Seven

CHAPTER 5

PIG. KISS. SIPS.

A summer breeze filled the outdoor throne deck, and the night stars twinkled brightly. Queen Sealyn's great-great-great-grandfather had the outdoor throne deck built for times just like this: bloody, dead bodies. Sealyn stood in front of the large throne chair made completely of jade. The entire deck was also made from slabs of jade sealed with gold. She stood in disbelief. Tybalt was dead. A soldier in her army fell victim to the curse. She grew tired of hearing the different stories from Jashun, Ashur, Doebromir, Brenna, and Lulana.

"Enough!" Sealyn said with too much force. The outdoors fell silent. "My apologies. Jashun, and only Jashun speak. Why were you at Tybalt's house?"

"To expose his treachery, majesty." Jashun shifted his stance. King Father Ryker folded his arms and looked at King Jace.

Sealyn tilted her head. "Why not come to the palace first?"

"Since he made threats against me, I wanted to make sure I was right that he would betray us all." Jashun wanted to make the queen see his loyalty. Queen Mother Graelynd dropped her gaze. She felt something was not right. She looked at her daughter, and she could tell Sealyn felt the same.

Sealyn looked at Tybalt's body again. "Just him speaking about this action would have been enough to send him to confinement, but you already knew that, didn't you?"

Jashun's eyes widened. "Yes, majesty, but…"

"You claim your conversation with Queen Corentine in the dungeons was a probe to trick her," Sealyn spoke with skepticism. "If this were so, you disregarded all protocols for taking on secret missions: informing your commanding officer, receiving written approval from him, then receiving a signed approval from your queen with her seal. We have this in place for instances just like this. Or you're lying, and Corentine was able to coax secrets from you that she planned on exploiting to her benefit." The night air stilled. "Which is it, Jashun?"

King Father Ryker smirked. He was proud of how Sealyn was handling the delicate situation. This would not be easy. They all watched Jashun cautiously. He wiped his sweaty hands on his pants. His head ached from the chair.

Jashun cleared his throat. "I—I guess I did not follow protocol." His stomach turned. This was not the hero's ending he was hoping for.

"Guess? You either know or you don't, Jashun," Sealyn corrected.

Jashun dropped his head. "I broke protocol, your majesty."

Sealyn knew it was a lie, but she needed to be careful. So much bloodshed had just occurred. Now she must weigh her options: out Jashun as a liar and traitor or …

"Lord Jashun, please rise." Jashun stood trembling. "I expected better from you, but considering today's battle, you showed bravery and fought gallantly. You are forgiven but with labor consequences. Report to your commanding officer in the morning with further instructions. Dismissed."

Jashun scurried away, not looking back. He heard Sealyn reward Doebromir with a medal of honor. He knew that honor came with a sack of coins too. That should be his money! He had resisted Corentine's 60,000 gold coin offer, and now Doebromir, who accidentally came across the treachery, was collecting his reward money. He heard Ashur received no punishment, only more training on protocols. Jashun spit. How could Sealyn do this to a friend? Should she not look past certain laws for her close peers? Of course not! Queen *Perfection* made a show of him. How would Brenna look at him now? He needed those coins more than ever. He paused, standing in front of his house for a long while, contemplating his next move. Doebromir patted his shoulder.

"Cheer up, Jashun. There was a dead body. She had no choice but to grant some type of punishment." Doebromir comforted.

"Sure. While you and Ashur look like heroes."

"Heroes? Jashun, we did what was right. Our duty. That is all." Doebromir smiled his big grin.

Jashun looked at the medal around Doebromir's neck, and a small tinge that felt cold ran through Jashun's body. He looked away quickly, scared of what that meant. "Goodnight, Doebromir. I'm sure tomorrow will be better." He lied to himself.

"That's the spirit! Besides, we're leaving in two days. Everything changes after that."

Doebromir was right. The battle for Len Nove was close. What would the Elysian forces face once they arrived? Would they be welcomed for coming to their aid, or would they be met with an unknown army? What about Stoltland? Would they have made their way to Len Nove? Once the Elysian armies crossed the border, no one would be able to hide their intentions. The world would know Elysium was coming.

Sealyn watched as the guards lifted Tybalt's body away. His body would be burned, and the ashes would be sent to Reformation Rock. No one would mourn him. He was a traitor. Sealyn was overwhelmed. She needed to prepare her armies for their leave, but it was the middle of the night.

Jace grabbed Sealyn's hand. "My love, it's time for sleep. We all need it."

"You go. I need to clear my head."

Jace hesitated, then kissed Sealyn's cheek. "Don't stay up too late. You need your strength." Sealyn's parents and other council members bid her goodnight.

She was alone, alone with Tybalt's blood. How was she to explain this to Norella? She watched as the maidservants poured water over the dried blood stain and began scrubbing. She turned away. She wanted solitude. She darted in the direction of the old war room. She had sealed up the entrances that were exposed during the Battle of the Betrayals, so she made her way to the newly finished Garden Library. She looked at the tapestry that once had Jace pressed against it with the dark mist choking him. She kept that tapestry to remind herself never to trust Corentine.

She pulled back the tapestry and pressed one of the stones. The bookshelf beside the tapestry creaked open slowly. She stepped inside and closed the door, then stomped her feet. The white fireflowers sprang to life with beams of light shining up on the old stone walls. She smiled, thinking of the time her friends went running down the other secret passageways after her coronation.

When Sealyn entered the old war room, she felt a cold chill rush down her back. Bookcases and trunks from before the Second Chance were everywhere. Before she broke the curse and resurrected the old magic, this room barely had anything on the walls, but now, almost every inch had a bookshelf with books and scrolls. Trunks filled with correspondences were scattered around, but so were blood stains from her family and friends. They tried to clean those spots, but for some reason, the faded crimson remained.

This still did not settle well with her, but the most pressing scene was the cross-legged body on the broken stone table. She walked closer and saw the man breathing. Thank Creator she didn't have to deal with another dead body. The lighting was not the best in the old war room, but she thought she recognized the figure.

"I wondered when you would make your way here," the body said.

A rush of excitement and relief ran over her. The body sprawled out on the table was none other than the one and only Lord Char.

"Welcome back to the land of the living, dear cousin," Sealyn jeered.

"Is it? You look more like a ghost. In my professional medical opinion, I advise more sunshine with a bit more ale and a few more bedroom getaways with your king," Char laughed.

"Char!" squeaked Sealyn.

He sat up, swaying and hiccupping. "Don't act like that isn't the best advice you've evers gotten."

"Evers?" Sealyn giggled. "You're drunk. Good to see some things don't change."

"When your nurse brings you wine, you don't say no."

"That's because you ordered her to bring you the wine!"

"And then some, if you know what I mean," he wiggled his eyebrows.

Sealyn laughed. She laughed hard. She realized this was the first time she had laughed like this in such a long time.

"So dear couzoone," Char slurred. "What have I missed? I heard lots of disturbing sounds all day."

Sealyn sat in one of the unbroken chairs. "Well, first, I'm cousin, not a couzoone. And second..." She told him all the gruesome details about the battle with the giant wolf-like creature, her riding Dun, the green arrows, and the power shooting from her hands. Then she told him the details about Tybalt from the many viewpoints of Jashun, Ashur, Doebromir,

Brenna, and Lulana's shocking accounts and about Jashun's punishment. She paused to take in Char's facial expressions. It looked like he was in pain, but instead, he burst into a fit of laughter.

"What could possibly be so funny?"

Char inhaled deeply, trying to compose himself. "I'm sorry. I'm sure I should be focused on the monstrous wolf and all the men who lost their lives and perhaps feel some which way about Tybalt's death, but can we just take a minute and discuss that Lulana definitely has the shivers for Ashur?"

Sealyn's mouth fell open. "Blessed crickets. I think you're right!"

Char fell back into another wave of laughter. She joined Char in his deep laughter. Char gave Sealyn his glass of wine, and the two sat sipping the delicious liquid for long, silent minutes.

"All right, Sealyn. You came in here for a reason. How can I help?"

Sealyn sighed. "I just need some solitude and maybe some clarity on what to do. What the next steps are and how to prepare for them."

Char chuckled. "Is that all? Let me see," He grabbed his chin and strummed his fingers on his lips. "Stoltland apparently has large scary wolves fighting for them now. Corentine is trying to turn soldiers against you to spy on Jace. Tybalt is, or was, a traitor. You embark on the journey to Len Nove in two days to break a curse that hasn't been broken in thousands of years with an army that hasn't fought in an ice territory." He paused for dramatic effect.

"Is that all?" Sealyn mocked.

"Good news is, Tybalt's dead. Mark 'deal with the traitor' off your list."

"Char!"

"Sorry. Sorry," Char lifted his hands in surrender. "I'm deeply saddened that our personality-of-a-stump friend is no longer with us."

Sealyn giggled. "Why is it that under the gloomiest of circumstances, you can find humor?"

Char smiled his wicked smile. "Because you and I have dark humor. It's the only way to heal sometimes. When you can find a way to laugh, then you have found hope—and that's all it takes to move forward."

"I'm shocked. I didn't know I was in the presence of a great philosopher."

Char gave a pompous laugh. "I'm the philliest philosophering philosopher you'll ever meet."

"I'll be sure to pass that along to the scholars," Sealyn paused. "Char, are you sure you don't want to come with us to Len Nove? Your presence would be greatly appreciated."

Char shook his head. "My dear, I might be young, but my fighting days are over. I don't care if I ever see another adventure again. I've made my peace with it, and I plan on growing fat and old. While you all are off fighting to save the world, my comings and goings will be at *Liquid Courage* with Sakul."

Sealyn smiled. She understood. Char nor Sakul signed up for the fight that had been thrust into their lives. She would miss them terribly, though. She felt slightly guilty for seeing the adventure die from Char's green eyes. "I like the longer hair. Keep that up, and you might start looking like Jace's twin."

"How dare you offend me like that!" He stood, hands on his hips. "I'm much better looking than that ragged horse." Sealyn chuckled. "How about I offer this? I will attend the next couple of days' meetings. I've been reading several of the unhidden books and scrolls in here. They have quite a lot to stay about strategy. I can offer you that."

"So you're finally ready to come back to society and stop hiding in your room?" Char bowed. "Then I will consider it an honor to have the great philosopher Char, a scholar of ancient military tactics and female persuading, join our councils."

The night before a major excursion would include a grand celebration send-off. The palace would fund and provide hundreds of tables of rich foods and drinks throughout the market. The greatest musicians sat near the square, creating uplifting music, while the people danced to their favorite songs. The send-off created an odd, emotional gathering. People were scared but wanted to give the soldiers a memorable night, so no one discussed their fears. Instead, loads of laughter, dancing, eating, and drinking filled the evening.

Favien let his dark brown beard grow thick for the quest. He hoped it might provide just a slight bit of warmth. His green eyes sparkled, and his stomach growled loudly as he took in the scrumptious smells of the spread of meat: fowl, goat and lamb, fish, shellfish, and wild game. Each table had different types of meats prepared in several ways. The aroma was undeniably captivating.

"Oh my, Favien," exclaimed Sakul. "You better fix that loud growling noise."

Favien laughed. "I'm about to. Look at this spread! I wish we could eat like this on our travels."

"As long as you leave me all the crab legs, then you can take the rest with you," Sakul joked. He placed two massive clusters of crab legs on his plate. Sakul wore his deep green tunic with brown leather pants. The fireflowers' lights glowed across his ebony skin.

Favien placed a rack of lamb ribs and several shaved beef pieces on his plate. "Sakul, I wish you were coming. The journey would be much more entertaining."

Sakul smiled. "I'm sure it would be, but adventure is not in my blood. Besides, Sorcha needs me here." He looked toward Sorcha, who was adding a scoop of potato mash to her plate. "The wolf really shook her. This is the first time she's left her room since that day."

The gentlemen moved to the cooked vegetable tables. Favien added some roasted carrots with honey to his plate. "I hate to hear she had such a hard time, but I'm glad she's out. She'll enjoy tonight."

"Don't take too long, friends," chimed Jace. "You're missing the theater acts now! Hurry and fill your plates, and come join us." Jace trotted off and took his seat next to Sealyn, and kissed her cheek.

Favien nudged Sakul. "He's fitting in nicely, huh?"

"He is. He makes Sealyn so happy."

The performers made sure only to perform comedy skits for this night. Send-offs never included reenactments of past battles. The crowd cheered at the announcement of *The Princess Pig*. This performance was a crowd favorite. In the tale, the king was short and large with barely any teeth left, and his vision was so bad that each time he tried to kiss his betrothed, the princess would lift her pet pig to his lips, with the king never knowing the difference.

Before the performance began, Char jumped onto the stage. Sorcha's heart leaped. The crowd cheered. "My fellow Elysians! It is good to see you all looking so well this evening. Before we get started, I propose a challenge." He paused for dramatic effect, then winked. "Yes, a drinking challenge." The crowd cheered, banging their pints on the tables. "Here it is: every time the king kisses the pig, you take a sip of your ale!" The crowd cheered again. "Shall we have a demonstration?" They roared in agreement. The princess actress brought the pig forward, and the king actor kissed the pig. Char raised his drink, saluting the crowd, then sipped his ale with the crowd. "You all are fast learners. Now, let the entertainment begin!" Loud clapping erupted.

Sealyn enjoyed the theater, but it also gave her an opportunity to crowd-watch. She often did this at big events. Becoming part of the shadows allowed her to see the hidden truths. Tonight, everyone would be fixated on the performance so that she could gaze around the crowds and notice anything suspicious. She had felt a dark presence all day, so she needed this time to see potential dangers. She excused herself to *Nijeel's Choice,* where Nijeel always kept her dark green cloak. She changed quickly and kept to the shadows, scanning the market. What was this presence she felt? Was it just nerves, or could the darkness be here?

The king kissed the pig. The crowd cheered and drank.

Sealyn observed Favien sending a few glares at Ashur. Favien said he understood why Ashur killed Tybalt, but Tybalt had been a good friend to Favien. Was Favien holding onto anger? Could this cause trouble among the troops on their quest?

Another drooling pig kiss. Clanking pints and drinks.

Scanning the area, Sealyn saw Sorcha clutching Char's arm, Jace and Finn laughing at the performance, Doebromir glaring toward Jashun, Lulana's cleavage becoming more noticeable with each drink, Pinx and Norella giving worried glances toward Jace and then to each other, Mimby sliding her hand up Hueweyn's arm, Max and Madilina arguing, and Jem looking angry at Jace. "You can certainly find out a lot from standing in the shadows," she thought to herself.

The crowd cheered and drank as another pig kiss occurred.

Something was missing. What was it? She saw Aerrick and Raquel sitting with their children, enjoying the performers. The royal family sat together, all enjoying the show as well. From the Council of Wisdom, Lord Stev and his wife, Lady Song, sat with three from the Council of Lands: Lord Rav—representing Korpam, Lady Adma—from Glantania, and newly appointed Lady Jadelyn for Shunal. Jadelyn's sister, Runihura, said she couldn't handle her responsibilities, so she returned home, but

Jadelyn was willing to take her place. The elders seemed to be encouraging the non-green-eyed. Who was missing? She felt a cold prickle go down her neck. Someone was watching her.

Pig. Kiss. Sips.

Sealyn's heart began to race as she continued to walk in the shadows. The palace Nichts sat on top of the tent with the best view of the stage. Maekel and Trent were snuggled together, which made Sealyn happy. Stawyer was seated with his wife and kids at a table near Aerrick. Someone important was missing, yet that feeling of someone watching her was still very present.

Laughter. Pig. Kiss. Sips.

Sealyn's heart pounded. She felt a coldness near her. She looked toward the entrance of the market near *A Brother's Bond*, and there she saw a hooded figure. Who was that? The cloak looked almost black, but it was a shade of green. Sealyn felt like she and the hooded person must have locked eyes because the figure's head jerked slightly, and she thought she saw—no, that could not be so. She moved quickly in the same direction and saw the hooded person join three others, then they mounted black horses and rode off into the night. Coldness shivered down her spine.

Pig. Kiss. Sips.

Sealyn's heart stopped. She realized who was missing. She shouted toward Tilmond, but he could not hear because of the crowd noise. She quickly ran to the guards stationed near the entrance of the market. They were standing but were asleep. Asleep? How could they sleep through such loud noise? She shook them, and they fell over. She gasped. What was this?

Jdru came running out of *A Brother's Bond* in nothing but a blanket. "Who's out here trying to break in?" Jdru shouted, waving a shovel while clutching the blanket around his waist.

"Jdru?"

His eyes bulged. "Sealyn? What in the king's graves are you doing?

She cocked her head. "I could ask you the same question."

Moonlight bounced off Jdru's bald head, and his cheeks above his reddish beard turned pink. A sudden scurrying sound came from Jdru's shop. They both watched as the beautiful blonde, Axe, ran across to *Liquid Courage* in only a blanket as well. She stopped and bowed to the queen. "Sorry, majesty," Axe said in a hushed voice, then the barmaid ran inside.

Sealyn jerked her head to Jdru. "Well, that answers my question." She grabbed his arm, pulling him inside his shop. "Get dressed and quickly," she ordered.

Jdru wasted no time clothing himself. "What's going on, Sea? What happened to those guards?"

"I'm not sure. I tried to wake them, but they just fell to the ground."

"And that didn't wake them?"

"No. Something's not right."

"Ok, you can turn around, Sealyn. I'm dressed. What do you need me to do?"

"Is Barm in the tavern?" Jdru nodded awkwardly. "Good. I need you to run inside and tell him to go alert Commander Tilmond and tell him to come urgently to *Avondelle's Apothecary.*"

Jdru winced. "The apothecary? Sealyn, what's going on?"

"I only have a hunch, and it's not good. Now hurry. I'll wait for you outside. I don't need to go there alone. You'll come with me."

Jdru hurried back out of Liquid Courage to meet Sealyn, and Barm raced toward the royal table. The royal cousins raced to the apothecary. Sealyn froze at the sight of the broken door. She barged inside.

Jdru tried to grab Sealyn, but she skated by. "Sealyn! No! Wait!"

Sealyn stood over Temm's short, convulsing body. White foam oozed out of his mouth and dripped over his light brown beard as his face turned purple. Jdru tried to lift Temm to help him breathe, but it was too late. His convulsing stopped, and his eyes glazed over. He was dead.

Sealyn screamed. "No! Zuri! Zuri! Zuri, please answer me! Zuri." No response came. Sealyn ran to the other side of Zuri's center counter and found Zuri lying on the floor, unmoving. "No. No. No. Zuri, please wake up. Please wake up." Sealyn cradled Zuri and tried to shake her awake.

"Sealyn! We're here. Where are you?" yelled Tilmond. He had several guards with him, along with King Father Ryker, Max, Doebromir, Favien, and Jace.

Sealyn sobbed. "We're back here. Help her! Please, someone, help her! Where's Dun?"

"He only answers to you. You must summon him," answered Max.

Sealyn focused on everything she had left, willing herself to find that connection she and Dun had. She sent her silent plea to him. Within seconds, a blazing green fire streaked in front of the apothecary windows, and Dun's massive presence was there. Tilmond scooped Lady Zuri into his arms and laid her on Dun's green feathery back. Sealyn climbed up behind Zuri, and Dun, in a whoosh of wind, soared in the air, flying to the palace.

CHAPTER 6
WAKE UP!

During the night before a send-off and every night of the quest, the queen requires the military to sleep in their leather uniforms. This allows for on-time departures and helps soldiers put on their armor faster in case of sneak attacks.

The giant phoenix cradled Zuri in his wings, expelling as much energy as he could. Madilina brought Dun buckets of water to help with his energy loss. The palace closed off the throne room to give Dun plenty of room and privacy. As instructed, the palace staff brought in

the healing plants and surrounded Dun with them. They sang their enchanting melodies, giving hope to everyone.

Sealyn paced in her bedchambers as Jace stepped towards her. Sealyn gasped and rubbed her temples. Jace steadied her. "Sealyn, are you well?"

"My head suddenly became dizzy. I feel a headache coming on."

Jace held her closely. "After what you've been through tonight, I don't doubt you have a headache."

"Jace, I saw four cloaked individuals ride off from the market's entrance."

"Do you know who they were?"

She shook her head softly. "No. The hoods shadowed their faces. I feel like they had something to do with the guards being in a sleep coma, Temm's death, and whatever is happening to Zuri." Her voice cracked when she said Zuri's name.

Jace hugged her tight again. "I agree. I need to tell you something more." He paused, and Sealyn leaned back to stare into Jace's grey, stormy eyes. "Commander Tilmond reported that ten other guards were found in a sleep coma. Their bodies were hidden outside the walls of the market."

Sealyn walked to her bedside table and pulled the bell chord for Maekel. "My love, there's a reason they went for Zuri. There's a reason they went for the apothecary."

"You have an idea. Don't you?"

Sealyn nodded, then Maekel fluttered through her door. "My queen, hows may I helps you?"

"Thank you for coming, Maekel. Would you please bring me some willow bark tea for my headache?"

"And some for me too, please, Maekel," interjected Jace.

"Jace, do you not feel well either?" Sealyn questioned.

"To tell you the truth, I don't. I don't know if it's from the drinks or something else. I'm sure it's the ale. Char's ridiculous pig game. I blame him for every headache I have."

Sealyn chuckled. She understood that quite well. "Maekel, please bring us both willow bark teas and a report on how Zuri is doing."

"Right aways, majesty!" squeaked Maekel.

"Oh, and Maekel, I had an interesting visit from Trent this evening," Sealyn grinned.

Maekel's wings fluttered rapidly. "Yes?"

"Funny. That was exactly my response to him."

Maekel looked confused. "Majesty, whats do yous mean?"

"He asked if he could have my blessing to marry you," Sealyn said with such happiness.

"Ands you saids yes! Ands you saids yes! Oh, mys queen! You've mades me the happiest creature alives! Thanks you!"

Sealyn smiled. "Only the best for you, my dear friend." Sealyn grasped her head again. Jace immediately ran to her.

He looked at Maekel. "Please hurry, Maekel. We need those teas."

Maekel flew out the door. Jace scooped Sealyn into his arms and laid her gently on the bed. He was worried. What if this was not just a headache? What if this was a side effect to something those hooded killers did? He felt her head. She was burning up! He rushed to the wash bowl and brought her a wet cloth for her forehead. Jace suddenly felt dizzy, too. His vision started to blur. Why did he participate in Char's pig game?

Jace knelt beside the bed and held Sealyn's hand. They felt each other's touch, but their grip started fading. Darkness clouded their vision, and their fingers slowly slipped away from each other. Jace fell to the floor into a deep sleep along with Sealyn. Sealyn's hand drooped over the bed, motionless. The halls of the palace, the market, and all of Avondelle went silent.

He heard birds singing. He felt the sunshine on his face. The cooler air made him shiver. Was he outside? Finn slowly propped himself on his elbows and blinked his blue eyes. Where was he? He recognized nothing about this landscape. He was terribly thirsty and ravenous for food. He saw movement a few feet in front of him. He stiffened, then he saw Lady Sorcha lift her head from the tall grass. Grass and twigs were tangled in her black curls. What was he doing in a field with Lady Sorcha? They both stared at each other, confused.

Finn heard a groan to his right and looked to see Ashur trying to stand to his feet. He was very unsteady. Was he dreaming? Behind him, he heard Lady Pinx cry out. She was trying to wake someone. Suddenly, he saw Lady Norella rise next to Pinx. What was happening? He stood and helped Sorcha to her feet while Ashur assisted Norella and Pinx. They crowded around each other, hoping one would start the conversation to figure out exactly what happened. They heard a loud cry for help.

"Someone! Anyone! Please help! I'm slipping!" the voice yelled.

Ashur and Finn sprinted to the edge of a cliff and slid to a stop before looking over. They leaned over and saw Jace hanging onto a small ledge a couple of feet below. Ashur instantly dropped to his stomach, extending his arms. "King Jace, grab my hands. Finn, hang onto my legs. Don't let me go over!"

Finn sat on the ground, grabbed Ashur's ankles, and braced his heels into the rocks as best as he could. The ladies locked their arms with Finn's arms, but Ashur started moving forward.

"My foot is slipping," Finn cried out.

"I'm going over!" yelled Ashur. The ladies screamed and pulled Finn, but their feet kept slipping on the rocks, too.

Jace looked into Ashur's green eyes. He could not let Ashur and Finn die because of him. He started loosening his grip. He hoped Sealyn would forgive him, but he had to think about others before himself.

"Don't you dare!" Ashur screamed. "My king, stay with me!"

They heard footsteps running, then a whoosh over the cliff. The ladies looked up to see two men diving over the cliff with ropes tied around them. Did they really just see people dive over a cliff? Jace felt strong arms encircling him, then watched a figure grab Ashur's arm. Next, they heard them yell, "Now!"

Suddenly, the four men were pulled back to solid ground. Once Jace was released, he stared into Lord Stawyer's green eyes and then embraced him. Lord Rielen, a cousin to Queen Sealyn, son of Lord Ryland, helped Ashur to his feet.

Jace embraced Rielen. "Rielen, are you hurt?"

"No, my king, but that was an exhilarating rescue!" Rielen loved adventure. Heights never bothered him, so he took every opportunity to seek adventure. He was thrilled when Sealyn invited him to join the caravan for Len Nove, but now, he had no idea what was happening to them.

"Where did you get the rope?" asked Finn.

Stawyer pointed to the three military wagons. "I woke up in the back of that covered wagon. When I checked the other wagons, I found Lord Rielen in one, and," he waved to the thick brown-headed rider on a white horse. "Lord Prince Ezen was in the other."

Ezen trotted over to the group with his horse. "Mornin', everyone. Hope no one's too scraped up?" Ezen was tall and had dark brown hair and a big bushy beard. He had the personality of his father, Prince Tovin, in that he never met a stranger. He was one of the kingdom's greatest trackers.

Jace exhaled. "Excellent timing, Lord Prince Ezen. I appreciate the rescue."

"Call me Ezen, Jace. We're in the wild. No need for formalities."

Sorcha could not take much more. "Enough with the pleasantries! Can we please figure out what in all Creation is going on? Where are we? What are we doing out here? How did we get here, and why can't I remember how I got here?"

Ezen jumped down from the horse. "I think it's safe to say, Sorcha, that no one has an answer to any of those questions."

They heard other sounds. There were more screams from others, but not nearby. They looked across the large canyon where water flowed rapidly. They were shocked by what they saw. Max, Doebromir, and Favien were fending off a giant *glatomont. The aggressive bird had long, skinny legs with fish-like scales and stood around seven feet tall, but its wings were small. Its beak was long and sharp.

Favien ducked and rolled under the bird, slicing its left leg. The glatomont squawked in pain. They also saw Commander Tilmond, Jem, and Jashun running to aid the others. They looked like they were covered in blood, then they noticed the other lifeless glatomont. Lady Madilina and Lady Rivers were hiding under one of the covered wagons with swords ready. The six surrounded the large creature. It lunged forward, trying to make a stab at Doebromir. Doebromir threw himself to the ground to dodge the sharp beak, but the creature kept running. It jumped off the cliff and plunged into the racing waters below.

The eight lined across the edge, staring below, then looked up and saw the others across, staring back at them. They all started yelling, trying to communicate, but the distance made the echoing hard to hear, especially with the rushing water. Stawyer ran to the wagons and grabbed the signal flags. He raised the blue flag, signaling they were all safe and unharmed. Max did the same. They all felt better knowing no one was hurt. Now what?

Jace panicked. He did not see Sealyn. Where was she? Was she back at the palace? He hoped she was. He prayed she was waking up in their bed to a warm cup of coffee and a delicious breakfast, celebrating with Maekel. But, what if she was not in the comfort and protection of the palace? What if she was also out in the wild? Would she be alone? Her best warriors were already accounted for, so who could she possibly be with?

Sealyn blinked her eyes. She was sure she was not actually seeing tall, thick blades of grass, but the smell was undeniable. She was definitely outside. She slowly stood and looked around the vast sea of green grass. The blades stood as tall as her thighs. When the wind blew, the field looked like sea waves billowing through. She listened closely for any sounds, but it was eerily quiet. She saw a large, covered wagon with three horses hooked to it. The horses were enjoying the juicy grass, chomping quietly.

She made no sudden movements to the wagon. It could be a trap. She scanned the horizon; only hills of tall green grass lay in front of her. She could see a forest in the distance, and then she heard a noise. It was human. She hoped it was Jace or Commander Tilmond or a palace guard. Another sound came from the opposite side. Perhaps multiple guards were here with her. She crouched low to see who was emerging.

She saw two tall young men stand and look confused at each other, and her heart sank along with her hope of brilliance. She stood. "This has got to be the worst joke in all of history!" she barked.

"Sealyn!" cheered Char. "What a delight. Since I'm guessing you're just as lost as we are, why don't you cook us up some breakfast? I'm famished." Sealyn rolled her eyes.

Sakul raised his arms gently. "Sealyn, please, please tell me you know what is going on." Sealyn looked down. "Sealyn? You have the plan to get us out of here, right?"

Char patted Sakul's shoulder. "Of course she does! She's Sealyn. She can get us out of anything because she knows what's going on. Don't you?" Sealyn started to shake her head. "Sealyn, at this point, I'd take a lie. Lie to me. Tell me you know how we ended up here and how we're getting back to the palace."

Sealyn sighed. "If my memory is correct, then we are in the Blissendelle Territory. I remember the drawing of the grass fields to the right of Sallen."

"Sallen? Blissendelle? This is extremely far from Avondelle!" Sakul panicked.

Char sighed deeply. He realized something horrible must have gone wrong for them to be in the middle of the grass fields in Blissendelle. As much as he did not want another adventure, he was in one. "Well, there's literally only one thing we can do." Sealyn glared incredulously. "Go to Sallen and visit the kingdom-famous tavern called *Betty's Boots*. It has the greatest ale you'll ever taste, and the roasted chicken is literal perfection."

"Char! We're not going on one of your many tavern-touring excursions. This is serious. I must get to Fort Kippen," Sealyn urged.

Char smirked. "My dear sweet cousin, you seem to be mistaken. You're not in charge. It's two against one." Sakul's eyes bulged. "We're taking that wagon to Sallen with or without you. Decide."

The last time Sealyn was given two choices, she chose war against Stoltland. Now, she was faced with traveling alone or traveling with two men who would most likely end up as tiger dinner. She realized that Sallen could be an opportunity to enlist several Nichts to send messages to the palace. She needed to know if they were the only ones abducted. Had they been abducted? She still had no idea what to call what happened to them. "Fine," she said with bitterness. "We'll go to Sallen." Char high-fived Sakul. "On one condition." She narrowed her eyes at Char. "Char, you have to drive the wagon while Sakul and I ride the horses."

Char winched, knowing what pain lay ahead on that rough wooden seat with the bumpy road. He would be sore for days, and Sealyn knew it.

The dirt and rock crunched beneath their feet. This was the king's road. It led to Avondelle from the borders of the Blissendelle and Clarien territories. The palace had markers along the road to let travelers know the direction of the capital. Lady Adalina read the next marker. "It says one mile! We're only a mile away from Avondelle!" She smiled at Rav and Hueweyn, then locked arms with Adma and Jadelyn. "We can do this!" Adalina encouraged.

Adalina fidgeted with her hands. Small twigs and leaves were tangled in her long black hair, and her brown pants were covered in mud. She was extremely worried about reaching the palace. How would she explain to everyone what happened? Her almond-shaped green eyes fought back tears. They had chatted about what they could remember. They remembered the market with all the tables of food, the dancing, the performances, the drinking, the laughing, and then something occurred to capture the military and king's attention. No one knew what.

"I did make it back to my chateau," Adalina recanted. "But I don't remember much after that."

Jadelyn's yellow eyes sparkled. "It was the same for me. Can we all agree it is possible that we five blacked out and randomly met up along this road, then continued having fun until we passed out? This sort of thing happens all the time in Shunal."

Adma was out of breath. They had walked ten miles already. She was sweating and hungry. Although her time spent in Avondelle had helped her lose some weight, she was not healthy yet, and this walk was making her life miserable. "I usually don't black out," she gasped. "I can handle my ales easily." She took in another deep breath. "I can drink twice what normal people drink and not feel a thing." She inhaled so deeply that the group thought she was going mad. "So I don't think that's it." She gasped and coughed and patted her oversized chest.

"I lose things when I have too much wine. Documents. Tools. Shoes, but not myself, so I must agree with Adma," Hueweyn said. He brushed back his shaggy brown hair that hung in his face.

Rav sighed. "I sleepwalk sometimes." His shy, orange eyes looked down. "But not for miles. This seems like something greater is at stake. Besides, Zuri would have stopped me."

This piqued Adalina's interest. "Zuri? I don't recall seeing Zuri with you at the party. Did you two have a falling out?"

Rav stopped walking. The rest of the group paused with him. "I saw her at her shop before the party started, but you're right. She wasn't with me for the rest of the night. Nor was she in my house. I think I remember feeling worried, like I was waiting on an answer to her condition."

"Condition?" questioned Jadelyn. She tossed her bright blonde braid behind her head. Her pale yellow dress was now covered in dirt stains.

Rav was sweating and combed his brown fingers through his raven black hair then paused. He suddenly remembered blips of memories: being escorted to the palace, Sealyn crying next to the green phoenix, Zuri wrapped in feathers, changing into his battle leathers, then darkness. "Zuri's hurt! She was poisoned! I must know if she's alive! I can't lose her. We were planning a life together. We didn't care that we were from two different kingdoms. We were going to make it work, just like our king and queen."

Adalina put her hand on his arm. "Easy, Rav. We're almost to Lady Raquel's house. I'm sure she can help us get to the palace faster."

With the aid of Lady Raquel's horse-drawn wagon, the group made quick time to the palace gates. They dashed up the steps and into the throne room. There, Dun was sleeping with Zuri still cradled in his wings. Her breathing was steady, and her beautiful ivory skin had returned to normal color. Rav grabbed his chest and hit his knees, then he brought his hands to his face and quietly sobbed in relief. Adalina felt a tinge of pain seeing his reaction. What kind of love was this to bring a giant man to his knees?

They heard what sounded like dishes clattering, so they silently walked into the breakfast room, and, to their surprise, they found the royal family sitting around the table in heated discussions. The rounded room came suddenly still when the royals caught sight of the group. Siany jumped up and ran to Adalina. She embraced her so tightly that Adalina made a grunt.

Siany pulled back. "My apologies. We're just so thrilled to see you all safe. Tell us. Where is Queen Sealyn?"

Adalina blinked in confusion. "Queen Sealyn? What do you mean?" She looked around the room at the concerned faces.

King Father Ryker stood. "What she means is that Queen Sealyn, along with King Jace and several other members of the

Vinurs of the Court and military leaders, went missing last night—same as you all."

"You mean this isn't history's worst hangover?" questioned Jadelyn.

Lady Princess Anadelvia smiled slightly. "No, my dear. This is far from that, although it may feel like a hangover. Please join us for some fitting nutrients. You all must be famished." She motioned for them to sit. Adalina idolized Lady Princess Anadelvia. She quickly took the empty chair next to her. She tried not to stare at her porcelain skin, perfectly combed short blonde hair, and petite figure. She wore a tight-fitting velvet pink and light green dress with sheer sleeves. Adalina made a mental note to request all her future dresses with sheer sleeves.

Hueweyn cleared his throat. "Your majesties, can you tell us what happened?"

Ryker was too upset to speak, so Queen Mother Graelynd spoke. "Well, what we've gathered so far is hooded figures slipped past the guards and stole a heavy sleeping powder from Lady Zuri's apothecary. During the break-in, they encountered Lady Zuri and Lord Temm. Temm defended Zuri as best as he could, but they held him down and poured poison down his throat, killing him. They used the same bottle on Zuri, but there was not enough to kill her as fast. This is when Queen Sealyn and Lord Jdru," she pointed at Jdru sitting next to his father, "found Temm and Zuri. Commander Tilmond's team arrived shortly after but was not able to revive Temm. Dun flew Sealyn and Zuri to the palace. He's remained with her in his wings ever since. She will make a full recovery." Adma patted Rav's shoulder, hoping this news would calm him. Graelynd continued, "Upon reviewing Zuri's inventory books, several bottles of this sleeping powder were missing. This indicates that more bottles were stolen earlier, which proves that someone poisoned all the ales and water that the celebration distributed during the send-off."

Hueweyn gasped. "We were poisoned?"

"Everyone?" asked Jadelyn.

Graelynd nodded. "Everyone, I'm afraid."

"That still doesn't explain where the queen is," panicked Adalina. She fidgeted with her hands again.

Prince Adomin set his black coffee down. "This is where we hope you all can share some light. Where did you wake up?"

The five recanted their tales and hoped their stories would help the royals figure out where their friends were. Everyone sat quietly once they were done. Nothing was solved; only more questions were asked.

Maekel fluttered in the room carrying a sealed scroll. "Majesties. I'm sorrys to bothers you, buts Queen Sealyn tolds me to gives this to Princess Siany onces they lefts on the quest, but I figureds since they're gones …" She dropped her head and sniffed, then handed Siany the scroll.

Siany quickly opened the scroll. "It's her declaration nominating me to rule in her stead during the Len Novian quest." She gasped. "She also states that King Father Ryker will also rule with me, and Queen Mother Graelynd is to be my advisor." She blinked, and a tear rolled down her cheek. Her sister trusted her enough to leave the entire kingdom in her hands. Her heart ached even more now to know where Sealyn was.

Prince Royce stood and held his gold goblet in the air. "A toast to our new interim queen. May your judgment be wise and your mercy be pure. Blessings to you, darling Siany." Everyone raised their glasses to Siany.

As Royce sat, Ryker stood. "We can't waste any time. We must make smart, quick decisions. All men seated here, meet me in the war room. Start organizing teams to scout military inventory and search parties. Siany, you need to be there too. Graelynd, my love, work with the ladies of the court to organize a list of who's still here and who's missing." He looked at Lady

Princess Nanceline, Prince Adomin's wife. "Nanceline, please work with your daughter, Anadelvia, and the rest of the royal ladies seated here to organize food services for those who have family missing and for the search parties. Maekel, bring me as many Nichts as you can find to the war room. We will meet back here for dinner. You have your tasks. Make your kingdom proud."

Diary Entry,

To myself--you're the only one I care to talk to because I'm basically speaking to me, and ME is the only one making sense right now. Everyone in the palace has been complete idiots. I'm more on edge today than ever. Maybe it's because I didn't sleep well.

I dreamed of **him**.

N.C.M.

Why does **he** still torment my dreams after all these years? Is it my lies? Is it because I refuse to tell my son the truth about his birth?

Why would that matter? Jace doesn't even care about us anymore. He has his pretty little perfect doll, but they're both stupid enough to believe they will have a happy life. The prophecy will stop that if I don't get there first.

My plan is foolproof. There are too many angles for Elysium to protect itself against.

And if by some miracle all plans fail, then my last backup plan is secured. I hate that plan. It means the sea. It means **he** could become a problem—again.

From myself,

The Queen of All Queens, Corentine

CHAPTER 7
LIVING GRAVES

The fires crackled and popped. The rabbits Doebromir and Jem had killed and skinned earlier slowly turned over one of the fires, making everyone's mouths salivate. Rivers stirred the vegetable and potato stew over the second fire while humming her favorite Elysian military tribute song. Rivers has always been a positive person, which made her teammates enjoy her company during the hard times even more. She pulled her several rows of rickracks into a golden ponytail tied with strips of leather. She was short, but her muscular strength made up for what she lacked in height.

Madilina drew lines in the sand with a stick, waiting for the delicious-smelling rabbit and stew. She looked at her husband, Max, who was sitting in between Favien and Jashun at the other fire. He had such a worried look on his face. She wanted to comfort him, but she knew he needed time to come up with a plan before he would accept comfort.

Tilmond sat down beside Favien and patted him on the back. "Favien, it's going to work out. You can see that Pinx is safe across the canyon."

Favien gazed across the canyon, seeing the other group sitting around their fires, eating as well. His heart ached to be the one sitting next to her. "I know, Tilmond, but being the one not protecting her is not easy."

The ladies walked over to the rabbit fire with the stew and poured the mouth-watering liquid into each bowl. The group ate in silence, satisfying their hunger.

Jashun sat his bowl and rabbit bones down and rubbed his hands together. "Well, let's figure out our plan."

"I agree," Max said, eyeing Madilina. "We can't sit around expecting a rescue team."

"My opinion is to head north and meet up with the other team at the end of the canyon, then carry on to the closest village for replenishing supplies," Favien advised.

Tilmond nodded. "I think that's an excellent plan. We'll signal to the other group to move out and head north. I'm still baffled that our caravans are packed with everything we arranged for the Len Novian quest."

"Me too. It's almost like someone wanted to teach us a lesson but still wanted us to journey to Len Nove," Max said.

"A lesson?" questioned Rivers. "Why would someone want to teach us a lesson?"

Max shrugged. "No idea, but think about it. Whoever did this had plenty of time to kill each one of us but instead left us here with all the supplies needed to make it to Len Nove."

"That makes all this more confusing," Doebromir said while scratching his bald head. "Regardless, I think we should leave behind an Elysian marker just in case the palace sends scouts to locate us."

The two groups cleared the fires and left their Elysian markers, then headed north. What mysteries lay ahead? They were marching off course with way fewer people needed to conquer Len Nove. They had a hidden enemy and no way of knowing if their queen was alive. What other problems would they face? Doebromir, Max, and Tilmond rode the horses, and Jem, Jashun, and Favien drove the three wagons. Rivers sat in the last wagon with her bow and arrow ready to defend, while Madilina sat in the middle wagon. Doebromir trotted beside Jashun. "Jashun, at some point in this journey, you and I will have that talk." He kicked his horse and rode to the front of the caravan.

Jashun's heart dropped. Would Doebromir find out his secret, or perhaps he already knew? He had to make peace with the idea that if Doebromir tried to kill him, he would have to kill him first. Could he do that? Could he really kill a comrade-brother?

Char pulled on the reins and stopped the wagon. He stared across the open terrain. As far as the eyes could see was green moss. A stream was to their left with a family of deer drinking water. He tied the reins and jumped down. Sealyn dismounted her palomino horse and petted him. Sakul rolled out of the back of the wagon and puked.

"Oh, gross, Sakul!" Char bellowed. If there was anything Char hated, it was puke.

"It's all your crazy driving's fault, Char!" Sakul yelled

Char's mouth gaped. "My driving? How dare you! I'm a perfect driver. It's the road, or lack thereof, that's the problem." Sakul swished water in his mouth and spit.

Char walked to Sealyn and pointed in the distance. "Look out there. Do you recognize that type of green moss?" Sealyn's eyes glistened and then looked back at Char. "Oh, yes," Char said with eagerness. "That would be Springy Turf Moss!"

Sakul stood waving his arms. "Nope. No, no … no, not happening."

Char bounced his eyebrows. "C'mon, Sakul. Where's your sense of adventure?"

"I remember you all telling stories about that springy moss. It's infused with magic. Not happening."

Sealyn drifted to her first memory with Springy Turf Moss. Her father gifted her and her cousins a large section of the gardens with Springy Turf Moss. The children were at a loss as to what to do with the giant circle of moss, then King Ryker stepped onto the moss and began jumping. The children stood in wonder. They ran to the moss and began jumping with the king.

Soon the whole family was bouncing for hours, seeing how high they could bounce each other.

Sealyn chuckled to herself. "Char, do you remember the last time we jumped on that moss?"

"Don't start with me, Sealyn!"

Sealyn gave him an evil grin.

"I'm warning you, Sealyn! You start sharing stories like that, then I'll share your stories too."

"That's not fair that you both know the stories and I don't," whined Sakul.

With the stakes as high as they were, they needed to laugh. They needed to give their bodies relief from the stress they were under, so without wasting more time, Sealyn shared the embarrassing truth Char didn't want anyone else to know. "Just call Char Lord Pee Pants!"

"Sealyn!"

Sakul laughed. "Pee pants? Now, I have to know."

"Siany, Jdru, Audayia, Char, and I were jumping on the moss. We were playing a game where Char was a Stoltland soldier, and we were the king's guard protecting the realm. We jumped around pretending to punch and kick Char, and, of course, being the great actor he still is, he would fall on the moss in pain. Well, we pounced on him and started tickling him. Char couldn't stop laughing, nor could we. He laughed so hard that he peed himself. We all ran off the moss, and there was Char still laughing in his pee. We never jumped on that moss again."

Char stood there pouting while Sakul wiped tears of laughter from his ebony cheek. "Yes, yes, I peed myself. Can we all move on?" Sakul still laughed. "I would like to redeem myself. Let us have a go at jumping on the moss now?"

Sealyn hesitated. She didn't want to leave their wagon and weapons, but again, they needed fun to relieve their anxiety. Besides, how many opportunities would she get like this being queen? "Fine, but not too long."

"I'll race you there!" Char took off running down the hill and leaped onto the moss. He felt like a child again. He loved remembering his childhood with his cousins. Those were his favorite memories. His family meant everything to him.

The three of them bounced and bounced on the sponge-like green moss. For the moss to have its magical bouncing properties, it must live near a water source that constantly keeps it damp. They splashed and jumped their way around the moss hills. Sealyn's spirits elevated as she jumped with her friends. She finally laughed, and it felt good. She took a moment to watch

Char and Sakul engage in a battle of who could bounce the other the highest. She shook her head and wondered how she ended up on this adventure with these two.

Suddenly, she heard a fluttering noise. She motioned for Char and Sakul to stop. "Shhh!" Sealyn hushed. "I think we're being watched." They looked around and saw nothing.

Sakul dabbed sweat from his bald head and whispered. "I don't see anything."

Sealyn's eyes narrowed. "It's more about what you don't see that worries me." Her heart pounded. She could feel eyes watching them. It was several pairs of eyes, but where were they?

Char walked to Sealyn and spun her around. "I think your paranoia has gotten the better of you."

It was definitely wings, but she saw nothing in the sky, then up from the grass edge fluttered several Nichts. Sealyn gasped. These were not just any Nichts. These were Earth Nichts. They chose to live outside of any city or village. They did not like disruption. Earth Nichts were larger than most types of Nichts, almost the size of small human toddlers.

Sealyn looked at the five Nichts staring at her. "Hello. We mean you no harm. My name is Queen Sealyn Araelien from Avondelle, and these are my two companions: Lord Char

Araelien and Lord Sakul Moordon. We come in peace. Who are you?" She hoped her words came out soft and welcoming. Char and Sakul finally joined beside Sealyn.

Brown eyes narrowed. "I am Obeesi." His black hair was twisted into several long sections and tied back with long blades of grass. He had dark skin with shaggy facial hair and large muscles, which were evident since he wore no shirt, only long black pants. "These are my brothers, Grant and Basalt, and these are my sisters, Ivy and Rose. We are of the Glinstone Clan."

Sealyn nodded. "It is a pleasure to meet you all. How many clans are in this area?"

"Four: Willowmint Clan, Luna-River Clan, Clayvine Clan, and again, us, the Glinstone Clan," Obeesi grunted.

Sealyn was fascinated by the Earth Nichts. She loved their shimming green wings and reminded herself to tell Maekel everything she learned. "We didn't mean to disturb you. We're passing through to Sallen."

"Sallen," questioned Grant. "Why are you heading north?" His light brown eyes narrowed. He, like both his brothers, wore no shirt, only black pants, yet he had a satchel strapped across his chest. His black hair was shaved on the sides and cut short on top, while the other brother, Basalt, was bald.

"That is classified information, Grant," Sealyn said sternly. She did not want a fight with the Nichts but needed to assert her dominance over all who lived in Elysium.

"We understand, your majesty," hummed Rose. "Forgive my brothers. They can be a bit harsh." Her long curly hair reminded Sealyn of Sorcha's curls, and her heart ached for her best friend.

"No worries. Forgive me, but you all don't sound like other Nichts. Why is that?"

The bald Basalt decided to chime in. "Because we choose not to. We decided to let go of the past and embrace new changes. We chose to speak the language of those who saved us, and we chose to live freely among nature. We are not here to harm you or hinder your journey, majesty. We're here to thank you."

Sealyn was shocked. She always heard such harsh stories about the Earth Nichts. Why would people spread such rumors? She decided at that moment that she would never believe another rumor unless she saw it for herself.

Ivy smiled shyly. "Majesty, could you do us the honor before you go and have dinner with us?" Ivy had such a sweet face. Her skin was lighter than her siblings, and her curls fell perfectly around her face. She had such blinding beauty. She wore a dark green top with black leather pants. Sealyn was weary of the black clothing. Why would they wear Stoltland's colors? She wanted to find out.

"How could we refuse such a wonderful invitation?" Sealyn cooed. "You lead, and we'll follow with our wagon."

As they approached the Earth Nichts' camp, Sealyn was amazed. There were so many. Four giant oaks stood enormously tall and thick, thicker than normal oaks. She suspected the Earth Nicht magic played a role in the oaks' sizes. She saw different colors and designs at the base of each tree. One tree was orange with green and white triangles that bordered the edge of the orange on top and bottom. They painted a green tiger on both sides of the door. The tigers stood on their hind legs, facing the door with their front paws stretched out. Why would Nichts paint with the Korpam's color orange and use its animal symbol, the tiger?

Another tree was painted with yellow stripes with a giant green snake that was drawn to appear to slither "in and out" of the vertical stripes. Again, why did they specifically use another kingdom's color and animal symbol? Sealyn's spine went cold.

The next tree had a giant purple bear painted on it, but the last tree made Sealyn stop moving. Anger boiled inside her. The last tree had a large black dragon eating a black horse. She whirled and faced Obeesi. "What is the meaning of this?"

Obeesi looked confused. "Meaning of what, majesty?"

"These colors. These drawings. Why would you paint your homes in our enemies' colors?"

Ivy fluttered forward and put her arm on her brother's. More Nichts gathered around. Ivy spoke softly. "My queen, we have a dark past. Each clan you see before you was once enslaved by one of the kingdoms shown here. Korpam enslaved the Willowmints, which is why they painted with orange and drew the tigers. The Luna-River clan were slaves to Shunal; the snake and yellow color. Glatania owned clan Clayvine, and we were slaves to…"

"Stoltland," Sealyn gasped. "Oh, Ivy. I'm so, so sorry. Please forgive my ignorance."

Ivy smiled. "There's nothing to forgive, majesty. Because of your grandfather and your family's continued support of the Nichts, we live in peace, in freedom. We chose to paint our past never to forget, not to harbor hate, but to remind ourselves always to be grateful."

Char sniffed, and Sakul wiped tears. Sealyn tried to compose herself, but tears welled up. She choked out her words. "I'm beyond impressed. You all have risen from living graves to thriving legends. I'll forever be in your debt of perspective. Thank you for sharing your story."

Ivy beamed and fluttered her wings. "Will you join us for dinner?"

The three sat in the middle of the four giant oaks and watched the different clans work together to make a large meal to feed all the members and them. The Willowmint clan had light brown skin with red undertones and dark, long, silky hair, whereas the Clayvines had pale skin with bright red and orange curly hair. The Luna-River clan looked unique. They each had bright white hair and olive skin. What a beautiful sight of sparkling wings and teamwork.

Char, Sakul, and Sealyn ate with the Nichts and enjoyed the delicious roasted vegetables and sweet breads, then the music started. What sweet songs. Char and Sakul joined in the dancing while Sealyn clapped with her new friends. Being here made the quest seem so far away. Sealyn felt safe, then instantly felt alone. Tears started falling. She missed Jace. She wanted him to see the beauty she was watching. Where was he? Was he safe? Was he hurt?

Ivy placed her hand on Sealyn's shoulder. "My queen, can I help?"

"I wish you could. I have no idea if my husband is alive. I feel he is, but I want to know he's safe." Sealyn went on and shared their story of how they ended up on this journey. The music stopped, and the rest of the Nichts listened to Sealyn. The Nichts trembled with the thought that their royal family could be in danger.

Grant spoke loudly. "Queen Sealyn, I offer you our services. We will cover the skies and find any signs of our king. You have my word."

"Oh, Grant. I could not ask that of you. I know your clans requested to live in peace and not to be disturbed."

"Disturbed? We will have no peace if our king is in danger," huffed Obeesi. "At first light, our best warriors from each clan will fly out. If the king is out there, we will find him. This means we all need our rest. You will be safe to sleep here. We will have guards to watch through the night."

The Nichts scattered to their designated trees, and Sealyn, Char, and Sakul laid in the thick grass beneath the tree branches. Sealyn finally felt hope. She could sleep better this night, knowing they now had a way to find Jace.

CHAPTER 8

MY DEAREST MAEKEL

Purple Ella tried to climb into Queen Mother Graelynd's lap but couldn't make the jump on the couch. With little effort, Graelynd leaned over and picked up the fuzzy exiguum. Ella curled next to Graelynd with her trunk resting on Graelynd's arm. Graelynd welcomed the distraction the tiny creature gave. The garden library's restoration was finished, but Graelynd still felt uneasy being in the room

where she almost lost her daughter and son-in-law. Now, she sat trying to organize the chaos of the disappearances.

She gathered with Adma, Adalina, Jadelyn, Brenna, and Lulana. They had composed a list of all the missing. Twenty Elysians were missing. She was relieved that no one else in the capitol nor anywhere else in Elysium had reported any missing persons. She wanted to do more. She wanted to ride out with the search parties but knew she had to remain inside the palace grounds.

Lady Novaly walked in carrying scrolls and books, and above her flew Maekel.

Graelynd stood. "Lady Novaly, how wonderful for you to join us. I had heard your studies were over and you would join us soon. I just didn't know it was this soon."

Lady Novaly set the scrolls and books on the small table before the fireplace and embraced Graelynd. She loved Graelynd. She was like a mother to her since her own mother passed away as a young girl. Novaly wore a flower crown of gardenias on top of her thick red hair, which was styled in two large braids with ribbons and flowers. She had pale skin with a beautiful, round face.

Novaly was of the Vinurs of the Court for Princess Siany. The rest of Siany's Vinurs were away studying in Port Rowlin. Novaly was the first to finish all the studies Princess Siany required. She was very intelligent but sometimes lacked awareness of reality.

"Dearest Queen Mother, how are you? I'm so sorry to hear about the disappearances."

Graelynd shook her head. "Going days without knowing if your family members are alive or dead is the worst form of torture, so any help you can offer is welcomed."

Novaly sat next to Graelynd and tickled Ella, who was delighted at the attention. She slung her trunk in Novaly's lap and waited for more pets and tickles. One of the many fascinating characteristics of exiguums was their laughter. They sounded like a child first learning he can laugh. Ella's fuzzy, purple trunk stretched across Novaly's rose gold dress, which was adorned with a light green sash and matching sheer sleeves. Adalina eyed her sleeves.

"Hello, Novaly. I'm Adalina. I'm part of Queen Sealyn's Vinurs of the Court. It's lovely to meet you."

Novaly smiled shyly. "It's a pleasure to meet you--to meet all of you."

"What a lovely dress. It matches your bright red hair," remarked Brenna. She eyed Lulana.

Lulana sneered. "What an interesting flower crown. Is that the fashion in Port Rowlin?" Brenna and Lulana giggled.

Novaly frowned. "No. It's my fashion."

"Ignore the pettiness of these two Vinurs," barked Jadelyn. "I think you're quite lovely, and that's probably what they're upset over. Jealousy. It's so childish."

The room gasped and stilled.

"Lady Jadelyn, may I remind you that in Elysium, the accusation of jealousy is the highest level of crime and is taken paranoidly serious," Graelynd scolded.

"My apologies, your majesty. I sometimes forget envy is Elysium's curse."

"What is Shunal's curse?" asked Adalina. "I always forget the curses for each kingdom."

Jadelyn shifted uncomfortably and rubbed her arms. Adalina thought she heard a weird sound coming from underneath where Jadelyn rubbed. Jadelyn's yellow eyes filled with tears. "Greed."

"No tears, darling," Graelynd comforted. "We don't let the past define us. Remember, you're a gift to this world, and the world needs you—all of you. Let's focus on finding everyone."

"Uh, majesty?" squeaked Maekel.

Graelynd's heart could barely take looking at Maekel. She knew how much Maekel loved Sealyn. "Yes, Maekel. How can I help?" Maekel's eyes teared up as she handed her a scroll with Sealyn's seal. Graelynd gasped. She tore it open, hoping this was news of where Sealyn was, but it was dated before they vanished. She read the scroll and began to weep. She looked up at Maekel, who was already crying.

Novaly reached out for the scroll. "May I?" Maekel nodded. Novaly began to read the scroll to the group.

My Dearest Maekel,

You are the ultimate companion, a sister of a different bloodline. My passion is for your heart's desire to be granted. I never want anything to stand in the way of your joy. I cannot discern how long this quest will take, and perceiving how much we do love each other, I know you would put off marrying Trit so that I could be in attendance. I cannot allow this. Maekel, I'm ordering you and Trit to participate in this year's Nicht wedding season. When I return, I want to see that you're married and hopefully with a little one ready to blossom. This is my royal decree and permission for you and Trit to be married. Now, sit and have a cup of tea before you pass out. I'll see you soon.

With Love and Adoration,

Queen Sealyn Araelian

Sniffs could be heard from each lady in the room. Maekel kept shaking her head. Graelynd tilted her head. "Maekel, there's only one thing we can do with this, and that is to obey the queen's orders."

"Majesty?"

"It means we must plan a royal wedding!"

King Father Ryker paced with his hands behind his back in the military courtyard. He hated waiting. Patience sometimes evaded him, especially when circumstances were out of his control. Lord Jdru approached his uncle.

"Any news?" Ryker questioned quickly.

Jdru shook his head. "The team is still not back. I'm sure they decided to cover more area, but I thought while we waited, you might want to spar?" Jdru handed Ryker his sword. Ryker's lip curved upward slightly and nodded. The two took their positions and began a friendly sword fight. Other soldiers began watching. They needed this distraction.

Horns blared, signaling the search party they had been waiting for was arriving. Several minutes later, the clatter of horse hooves entering the barracks echoed. The team consisted of twenty riders and one wagon for aiding possible wounded. The leader of the team dismounted his black horse and walked to Ryker.

He bowed. "King Father Ryker, we finally have news!"

Ryker smiled and squeezed the soldier's shoulder. "Captain Graegory, please continue with the news."

Graegory's green almond-shaped eyes sparkled. "Yes, majesty. We found the Elysian marker, and look what was buried below." He handed the scroll to Ryker.

Ryker's eyes scanned the letter for news of his daughter, but there was none. He read the note from Doebromir stating the names of his group and the other group. He was happy Jace and the rest of them were safe and unharmed, but his heart ached for news of Sealyn.

"Thank you, Captain Graegory. I am pleased with this news."

Graegory nodded. "I'm sorry Queen Sealyn still hasn't been found, but I'm confident our soldiers will find them."

"I agree. We have some of the best trackers in all seven kingdoms. I'm happy for you, Graegory," Ryker said while patting Graegory's shoulder. "I know Lady Pinx is your sister, so you must have been worried about her and Lord Favien."

Graegory swallowed the lump that had been forming in his throat. "Yes, majesty. I'm relieved to know she's safe." He hesitated but continued. "She asked me to escort her down the aisle for her wedding."

"Did she? Not your father?"

Graegory remembered the night after the Green Phoenixes won feydom. Pinx and Favien came late to his parent's house to celebrate. Favien passed out quickly in his father's rocking chair, so he and Pinx snuck into the kitchen, trying not to wake him. He remembered vividly his sweet sister asking him to walk her down the aisle. "She wants both. Pinx is sweet like that. I was so honored when she asked that I picked her up and twirled her around our parent's kitchen, then we knocked over Mother's fresh-baked apple pie. We laughed and ended up sitting on the floor and eating the pie," Graegory choked up, thinking about his sister and how he promised to protect her. "We talked all night about our hopes and dreams. She's my favorite person, so I don't ask this lightly, my king. I believe we should continue the Len

Nove mission. I ask you to send out all soldiers who were trained and assigned. Along the journey, we can have several scouting parties that will keep their distance from the main caravan that will keep searching for Queen Sealyn."

Ryker paced and looked at Jdru. He saw the concern in Jdru's eyes he had for Sealyn but also for his brother, Char. No matter how much those two fought, they had an unbreakable brotherly bond. Jdru nodded at his uncle.

"Very well. I will speak with the interim queen. In the meantime, ready everyone for the quest."

Jdru stepped forward. "I want to come too. Please don't argue. He's my brother, and Sealyn's like my sister."

"I can't argue with that!" Ryker mounted his horse and rode toward the palace. He wanted to join the search but could not disobey the queen's orders. He wrestled with his anger the whole ride. At the palace steps, he paused and released his anger. He accepted that as a parent—there comes a point in time when he must trust that he did his job preparing and teaching his daughter everything she needed to survive; whether she listened or not— well, that was a whole other thought that he did not want to deal with.

Queen Corentine,

The Fire and Ice Nicht slaves are working remarkably well. The ice that was on the streets has completely melted, along with the homes and shops. We found the catacombs. They are unlike anything we could have imagined. The old magic cannot be undone there yet.
The next shipments of the barrels of ice will depart by end of day. The Ice Nicht slaves are weak but capable of handling the journey. If you can send more Nichts, please do.
Source still evades us.

Loyally,
Commander Malum

CHAPTER 9
COMPLETE CHAOS

Finally, the end of the canyon was in sight. Doebromir pulled his horse to a halt and checked the map. They were only a half day's ride away from Sallen. He could almost taste the warm Puffin Pies and sweet ale. He recounted Char's stories and could not wait to experience *Betty's Boots* for himself. He was the first one at the end of the canyon to scout for anything unusual. Luckily, they only experienced *misps, the small, scaley creatures that live only on rocky terrain, and escaped their attacks with minor scratches.

Once the two caravans joined together, they all gave each other warm embraces, evaluated injuries, and took inventory of their supplies. They agreed Sallen would be the best place to replenish and get a good night's rest, then continue to Fort Kippen. Tilmond, Jace, and Doebromir took the lead and gave plenty of distance to have their private conversations.

"Now that we're out of earshot, Tilmond, what do you think happened?" asked Jace.

Tilmond shook his head. "All I've been able to put together is that whoever did the poisoning did enough not to kill us and split us up enough not to ruin the quest."

"Not to ruin the quest?!" repeated Jace. "You're under the impression that we can still complete the Len Nove quest?"

"Why not?" shrugged Tilmond. "We have a good crew, and there might be more of us waiting in Sallen. Fort Kippen's soldiers could also be helpful."

Jace's eyes narrowed. "You're missing the key factor, Tilmond. Sealyn! Where is she? She's the way the curse will be broken, but if she's not on the journey there or even alive…" His voice cracked, and his mind trailed off.

Jace remembered a sweet memory of him and his bride. He knew Sealyn had been struggling with flashbacks. The guilt of that day was all-consuming to him as well. He wanted to help

Sealyn find moments of peace, so he tasked the Ice Nichts with a special assignment. A shallow cave revealed itself at the very edge of the Ever-Changing Mountain after the arrival of the Green Phoenix. It was deep enough for shelter from a storm, which was perfect for what Jace had in mind.

Sealyn had her soldiers prepping day and night for winter weather, so Jace felt this particular secret would be justified. The Ice Nichts had perfected the art of snowmaking. They enjoyed freezing Avondelle's nearby lakes and creating feet of fresh snow for the local children to enjoy. The site of tiny hand-sized creatures flying with beautiful wings creating snow was stunning. The children loved experiencing the winter weather during their summer.

Jace made sure the cave and its surroundings were empty and well-guarded. The Ice Nichts made fluffy, white, glistening snow in front of the cave's entrance, then iced over the outside and inside of the cave. Jace laid out several furs to create a cozy and soft floor in the cave. He brought several of the blue fire flower vines and hung them across the ceiling, attaching them to the ice hooks the Nichts customized for him. Several candles were placed on the ice shelves of the walls, and candlelight danced along the ice glass.

Jace finished lighting the last candle when he heard her voice, "Jace?" Sealyn called from outside the cave.

He ran to the entrance, "Right this way, my love." He stretched out his hand. Sealyn's feet crunched on the snow as she reached Jace's hand. She giggled and grasped it.

"Jace, what is all this?"

Jace grinned mischievously. "Well, my queen, you've been so focused on ensuring our troops can handle fighting in the winter, but what about staying warm at night?" Jace lifted his eyebrows twice quickly.

Sealyn giggled, "Jace, you can't be serious. Here? Now?"

"I'm only trying to be a good student of my queen's training." He escorted her inside the blue-lit cave until their feet were on the furs.

Sealyn noticed Jace's bare feet on the fur blankets. Her heart skipped. She turned and faced him, "I do love it when a soldier is proactive." She stroked his cheek and stared into those mysterious grey eyes. Jace wrapped his arm around Sealyn's waist, pulling her close and breathed in her intoxicating scent of gardenias and coconut. Jace's fingers traced Sealyn's lips, then he pulled her chin, embracing his lips with hers.

The two fell into one of their many passionate kisses. They both felt the electricity running through their veins. Jace pulled away, smiling and then lifted Sealyn into his arms. He carried her deeper inside the beautiful cave. He laid her gently on the soft, welcoming blankets and tucked a small pillow under her head. His love for her grew deeper with every kiss, every smile, every breath. His body needed her.

The royals locked in and focused on each other, not noticing the green glow in Sealyn's palms. Their passion even kept them from seeing the cave's end glowing with blue and green swirls.

"Jace!" yelled Doebromir. Jace shook his head. "Jace, are you hearing me?"

Jace blinked in confusion. "No, what did you say?"

"I said, you can't think that way. Sealyn is resourceful. She will know how to take care of herself. I'm sure the royal guard is already looking for her and may have even found her by now."

Jace nodded as tears welled up in his eyes. He wanted to go back to that memory and live there. He wished they had never left that cave. He promised himself that if he found her, he would take her back there immediately.

Favien raced to the front. "Tilmond, look behind the caravan! Is that a swarm of misps?"

Tilmond jerked his head and stared at the cluster of flying creatures approaching them. He looked ahead and could see Sallen. They were so close to safety and a soft bed. He squinted hard to see what the swarm was. "Those can't be misps. They've been in the air too long."

"Wait," Doebromir said. "Do you hear that? It sounds like the air creatures are saying something."

The cluster was approaching fast, too fast for them to make it to Sallen. Tilmond ordered the group to form defenses and wait for the pursuers. Finally, the caravan realized the flying creatures were Nichts- Earth Nichts.

Obeesi spoke first. "Greetings. Are you from Avondelle? Perhaps in search of Queen Sealyn?"

Jace's heart leaped. "Yes. Who are you?"

"I am Obeesi of the Glinstone Clan. Queen Sealyn sent us to find you and deliver a message. Would King Jace be among you?"

Jace choked on his words and thought his heart would beat out his chest. "I am King Jace." Saying "king" still felt like eating cotton to him, but he was slowly getting used to it.

All five Nichts bowed their heads and fluttered their wings. "Your majesty," Obeesi started, "It is an honor to meet you." He handed the scroll to Jace.

Jace opened the scroll eagerly and read aloud:

My dearest Jace,

My fear is that this letter won't find you, but my hope tells me it will. First, I love you, and second, I'm safe and healthy. You won't believe who I'm stuck with. I have no doubt if the Glinstone Clan Nichts found you, then you're heading toward Sallen, or they found you there. We are coming to Sallen, too. Wait for us there, and we will journey together to Fort Kippen.

And one more ridiculous request, because the two I'm stuck with won't shut up unless I write this: have four large ales waiting on Lord Char and Lord Sakul because they need them all.

All my undying love,

Queen Sealyn Araelien of Elysium

Sorcha burst out with a squeal and laughter, and the rest of the group joined. "Can you imagine what Sealyn has been going through with Char and Sakul?" asked Sorcha. She laughed more with tears of joy streaming down her ebony cheeks.

"All I know is now I want to celebrate, and now we can with the ease that our queen is safe!" cheered Doebromir.

"Someone should go back with the Glinstone Nichts to help protect Queen Sealyn," Jem advised with flashing red eyes.

Tilmond nodded. "Excellent idea. Jem and Stawyer, come with me to escort the queen to Sallen. Favien, Doebromir, Max, please lead the rest of the caravan to Sallen and protect King Jace," He saw Jace shaking his head. "*King* Jace," Tilmond emphasized the word "king." "You have a responsibility, and so do we. You will be reunited with her soon, but you must let us do our jobs to protect the kingdom."

This was the part of being king that Jace did not like. He reluctantly nodded his head, and the two groups parted ways. Jace felt hopeful and clutched the letter tightly as they rode toward Sallen. His mouth had a slight smile, knowing he was soon to see his bride, and as a bonus, Char and Sakul would be joining the journey.

Siany shifted her stance in front of the large crowd gathered in front of the palace. She hated giving speeches. She had no idea how Sealyn did this. Vomit loomed in her throat. This was also the exact reason she did not want to be queen: sending people to die for a cause. The crowd stilled, and a hush fell over everyone as Siany approached the royal family.

Her long, brown braid cascaded down her chest, and she breathed deeply. "My fellow Elysians." She began strongly, but then she heard a noise. It was obviously a recognizable noise to the hundreds of military men and women standing before her because they all turned around in unison. The royal guard drew their swords, and Captain Graegory yelled for the army to do the same.

Siany's mind went fuzzy. Were they preparing for battle? Surely not. Their borders would have stopped anyone from entering. Her mind was refusing to accept reality. Even the sight of hundreds of Stoltland soldiers sprinting toward her military would not snap her out of the denial. Lord Aerrick, Lady Raquel's husband, ran to Queen Regent Siany, scooped her into his arms, and ran inside the palace. Captain Graegory ushered King Father Ryker and Queen Mother Graelynd to follow Lord Aerrick. The rest of the royal family and Vinurs ran with Graegory.

Graegory barred the palace doors and turned to face the royals. His eyes caught sight of blood on Ryker's clothes. "My King!" Graegory yelled. "Are you hurt?"

Ryker looked down and saw the blood. He patted himself. "No, this isn't from me. Is anyone hurt?"

A groan and grunt came from the back of the crowded entryway. "That would be me, majesty." Prince Adomin walked slowly forward, holding his left shoulder, where an arrow was lodged in. Blood streamed down his arms and dripped off his fingers. Adomin's wife, Princess Nanceline, took her gloves off and pressed around the wound.

"Where's Dun?" asked Ryker.

Siany's head dropped. "He's gone."

"Gone?" Ryker yelled.

Siany shivered. "Yes, he and Lady Zuri left early this morning. He somehow spoke to my mind and said he would return when Zuri is safe with the others."

Ryker started pacing. "This is complete chaos!"

"Queen Regent Siany, I ask that we take everyone to safer ground," Lord Aerrick pushed. They paused and could hear the screams and swords clanging together. They had no idea who was winning. Siany froze. What was she supposed to say? Where were they supposed to go? Were they surrounded? She saw her father, who was still shaking his head, then she looked at her mother. Graelynd locked eyes with her and smiled.

"May I make a suggestion?" cooed Graelynd. Siany nodded. "Here's how this will go. Lord Aerrick, you will escort Queen Regent Siany, her cousins—Auralia, Saemelina, and Anadelvia, Kipnor, and the Vinurs of the Court to the old war room. Jdru, you will go with them and protect your cousin at all costs."

Ryker paused. "My love, Sealyn sealed the entrances to that room."

Graelynd chuckled. "You're still her Papa Bear, aren't you?" She cupped her hand to his cheek. "My dear, yes, she sealed off the old entrances, but your daughter created a new entrance. She thought her old mother wouldn't know, but a mother knows all about her daughter." She looked amused. "Next group, the Araelien bloodline—Lord Marin, Lady Ebbalee, Ryland, Shaenna, Lezlin, Quinten, Tintallina, and you, my love, Ryker. Lady Raquel will accompany this group through the ugly lady portrait and work with Lezlin on anyone who may incur injuries. Cian, you will be their protector."

Cian nodded but hated to be away from his wife, Lady Auralia, and his children, but he knew duty came first. He wondered if his skills as a Tackler in feydom would become assets in this fight.

Graelynd continued, "Lastly, the Dovinus bloodline—Grand Queen Karis, mother, please go with Kolt, who will escort Adomin, Nanceline, Royce, Toven, and Jaequel. Brandle and Menry, you both are the most skilled with surgeries, so you will be with this group as well. Please tend to my brother. We will go to the secret chamber below the gardens through the kitchen."

"Majesties!"

They all jumped at the sound of Maekel's greeting. "Maekel! Oh, good, you're safe," Siany sighed in relief. She was more overjoyed when she saw Trit, Milola, her chamber Nicht, and Rayn, her mother's chamber Nicht, flittering together in front of them.

"We cannots send for helps. The Stoltlanders are shootings down any Nichts that flies. We ares the targets," Maekel choked on her words.

Siany realized exactly what kind of attack this was. Stoltland came to take out the communication lines—the Nichts. Once they had achieved this, Avondelle would be completely vulnerable, and no one would know to come help.

"Maekel, make sure no more Nichts fly outside of these walls. We need to protect you all. Graegory, go to the roofs and see what soldiers are left. We need to know what is happening outside. Take Trit with you. Once you have the report, Trit will immediately come to me with the update, then to the other groups. Trit, you must always stay unseen." Trit nodded, and his brown eyes sparkled with bravery. "We've already wasted too much time. Everyone go!"

The groups took off running to their assigned locations. Graegory and Trit zoomed to the roof. Maekel and her companions went with Siany. Maekel wanted to make sure to keep her promise to Sealyn. Sealyn made her swear that if anything happened to her, then Maekel would keep Siany safe. She felt slightly uncomfortable that Sealyn had concluded the conversation with the words, "Also, Maekel, I know your Nicht secret, and because of that very secret, I know you are the only one who can shield my sister from death." Maekel worried, not because Sealyn knew her secret, but because the crown's life could one day fall into her hands. Would she be able to do what Sealyn thought she could?

Maekel's thoughts were interrupted by the two black armored soldiers in the garden library and a knife soaring through the air toward Siany.

CHAPTER 10
WHAT'S A TOR?

Jace paced outside Betty's Boots. He refused to go inside and celebrate without Sealyn. He needed physical proof she was unharmed. He could hear the others inside cheering and was happy they were enjoying themselves. Finally, his heart heard the clapping of Sallen's citizens. He knew they were celebrating their queen's arrival. Everyone inside Betty's Boots came stumbling outside to join in the cheering.

When Sealyn's caravan rounded the corner, Jace was the only person she saw in the crowd. Her face beamed with a huge smile, and she waved to him. She wanted to gallop to him but was afraid she would trample someone in the crowd, so she counted the seconds. She was about to be back in her love's arms finally.

Music began to play loudly once they were in front of the tavern. Sealyn dismounted her horse and flew into Jace's arms. She breathed in his scent of pine and leather. She did not realize how much her body needed him. How was it possible to miss someone this much? She wanted everyone to go away so that they could have a private moment. She knew it was not queen-like to show such affection in front of the public, but she threw the rules out of her head and pulled his face to hers. Their lips collided with passion and met with cheers from the people.

"I'm not about to stand outside my favorite tavern and watch you suck lips with our king, Sealyn!" Char mocked. "I have ales to drink, bread to eat, and women to…" Sealyn glared at Char. Char grinned. "And women to respect and treat to a lovely celebratory dinner."

Doebromir smacked Char on the shoulder. "First round's on me! Let's get to drinking, my friend!" The group gathered inside

Betty's Boots and took their time enjoying the savory food and fresh ales. Sealyn watched Jace laugh- real laughs. She loved that sound more than anything. She felt a chill run down her spine and looked out the window. A large shadow passed by. She knew that shadow. She leapt out of her chair and ran out the door, with her companions trailing after her.

Dun landed gracefully, yet the crowds of people still scattered at his intimidating sight. He slanted his wing for Zuri to slide down. She stood beside Dun in her dark blue leathers, looking like a fierce ice warrior.

"Dun! Zuri!" exclaimed Sealyn. "You're here!" She ran to Zuri with a hug, and then Dun wrapped his wings around Sealyn. She needed the feeling of his fortress wings. They were such a comfort to her. Sealyn stuttered through her words. "How? Why? What are you doing here? Are you well?"

Zuri laughed. "I'll take one question at a time, majesty. Yes, I've fully healed, all thanks to Dun." She turned and stroked a green feather. "We came ahead of your army. They were to leave for Len Nove by mid-day, so we left early to catch up."

Dun stiffened and locked eyes with Sealyn. The chill went down her spine again. She knew. "Go," was all Sealyn could get out before Dun took to the sky, heading for Avondelle in green flames.

"What was that about?" asked Max.

Sealyn looked to Tilmond. "Is there a room where we can all gather privately?"

A raspy, old voice spoke up. "I have a manor prepared for you and your guests, majesty."

"Betty!" cheered Char. "I was wondering if I'd see you. Come here, you gorgeous silver fox. I need some sugar."

Betty chuckled. "Oh, Char, you old scoundrel. He always makes me feel like I'm a young lady again."

"Thank you, Madam Betty," Sealyn said. "We would be most appreciative if you could lead us there."

Siany watched as the dagger sliced right through her heart and stuck into a book behind her. Her hand patted frantically at her chest, but there was no blood. She was confused. Was she dead? She looked at the soldier who had thrown the knife, and he looked just as puzzled as she did. He was looking not at her but at the knife sticking out of the book's spine.

"Where'd they go?" the dark-skinned soldier asked his comrade.

The other soldier removed his helmet, revealing bright blonde curls, and grabbed his knife from the book. "They were just here. How does a group vanish?"

"Corentine will kill us if we don't figure this out."

"Sweep this library clean. They must be here. I mean, we did see them come in here, right?"

"What if it was a spell? Someone made it look like we saw them to distract us?"

The Stoltland soldier scratched his blonde curls, and his black eyes sparkled. "That must be it. The little green witch cast a spell. Let's head to the next room." The two soldiers ran cautiously out of the library.

Maekel let out a deep breath, gasping for air. All eyes blinked in wonder. Siany wanted to discuss what just happened, but she motioned for everyone to silently follow her to the secret entrance to the old war room. Once they entered the room, Siany whirled on Maekel. "Maekel, you're a Translucent!" The room gasped.

Maekel's eyes filled with tears. "Majesty, please, please don'ts be upsets with me. I didn't wants anyone to knows."

"Maekel, there's nothing to be ashamed about. Your powers are some of the greatest powers recorded. Why would you not want anyone to know?" Siany questioned.

Maekel dropped her head. "Most of my kind weres forced on the fronts lines of battles or spies. I didn't wants that life, so I tries to keep it hiddens. I wanted to ones day be ables to decide for myself what to do withs my power, but it wasn't untils the last day I saws Queen Sealyn that I realized she hads been givings me that choice all alongs. She knews my secret and let me stays quiet about it. She nevers questioned me, nevers forced me to do anythings I didn't wants to. She asked me to protects you. She believeds I was strong enoughs, but I wasn't sures."

A tear slid down Siany's cheek. "You were very brave, Maekel, and you saved us all. Thank you."

Maekel smiled. "I can't creates a protection shield very fars, only ins close spaces. Since I was ables to touch you and you weres holding onto everyone else, we all becames translucent."

"Wow, that's amazing," cheered Novaly. She flipped her red braids behind her and hugged Siany. "Now what?"

Siany let out a sigh. "Now, we wait, but let's wait very close to each other just in case Maekel needs to save us again."

"You're serious? You're actually serious?" roared Max.

"Yes, this has to be done," snapped Tilmond. He stood from the brown couch and warmed himself before the fireplace. He towered a foot over everyone, so his presence was deafening.

Finn's blue eyes sparkled in the firelight. He looked at Zuri and then to Max. "Please, Max. Len Nove needs us. The curse must be broken."

Max shook his head. "I'm not questioning whether the curse should be broken or not. I agree that it needs to be. I'm questioning the sanity of going there with this group and no army to back us up." He leaned back on the brown leather couch and crossed his muscular arms. Max did not want to back down. He felt such loyalty to provide the safest plan of attack for the queen.

Sealyn leaned against a corner, watching her friends and comrades heatedly discuss the quest. Standing in corners was how she first learned to read rooms when her father was king. She could tell the room was divided. Some wanted to return home and start the quest with the army, but she knew from Dun that the capitol needed the army more than she did. Others wanted to continue forward and not lose time, and then there were Char and Sakul, who just wanted to stay in Sallen to eat and drink. What was the right move? She gazed around the room. The answer was here.

She looked at the clusters of people forming. Those who were extremely good at being stealthy: Jace, Finn, Pinx, Ashur, Zuri, Rivers, and Madilina. They could easily sneak around without being seen. The brute force: Tilmond, Doebromir, Stawyer, Jem, Favien, and Max. These men were trained in the ultimate combat skills. It was like having five men per one. If she needed diplomatic help, then she had Norella, Sorcha, and Jashun. Ezen and Rielen were amazing trackers, so navigation would not be a problem. They could do this. A smaller force might just be the way to win this battle. She knew what to do with Char and Sakul as well.

"That's enough," Sealyn said dryly. "We're going to Len Nove, and this is the group to break the curse." Sealyn gave a sly leer to Char.

Char froze. "O, for all the curses in the land, you have got to be kidding me!"

Graegory's arms felt heavy as he swung his sword again and again and again. The Stoltland soldiers seemed to keep appearing. He lost his three men who were guards for the far-right tower. It was just him. He slashed through another soldier, making him lifeless before he hit the ground. He left his sword in the dead soldier. Graegory thought he would have a moment to breathe until he saw two more soldiers enter the tower's rooftop. His shoulder was bleeding badly. He could barely lift it. The curly blonde soldier lunged forward, but Graegory managed to fend off the blow with his shield, but the other dark-skinned soldier quickly stabbed him in the thigh. He fell to his knees in agonizing pain and dropped his shield.

The two Stoltland soldiers walked in front of Graegory, laughing.

"How does it feel, little bird, knowing you're about to die?" They both chuckled.

The blonde-haired man moved his face almost nose to nose to Graegory. "Where's your Green Phoenix? No one to protect you now. What lies people spread about your mythological creature!" He smacked Graegory's face.

Graegory tried not to make a sound. He would not give them the satisfaction. He looked around, wishing for a weapon to be near him, but there was nothing--nothing but dead bodies and blood pools. He looked up and remembered the story of the twelve martyrs. They died this way. They died for a cause they believed in, and he was proud to die the same way. The dark soldiers drew back their weapons and prepared to swing, but a loud screech echoed throughout the territory. The screech was so forceful that it sent the two Stoltland soldiers flying off the tower, plunging to their deaths below.

Graegory blinked. The sound did not affect him. He looked up and saw Dun soaring above. Dun let out another blistering screech, and Graegory looked below and watched as blood poured from the Stoltland soldiers' eyes and ears. This gave the Elysians enough time to kill the remaining soldiers. The battle was finally over.

Graegory hobbled as fast as he could to Dun. The giant phoenix stood in front of the palace with sad, yellow eyes.

Graegory dropped on his hands and knees in front of Dun. "Dun, I'm so glad to see you." Dun nudged Graegory's head and wrapped one of his wings around him. Graegory felt his wounds healing. What great power this phoenix had.

"Thanks, Dun. I feel much better. I must go find the royal family," Graegory stood to leave, but Dun snapped his beak. "It's ok, Dun. I know I'm not completely healed. I'll return for more healing once I know the royal family is safe. You heal as many wounded soldiers as you can out here." Dun nodded.

Upon entering the palace, Graegory found the royal family and the Vinurs of the Courts gathering in the throne room. He was relieved that everyone was safe. "Majesties. I bring news. Dun has arrived. The battle is over, but at a great loss."

King Father Ryker shook his head. "How many?"

"Unknown, my king," responded Graegory. His almond-shaped eyes filled with tears.

Siany placed her hand on Graegory's shoulder. "Thank you, Captain Graegory. Your valiant efforts helped save our people. We must gather as much information as possible and see to the wounded. We will honor the fallen."

Hours later, the remaining War Council and the Council of Wisdom gathered. Fear and frustration echoed in everyone's words. Prince Royce watched each expression with concern. They were losing the morale battle. He needed to quickly think of a distraction to help contain the panic swirling in the room.

Prince Royce cleared his throat, "May I have the room to speak?" The room fell silent. "Thank you. I received a letter two days ago from my son, Lord Prince William." All eyes shifted in confusion. "He wrote for me to inform the royal family that he and my wife will be testing the new ships. He has several new designs that are all very promising. I expect great results."

"Thank you, uncle," Princess Siany nodded. "But what does that have to do with our predicament?"

He chuckled. "Absolutely nothing, but let's focus our minds on progress. The rest of the kingdom is still moving forward. Most likely, no one knows what we have faced yet. We can't lose focus because we're panicking."

Queen Mother Graelynd walked in carrying a tray full of sliced lemons. "I couldn't agree more, brother. After hearing all the arguing, I went to the kitchen to fetch what we needed." Siany squirmed in her chair. She knew what her mother was doing. "Everyone, take three slices of lemon." All obeyed. "Now, take a bite of the first slice." Their eyes grew wide and again obeyed. Sounds of spitting and scrunched faces were at each seat. "Now, what is the first task to complete?"

King Father Ryker enjoyed lemons, so he was the first to speak. "We need to establish exactly how these foul humans are invading our lands. They aren't crossing our borders, so how are they doing it?"

"I seem to recall reading several of the old magic scrolls that spoke about Tors," Lord Stev said.

Lord Ryland tilted his head. "What's a Tor?"

"A Tor is a special gate or bridge to other kingdoms," Stev informed. "They were created from the high enchantresses for faster access to each other. According to the old texts, each Tor is marked with the colors of the kingdoms."

"That's it!" exclaimed Ryker. "Stoltland must have figured out where their Tor for Elysium is. We must find it. If these Tors did not exist until after the old magic was released from Sealyn breaking our curse, then it must be among the several unveiled objects or landscapes."

Royce nodded. "Agreed. This is the first task. Identify all Tors of the kingdom, not just Stoltland's."

"Yes, send out several trackers to find the Tors, and Lord Stev, you will oversee searching the old texts for clues of their whereabouts. You may uncover a map. Take as many people with you that you'll need to get this done."

Graelynd smiled. "Great. Now, bite lemon number two."

Lord Quinten, Ryker's youngest brother, moaned. "Why are we doing this?"

"It's a focus technique. The sour taste distracts your thoughts enough for you to focus on the needed task, which has already worked. So, bite the lemon, Quinten, and get to thinking." Graelynd giggled. This reminded her of younger Siany and Sealyn, trying to finish their studies, but neither could stay focused. Her lemon technique was the trick, and watching her daughters' faces was very entertaining. She gazed proudly at Siany, but her heart ached for Sealyn. She wanted to protect her, and she had no way of knowing if she was safe. She knew she raised a strong daughter and needed to trust that.

Commander Malum,

You will have more Nicht slaves coming. We attacked Avondelle through our Tor. Though we lost several soldiers in the attack, our mission was a success. We managed to locate a large nest south of Avondelle. This particular nest was unnoticed by the palace, so it will take some time before they're reported missing.

With that said, I'm living up to my end of your request. Now, you need to deliver on my orders. Find the source!

Majestically, ,
Queen Corentine of Stoltland and the seven kingdoms

CHAPTER 11
THE SHIVERS

After four days of solid riding and barely sleeping, Queen Sealyn's comrades finally could see Fort Kippen in sight. The fort was ginormous. The walls stood forty feet high and were made from massive trees, with sharp points at the top. Three layers of tree trunks solidified with mud, sand, and clay created thick, impenetrable walls. Enemies could not figure out how to enter the fort, for there was no door. Fort Kippen never allowed outside guests to visit inside the walls, but what did exist inside was a thriving village.

Char leaned to Sakul and whispered, "Want to take bets on how we get through those walls?"

"No, Char! You already made me lose half my coins at that last card game at Betty's Boots. I'm not going to lose anything else to you."

"Silence, you two," hissed Sealyn. "We're being watched." Char and Sakul froze. Sealyn dismounted her horse and pulled the hood from her head. "You can come out now. We come in peace."

Two large figures cloaked in white furs rose from the ground. Char's mouth fell open. "They were right in plain sight!" Sealyn glared at Char.

The first stranger had long, black, twisted locks and ebony skin. His green eyes looked wild, like he had been in the wilderness for longer than any human should. He walked slowly to Sealyn. Jace quickly dismounted and stood beside her while Tilmond and Doebromir stood behind her.

"I am Ajorn, and this is Sune," Ajorn pointed to his pale, red-bearded companion. "Who might you all be?" He looked pleased with himself.

Sealyn smiled back. "Have the years really worn that much against me, Ajorn? It's me, Sealyn."

Ajorn let out a loud laugh. "I knew it was you! I was joking." He bowed. "I guess I should say Queen Sealyn now. You're much too royal for us to use our ol' nickname for you."

Char quickly slid into view. "Oh, please use the old nickname. I would just love to hear it."

"Don't you dare, Ajorn!"

The red, curly-headed Sune chuckled a grunt and said, "Penguin."

Char fell into a fit of laughter along with Sakul and the rest of the group. "Well, it's the gallows for you, Sune. Soon to be forgotten." Sealyn shot back at him.

"Good wordplay, Sealyn. I mean Queen Sealyn," Ajorn quickly corrected. "I assume you're here for the mission?" Sealyn nodded. "Then let's get you all inside. I'm sure you're freezing and in need of a proper meal. Where's the rest of the army?"

"That story will be told after a fresh ale," Sealyn patted Ajorn on the shoulder.

Ajorn and Sune escorted them to the far right of the main wall. Everyone in the caravan except Sealyn was confused. Ajorn looked back. "Everyone brace yourselves!" He looked up to the high tower at the corner and yelled the words, "All or none!" The ground began to shake, and the horses shifted their stances. The platform they were standing on slowly slanted downward, opening to a tunnel below the fort.

Ajorn enjoyed giving tours of the tunnels to new recruits, so he immediately began retelling the fort's history. "We have several levels of tunnel workings under the fort. Each level is reinforced with lumber and stone columns, and every level has a large meeting room for occupants of that level to enjoy. We are currently on level one, so it's a quick journey to the top."

They unloaded their horses and carts before entering the main floor. They were tired and needed rest and food, but their spirits lifted when Ajorn opened the massive green iron doors. Fort Kippen looked like a miniature version of Avondelle. Beautiful, tented booths, indoor bakeries, taverns, shops, and more were everywhere. Large copper cauldrons were stationed sporadically with warm, cracking fires, and above were several bridges that linked end to end but only for military purposes. The fort's perimeter was highly guarded with the latest technologies from Lord Prince William.

Centered at the far end of the fort was the grand banquet hall--home to Sealyn's childhood best friend, Lady Aellizzabelle, also known as Lizz. Sealyn's heart leapt once she saw the banquet hall. She was moments away from being reunited with her friend. The last time they were together was during Feydom. Sealyn chuckled to herself, remembering Lizz telling the tale of her running from the snakes she had mistakenly buried herself with.

Ajorn motioned for them to follow him. "Come. The general is waiting for you, and a table is being prepared. We were worried because you're two weeks late."

"A queen is never late," Sealyn jeered.

Sune laughed. "Still Punctual Penguin, I see."

They walked into the large banquet hall made of large oak columns and red brick floor and walls. They weren't expecting this. Three white marble fireplaces were evenly spaced around the square room. Couches and rugs were in front of each fireplace, welcoming their tired muscles. The center of the room had two long tables forming a "T," piled high with endless food and wine. They heard shouting, then loud sounds of running. "Stop that! Don't you do it! I'm warning you! Don't you dare jump—" Before the concerned mother could finish her sentence, two small boys leapt from the upstairs banister onto the banner ropes and slid down.

"Aunt Sea! Aunt Sea! Aunt Sea!" the young boys chanted in unison.

Char whispered to Favien, "Are those horrendous creatures saying 'antsy' or 'Aunt Sea?'" Favien laughed.

Sealyn kneeled and opened her arms wide, and quickly was tackled by Lizz's sons. Lizz ran down the stairs with her husband following behind.

"Queen Sealyn, I'm so sorry. They overheard me say you were here, and then I couldn't catch them." Lizz panted.

"No need to worry. These two are always forgiven." She gave them another squeeze, then stood and embraced her friend. "I've missed you. We have so much to discuss."

Music played softly while they feasted. Sitting across from Ajorn and Sune, Favien and Doebromir clinked goblets each time they began another ale. Sorcha savored the hot soup for her throat and blushed each time Sakul's hand brushed against hers. Sorcha was happy that Sakul came on the journey and seemed to be enjoying himself. She watched him laughing with Char, Ashur, and Max and could not help but smile. She was nervous about

Sealyn's plan, though, mainly because Sealyn had yet to share any details.

Jashun grumbled to himself while he ate. He felt insulted having to sit at the end of the table with the trackers. He did not care that Ezen and Rielen were of royal blood. They were just trackers. He should be sitting near Favien, listening to what the king and queen were discussing.

Sealyn stood and clapped her hands to silence the room. "I hate to interrupt your enjoyment, but I wanted to discuss strategies with General Matticus and Lady Lizz openly." A servant walked in quickly, handed the general a note, then scurried out. "General, is everything well?"

"Yes, majesty," Matticus pushed his spectacles up his nose. "I just received word that our commander and his scouting party have just returned with valuable information for you. He should be walking in momentarily."

A few strands of brown hair fell in front of Tilmond's face as he leaned to Jace and whispered, "Majesty, we will want to convince this commander to join us." Jace nodded in agreement.

The doors burst open, allowing the cold air to pierce through the warmth of the fires. In walked Commander Brehan. He stood six and a half feet tall and broad with solid muscle. He had long, sandy blonde hair twisted in rows and held in place with leather strips. His blonde beard still held flakes of snow, which matched the layers of white fur he was wearing. He had that same wildness in his green eyes that Ajorn did, except his had something that looked like pain in them. The ladies used only a few words to describe him: fiercely handsome.

Norella's mouth went dry at the sight of Brehan. She had trouble catching her breath. Their eyes locked, and she felt as though time decided to stand still, just for them, and then it was over. He blinked, kept walking to the head table, and sat next to General Matticus. Norella started breathing heavily and chugged the remaining wine in her goblet.

Pinx noticed Norella's behavior. "Norella, are you well?"

"I'm fine. Perfectly fine. Why wouldn't I be?"

"Well, maybe because your face is pink, your breathing is rapid, and you're chugging northern wine. Don't you know how strong the wine is up here?"

Norella's eyes widened, and she peered into her empty goblet. "I think bad decisions will be made tonight."

Zuri and Rivers laughed. Rivers finally caught her breath and said, "I think she has what Adalina says is called 'the shivers.'"

"I do not have the shivers over Commander Brehan!"

Pinx giggled. "Who said anything about him?"

Sorcha shushed the girls because Sealyn was getting to the part about her plan for Sakul and Char. They had already discussed the discoveries of Brehan, and now, it was Sealyn's turn.

"So your plan is to walk through the front doors of the palace and be welcomed in?" Brehan said incredulously. He shook his head at Ajorn and Sune. "Exactly how do you expect that to work, majesty?"

Sealyn stared at Char and Sakul with her sly smile. "With two drunk idiots."

Char stood up, pointing at Sealyn. "I knew it! You're going to use us as bait!"

"Precisely."

Siany's eyes teared up as she watched Maekel and Trit kiss to become husband and wife. Their sparkling wings fluttered with excitement. The palace court and Nichts cheered loudly. They all needed this. After such death and blood, celebrating something happy was the start of mending broken hearts. The timing was perfect for Maekel and Trit to join the Nicht Nexgen season. Elysians loved the ending of Nexgen. At the end of the season, hundreds of tiny Nichts are born from the Emangaton Flower.

The Emangaton Flower has hard outer petals that look like a tulip. These hard petals form a protective shell to keep the Nicht embryo safe and warm during the winter. Inside the shell are soft petals that are in circular rows like rose petals. The center has sticky, sponge-like tentacles that latch onto the embryo, keeping it in place and providing the nutrients it needs to grow. The entire flower collects sunshine, rain, salts, and minerals for the tiny Nicht. The roots even collect chitin from the fungi for the development of wings and scales for the wings.

As the weather warms, the outer petals fall, and the flower begins blooming. When spring arrives, all the developed baby Nichts flutter out of their flowers, creating a masterpiece of colors dancing in the sky. The joy on each parent's face is perfection. Celebrations last for days, bringing a fresh perspective on life.

Siany walked to the special Nicht tea table, where Maekel was seated with her family and friends. Maekel had her tea set from Sealyn on display but refused to use it. She only wanted to use that with Sealyn.

"Maekel, may I just say that you are a radiant bride, and I'm so happy for you both," Siany cooed.

Maekel blushed. "Thank yous, majesty! This is the happiest I'ves evers been!"

Adalina and Jadelyn joined Siany. "I bet you can't wait to start fertilizing," Adalina joked.

Maekel squeaked in embarrassment. Siany elbowed Adalina. "Adalina! Don't say that in front of Maekel's father!"

"My apologies," Adalina winked at Maekel, then locked arms with Jadelyn and skipped away to the dance floor.

"And on that uncomfortable exit, I did want to inform you that the Emangaton Flowers are almost ready. Lady Raquel has been preserving and tending to them nicely. Another week and the petals will be ready to accept," Siany tried not to blush at the insinuation.

The music stopped, and the crowd hushed as Queen Mother Graelynd walked to the center of the dance floor for an announcement.

"My fellow Elysians, I would like to announce that the bride and groom request everyone to join in on their first dance as a married couple, but before the music starts, I must share Queen Sealyn's gift to Maekel and Trit. Would you both join me?"

Maekel and Trit fluttered beside Graelynd. Tears started forming in Maekel's eyes. She had no idea how it was possible for Sealyn to send her a gift, especially since she had no knowledge about the wedding.

"Maekel and her esteemed family have been working tirelessly on saving the lives of so many Nichts from slavery from the pro-slavery kingdoms. We support those efforts. Queen Sealyn was made aware of such efforts many moons ago, and since then, she has been preparing homes and jobs for all displaced Nichts."

"What?" squeaked Maekel. She was in shock.

Graelynd giggled. "Yes, Maekel. We now have dedicated the amber tree grounds as a sanctuary for all formerly enslaved Nichts to live and recover." The amber trees were massive in circumference and height. They glowed amber at night from absorbing the sunlight, keeping predators at bay. "Some of the local Earth Nichts have been volunteering to carve beautiful spacious homes inside the trees, and *A Brother's Bond* has donated tables, kitchenware, and chairs for outdoor eating and cooking. Madam Bip and Lady Raquel have volunteered to teach gardening, and we have several volunteers to teach at the new school, such as Princess Siany, Lady Novaly, and Lady Pinx.

Queen Sealyn wanted you to know that all of Elysium will do what we must to ensure they have every opportunity to feel loved, wanted, and safe."

Maekel burst into tears. Her queen knew her too well. She did not want trinkets. She wanted her kind safe, and Sealyn gave her that. She missed her and wanted desperately to thank her. Trit hugged his beautiful wife and started softly spinning her.

"Let's dance, my beautiful wife. It's time to celebrate our new lives and the lives you've saved," Trit whispered. Maekel smiled and nodded. The band immediately started playing one of Elysium's favorite songs, and everyone joined the happy couple.

The room filled with joy and relief. Thankfully, Dun's recount of seeing Sealyn had given the royal family renewed hope, so they allowed themselves to enjoy the wedding celebration fully.

The Gelida Seas
Zykoan Port
Zelkath Port
Len Nove
Pantorian
Tholgerton
Ciderton
Golden Lake
Fort Kippen
Avondelle
Sallen
Elysium

CHAPTER 12

CIDERTON

Lady Zuri walked softly down the stairs toward the banquet hall dining area. The aroma of bacon, eggs, and fresh pastries filled her nose. She finished fastening her silver cape clasp and allowed the white rabbit fur to warm her against the cold morning air. She was glad all four fireplaces were roaring their heat. This might be the last royal breakfast they have for a while.

"Good morning, Lady Zuri," Char stood with a bow. "Care to join us for a fine breakfast?"

Zuri shook her head and laughed. "Your charms are starting early today, Char." She took the seat next to him.

"Well, fate has smiled upon me. I wished for a beautiful lady to sit next to me this morning, and look, you have arrived." Char bounced his eyebrows. Doebromir threw his half-eaten pastry at Char. "Watch it, Doebromir. I wouldn't want you to catch the reputation of wasting food."

Doebromir leaned his head back and gave a big laugh. "I doubt anyone would believe that rumor."

Sealyn stared down from the balcony, watching her friends enjoy their breakfast. Today would be hard for them to walk away from comfort and into the icy wilderness. She was asking them to risk their lives. They really had no idea what they would encounter. Blind faith is all she had. Lady Lizz leaned against the railing next to Sealyn. She nudged her to get a smile.

"All right, Sealyn. I've known you long enough to know when you're holding something back. You might as well share it with me now." Lizz took a bite of her Puffin pie.

Sealyn dropped her head and sighed heavily. "O, Lizz. You did always know me best." She lifted her head and began retelling Tybalt's betrayal and death, the mysterious way they began the quest, Dun's communication to her about Stoltland's attack, her doubts about Jashun's loyalty, and her fears of Stoltland's plans. "And lastly," Sealyn paused.

Lizz inhaled. "O, good, there's more."

"I'm a Luxen."

"A what 'en'?"

Sealyn snorted. "A Lux-en."

"Yes, you will have to explain that one."

"Someone who can channel and use the old magic for good. An undoer of the dark magic, if you will."

Lizz nodded slowly. "That's good, though, right?"

Sealyn shrugged. "To be honest, I'm not exactly sure. I can't control it. I tried channeling it while Char and Sakul were ahead of me, but nothing happened. I don't know what triggers it."

"Tell me about the scenes when you can access the power."

"Well, there was the giant wolf thing from Stoltland, and usually when I have flashbacks of the Battle of Betrayals." Sealyn liked talking to Lizz. Lizz was incredibly brilliant and often found different viewpoints than Sealyn, making her the perfect person to add insight to this situation.

Lizz tilted her head in thought. "Seems to me that darkness calls the light."

"What?"

Lizz leaned back to face Sealyn. "Think about it. Why would you need the old magic if you're not in danger? Perhaps, the access doesn't present itself until you truly need it."

"So I'm just supposed to trust that the next mythical creature we face, the old magic will graciously show itself at the right time?"

"I'm sorry, Sealyn. I know that's not very helpful, but consider that the old magic could be protecting you. If you could channel it all day, what toll would that take on your body? Maybe you're not strong enough yet to handle it."

Sealyn crossed her arms. "Definitely don't like hearing that, but truth is truth—no matter how much it stings."

Lizz nodded. "I would advise that the next time you feel afraid, give into the feeling of trust. Blind faith, remember?"

"Yes. Blind faith." Sealyn hugged her friend and whispered, "Thank you."

"By the way, Sealyn, your room was quite loud last night. Tell Jace our walls are not soundproof."

"Lizz!"

Favien finished saddling his horse and added a few extra provisions to his bag. He saw his hands shaking. How could Sealyn agree to let Pinx come on this quest? He shook his head in disbelief. This journey would be unlike anything they've ever faced, so where was the justification? He stroked the side of his chocolate horse, hoping she would not sense his nervousness.

Brehan, Ajorn, and Doebromir walked to Favien. Ajorn patted Favien's back. "All ready this morning, Favien?"

"Absolutely!" He tried not to sound too enthusiastic but wanted to convince them he was confident.

Brehan's eyes narrowed. "Is it usual to have non-military men and women on quests?" He watched Favien shift uncomfortably.

Doebromir spoke while still finishing a Puffin pie. "Sometimes, but remember, this wasn't our choice. It would be better if we had the original strategy to move forward with, but this is what the Creator has chosen for us."

Brehan nodded but was not convinced of Favien's confidence. He knew Favien's choices would be torn between

Pinx and his queen. "Well, we have only moments before we leave."

"I'm glad your team is joining us, Lord Brehan," Favien struggled to get out.

Ajorn smiled. "I wouldn't miss an adventure with Queen Sealyn. You know her father sent her here to train as a young girl. Oh, the stories we could tell."

Fort Kippen's horn sounded, and the caravan gathered underground at the first-level meeting plaza. It was time for the quest to begin. Sealyn felt her stomach flutter. They had trained for this, so why did it seem like they were walking into a trap? She could hear tiny whispers telling her not to go, but she had to, right? No other third-generation Luxen existed as far as they knew. She could not think only of herself. She had to think of the future generations. She silenced that slithering voice, which felt like swallowing air.

She looked at Jace, who, of course, was looking at her. His eyes softened. He reached out and dropped a necklace, made of leather with a single emerald stone at the center encased with a swirling silver cage, in her hand. She loved it. Whatever they faced, she could handle it with Jace by her side.

"Majesty! Majesty! Wait!" exclaimed an unfamiliar voice.

Lady Lizz whirled around to see her two high servants running toward them, out of breath. "What is the meaning of this? The queen's convoy is ready to leave."

Gasping for air, one of the girls replied, "My apologies, majesty. We meant no harm. We only aim to help on your journey."

"I'm sorry. We cannot take on further people for this quest," Sealyn said abruptly.

The servants both held their arms up in defense. "Oh no, majesty. We didn't mean to cause confusion. We found information that we think could benefit you on your journey."

Sealyn looked to Lizz for confirmation. Lizz nodded. "These two are constantly found in our libraries and have been tucked away reading ever since the unveiling happened. If they say you need to see something, then you do." Lizz motioned for the girls to give Sealyn what they had found. Sealyn opened the scrolled-up pages and read the first few lines. Her heart pounded.

"Names?" Sealyn questioned.

The one who handed Sealyn the scrolls quickly said, "Quinley, majesty." Her green eyes sparkled. She was a natural beauty with short, trimmed blonde hair.

"And I'm Revalyn, your majesty." Revalyn brushed back her black curls behind her ears and adjusted her spectacles. She had a sweet, lovely face with light freckles that danced across her nose.

Sealyn nodded. "Quinley and Revalyn, I appreciate your help. This will not be forgotten." The girls grabbed each others' hands and giggled together. They hoped their futures could lead to Avondelle one day, and maybe, just maybe, this was their first step.

The massive doors slowly dropped open, and Sealyn felt the rush of cold air brush past her skin. She could smell the frosty forest waiting for them. The caravan moved forward. Sealyn felt her palms warming. She kept repeating the words she saw written in the old magic: "I accipere onus." She repeated these words to herself over and over. What did they mean? She hoped the rest of the scrolls had the answers, especially about the word "onus."

What burden would she have to accept? Would she have to cross lines that her heart was not prepared to cross? If she did cross those lines, would she still be the worthy choice to break all seven curses?

Brehan held his fist in the air, signaling they were finally crossing Len Nove's border. Jem blinked his red eyes in disbelief. He never thought he would see any other place besides his home, and now he was on the quest to save all seven kingdoms. He saw the Elysians' confusion as they passed through the light blue haze that looked like a translucent wall. He knew the curse's haze well. Red haze filled the cities in his kingdom, except the areas where the rebels lived.

Ashur whispered to Jem, "Have you ever seen anything like this?"

"In a way, yes, but not blue. Red haze curses my land, but we don't have snow," Jem informed.

"I must admit, this is quite breathtaking," Ashur said, while gazing around the land of snow and icicles. Jem did the same and quickly looked behind and stared at Queen Sealyn. She was looking to her right, and seeing her beauty against the sparkling white background, Jem found the words escaping his lips, "Yes, quite breathtaking."

Tilmond rode past Jem and Ashur, slowing his trotting beside Brehan. "Commander Brehan, is that the abandoned village ahead?"

"Correct. That is where we will split our forces. Remember, the village was abandoned long ago, and it's strange." Brehan tilted his head.

"Strange?"

"It's hard to explain. You will see in the next few minutes."

The caravan arrived at the icy stone wall of the abandoned village. A large sign hung from a post frozen in place that read, "Ciderton. Len Nove's best-tasting cider." The entry for the wall was enormous, which was odd. Most openings for villages were only big enough for a single cart to pass through. The stone streets were slick from ice, but Brehan tossed Fire Salts in front of them, which would melt anything in a fifty-foot radius that is not too thick. The first building they came upon looked like a normal tavern except frozen, and the size was three times the normal size.

"Everything is frozen. Are we going to find frozen skeletons inside?" asked Char.

Ajorn shook his head. "No, Char. We use Somber Tavern as our headquarters when we make our monthly visits here, which is why the Fire Salts worked on the streets. It took years for the thickness of the ice to wear down. With that being said, we cleared out any unpleasantries a long time ago."

"So you're saying there were frozen skeletons in there?"

"Char! Not now," snapped Sealyn. She motioned to Pinx and Sorcha, who looked like they had swallowed old socks.

"I was only testing the waters to see if the tavern scene would be lively or dead inside," Char smirked, hoping to ease the tension. Sealyn shook her head. "No? Not even a mood for puns? Well, this is a grave day."

They slowly entered Somber Tavern. Ice fell from the rusty hinges. A cold silence welcomed the group. Brehan and Sune walked around the massive room throwing Fire Salts, then lit the big white and blue stone fireplace and the other small fireplaces. The tavern had a huge area with extremely large pillows on the ground near the biggest fireplace. Two oversized doors were at the end of that room, leading to an open field outside. Big metal bowls sat at the end of each pillow.

In the middle was a square bar with a full kitchen. Several bar stools were turned over or broken, but most of the tables surrounding the square were in decent shape. While the group took their seats at the tables, Finn and Zuri walked to the pillows. Zuri knelt and placed her hand on the damp, moldy-smelling fabric. She shed a tear at what these represented and looked up at Finn, who also had tears in his eyes.

Max and Madilina exchanged glances. They did not know what any of this meant. Why would a tavern have these pillows, and why would the pillows cause Zuri and Finn to cry? What had they stumbled upon?

Max cleared his throat. "Lord Finn, is it well with you that I may ask what the pillows mean?" Max was always curious. He never knew when not to ask sensitive questions but still asked.

Finn looked worried but gathered himself. He walked back to the group and leaned against the bar. "You've heard Lady Zuri speak about Len Novians and the Mammoths." They nodded. "Well, what you see here is how close relations were. After a long day's work, humans and mammoths would frequent the taverns for social interactions and rest. The mammoths would come through the open doors at the end over there and lay on the pillows. The bartenders would fill the bowls with refreshments, grains, and fruits. Live music would play inside and outside in the field. This was a happy place until …" Finn's eyes glazed, as if he were in a trance. Zuri put her hand on his shoulder.

"Until the curse. Our king broke the treaty, which cursed us. We know all of this because of books and the stories our parents would tell us," Zuri continued for Finn. "This is just the shadow of the heartbreak. You will see more darkness ahead." Zuri dropped her head. She felt her heart beating rapidly. She did not want to remember the icy catacombs. The torture of being lost and forgotten there was more than she could handle.

Char and Sakul popped up from behind the square bar with bottles of amber liquid. Char quickly pulled the cork and out poured the perfect smell of crisp apple ale.

"I'm guessing this has been aged and chilled to perfection," Char winked. Sorcha folded her arms and glared at Sakul.

Sakul set his bottle down quickly and raised his arms. "It was Char's idea to find drinks, but it does seem sad to waste something that smells so good."

Sealyn rolled her eyes and sighed. "Indeed it does. Let us bring back some happy memories to Somber Tavern. Jem, Jashun, and Doebromir, can you please bring the food and water from the sleds? Char and Sakul, you oversee ensuring we all get a taste of the ale, not just you two. Tilmond and Brehan, set up the maps on the far table, and when you're ready, instruct everyone on their tasks." Sealyn guided Zuri to sit at her table. She knew this had to be incredibly difficult for both Zuri and Finn; after all, this was their kingdom. Jace scooted his chair closer to Sealyn and wrapped his arms around her.

Norella scandalously eyed Brehan. "Commander Brehan, I've been studying the maps. Could I be of assistance?" Brehan hesitated. He looked scared and excited at the same time. He tried to force out words, but all he could manage was a nod. Norella beamed.

"Such a smart girl you are," Rivers chuckled.

"I agree. Although, I've never seen you put much effort into studying maps until now. I wonder why that is?" Pinx facetiously asked.

Sorcha cuddled close to Norella. "Maybe sitting extra close to a burly man is all the incentive our sweet Norella needed to find maps fascinating."

Char filled Norella's wooden cup with ale. "Burly cuddles, did I hear? I'd be more than happy to assist you there, Norella." Char wiggled his eyebrows.

Norella huffed and drank her ale in one gulp. "If you cackling hens don't mind, I'll be helping the commanders with our life-changing quest." She stood and left the giggling table.

While their people ate and drank, Sealyn and Jace walked outside the tavern for fresh air. Jace held Sealyn close and kissed her fingers lightly. Sealyn blushed. The way he looked at her made her heart beat faster. She could barely catch her breath sometimes. Jace leaned in and pressed a light kiss on her lips. The weather might have been cold, but that kiss was warm. They stared into each other's eyes for only a second, then the hunger for more took over. Sealyn knew moments like this would be scarce in the future, so she wanted every minute of their privacy to count.

Jace pulled back and rested his forehead on hers, breathing deeply. He winked and began to run with her. They ventured down stone stairs leading to a bridge over an icy stream. Jace leaned against the railing and pulled his queen close to his body. They drank in their love for each other, memorizing every freckle, every feature on each other's faces. Jace did not want this moment to end, but with a cracking sound, it did.

Sealyn quickly looked over the bridge into the frozen water. She saw black lines that looked like veins under the ice. A slight crack formed under the bridge, but where did the original force start? They looked further down the stream, following the crack. The ice looked like it was moving. Sealyn's hands started sweating.

"Should I remove the gloves?"

"I believe that is a wise decision, my queen," Jace replied, drawing his sword. He realized this was the first time he had drawn a sword since stabbing Drystan. A wave of memory rushed over him. He smelled the burning books and felt like he couldn't breathe. He saw Drystan's hand reach up to stop him, but the sword went through Drystan's hand and into his heart. Jace thought he was about to faint from the memory.

Another loud snap sounded, and then an explosion of ice. Jace quickly came back to reality. A *lorkin sprang forward, snarling and angry. Lorkins were normally pure white with blue eyes, but this one had a black streak down its back and tail and solid black eyes and claws. These reptiles were like crocodiles but have more blubber to handle cold temperatures. They are also twice the normal size of crocodiles and have an extra row of teeth. The lorkin charged toward Sealyn and Jace, digging its claws into the ice.

"Why is it coming at us? Aren't lorkins afraid of humans?" Jace yelled.

"This one looks infected. Look at the black veins on its belly," Sealyn pointed.

"I'm more concerned about its teeth!"

Sealyn dropped her gloves and saw her green palms. Her magic was ready and excited for a fight. Sealyn remembered the arrows she had fired before but knew Dun's magic helped her conjure it. She had to remember the old magic's words. She thought back to the dusty scrolls she had uncovered in the old war room with Char. The words "Arcus Sagitta" flooded her memory.

Sealyn moved her arms like she was holding a bow and arrow and spoke the words "Arcus Sagitta" and released the green light arrow from her bow. It found its target, but the beast was large and determined. It would take more than one arrow to kill it. Sealyn fired another and another. The beast gained speed, bleeding black blood. It was finally close enough to make a deadly jump. The lorkin pushed hard from the ice soaring at them. Sealyn quickly spoke the word "Ensis," and a large green sword appeared in her hands.

Jace and Sealyn braced for impact. They held their swords, praying their weapons wouldn't miss the lorkin's weakness. Jace's sword sliced through the head, while Sealyn's sword stabbed through the throat. The large beast crashed on top of them, breaking the fragile bridge.

"Sealyn! Sealyn! Queen Sealyn!" Tilmond yelled. The group ran to the broken bridge, seeing only the last seconds of the fearsome lorkin's attempt. Tilmond, Jem, and Favien quickly jumped into the rubble. "Jace! Sealyn! Answer me!" Tilmond panicked.

Doebromir, Sune, Ashur, and Brehan rolled the creature away. Finn and Stawyer quickly aided Jace to his feet. Jace could not speak. The creature knocked the breath out of both him and Sealyn. Tilmond did not want to move Sealyn, fearing something may be broken. He motioned for Sorcha to inspect her. Zuri made fast work of bandaging Jace's cuts.

Jem cupped the back of Sealyn's neck and helped her sip water. Tilmond noticed the way Jem was looking at his cousin. He did not like it. He hoped it was just fear of losing his queen rather than anything more.

Sealyn finally stood. She felt dizzy, and her hearing seemed muffled, but she was only bruised with a few cuts. She looked at the diseased creature and felt sorry for it. The black veins had to mean something, and she feared what it could mean.

Ajorn jogged to the group. "I surveyed the area from where the creature crawled out, and it's now resealed. I don't see any signs of more."

Brehan shook his head. "We've never encountered a lorkin like this. Normally, they stick to eating their fish."

Sealyn stood over the creature. "Did you see these black veins?" Brehan knelt beside the lorkin, ran his gloves across the dark lines, then dipped his fingers in black blood. He sniffed the blood and looked at Sealyn with concerned eyes. "It smells rotten, doesn't it?" Sealyn asked. Brehan nodded.

Ajorn saw the look in his commander's eyes. "What does this mean, Brehan?" Brehan shook his head.

Sealyn sighed. "It means we're not the only kingdom here for Len Nove."

Prince Haedon,

I haven't received enough progress reports. I sent you up north to ensure the proper growth of this new army. I want those beasts controlled and multiplying. With this letter, I've sent you the book to aid this project faster. It was found in one of the new caves off the Obsidian Shores.

This is the old dark magic, Haedon. Commit to it, finally, and you will be announced as the heir; disobey, and you will be forgotten as your stepbrother, Jace.

Draco Fetura is the book to your redemption, especially Chapter 6.

Remember our deal. You want that harlot of a woman. I want my dragons!

Regards,
Queen Corentine of Stoltland and of the seven kingdoms

CHAPTER 13

SURZEES

Beautiful autumn leaves waved at each passerby in the market. Feydom was days away, and Siany was amazed at the resilience of her people. They still wanted to celebrate Perdonair, and what better way than making sure Feydom still carried on? They decided not to have a Black Pheonix team, so those team members were able to join the other teams.

Siany also decided to make the market more protected and durable. She petitioned Prince Royce, Lord Hueweyn, and Lord Rav to construct permanent stone buildings for the people's businesses instead of the tented, wooden booths. She knew the undertaking would be huge, but her people needed a project during their healing.

She sat at her writing desk in her sitting room, glad for silence. Her peace was quickly interrupted when her Nicht, Milola, came bursting through her door.

"Majesty, I brings good news!"

"Finally. Do tell me."

"More thans half of the buildings are completes, all the woundeds are finally ups and walking, and the army has secureds Stoltland's Tors."

"Excellent news. I must check on Madam Bip and Lady Novaly with the protection potions."

Milola fluttered her wings and brushed back her blue hair from her eyes. "I overheards Lord Hueweyn says he was goings to meets thems for lunch at *Mimby's Morsels*," Milola giggled. "You knows Hueweyn likes to see Mimby oftens."

Siany shook her head. "Leave it to you to still find romances to swoon over in these hard times. Let's make a day of it. We'll go to *Mimby's Morsels* for lunch and inspect the buildings and potions. Invite Lady Adalina, Lady Adma, and Lady Jadelyn. Make sure Maekel is with us."

Milola tilted her head. "You don't wants to invites Lady Brenna and Lady Lulana?"

"No. They seem to be more about gossip than helping us put the kingdom back together. It's annoying, really."

"Understoods, majesty. I'm exciteds for you to sees the improvements."

Siany and her group joined Hueweyn, Rav, Madam Bip, and Novely at their table. She enjoyed the social scene. This was something she missed. She forgot how much fellowship is needed to keep everyone hopeful. Her heart ached, though; she missed her sister. Sealyn was the chatty one at the tables, entertaining people with past adventures. She and Char were excellent at making people laugh. She looked forward to the day when Sealyn would return. Siany hoped Sealyn would love the upgrades and how she conducted the kingdom in her absence.

"We think you will be impressed with the new potions we've been brewing, majesty," Madam Bip began. "I've uncovered several new magical root systems. They're proving to make some potent concoctions."

Novaly giggled and patted her red eyebrow. "Concoctions is right. I lost an eyebrow to one of the potions, but Bip was able to make a potion for hair growth. We haven't figured out how to slow the hair growth, so I must trim that one eyebrow every few days." The table laughed.

Nijeel entered *Mimby's Morsels*, looking like he had an important mission.

His coffee-stained apron had fresh spills, and his bald brow was sweating. His glasses were even fogging. Nijeel was definitely busier than normal. Mimby rushed to greet Nijeel with a large basket of food. Her copper skin was sweating too. What was going on?

Siany rose and walked to them. They bowed hastily. "Good afternoon, Sir Nijeel."

"Good afternoon, Princess Siany or Queen Siany or majesty?"

Siany laughed. "It's ok, Nijeel. I'm just concerned about why you both seem so frazzled?"

"It's the diplomats. They always send several guards before their arrival to ensure safe passage. They seem to be extra ravenous from their travels," Nijeel informed.

"Diplomats!" gasped Siany. She had forgotten all about them. Diplomats from Blissendelle, Hill Chimes, Clarien, and Seanove were attending this year's Perdonair celebrations. These Elysian territories happen to have diplomats with eligible sons for Siany as well. How clever. Siany needed to prepare herself.

Lady Adalina gently linked her arm with Siany's. "Oh, we're excited to meet everyone. We've been decorating the palace for days. It's like a battle never took place there." Siany cringed. "Luckily, our majesty ensured we would have everything in order for them." Adalina smiled at Siany. She could see Siany's expressions of overwhelmingness, so she wanted to help. "If the soldiers are already here, surely they have sent word to the palace about when the rest of their party will arrive. Why don't we return to the palace for the good news? Jadelyn and I can visit with the soldiers, find out more details, and express a welcome from you if you permit?"

Siany nodded. She was relieved to escape back to the palace but hated missing the market tour. She needed to organize her schedule better. Being caught off guard like this was not good. What else had she forgotten? Now though, she had to have her wits about her. Diplomats were coming, and they would want to know the state of their kingdom and if she was finally ready to choose a husband.

The convoy split into three groups and dispersed. The morale was low. They now knew that Stoltland was here and gaining control of Len Nove fast. The infected lorkin proved that. Their plan of two drunk idiots walking through the front door of the palace would most likely fail, but it was the only plan they had.

The further they traveled, the more snow they encountered. Teeth chattering and toes freezing, the groups pushed on. The sled dogs and horses made fast work through the snow. The forests, lakes, and ancient ruins looked beautiful, covered in glistening white, but the blue colors dominated even more than the white. Blue trees. Blue haze. Blue stones. Blue flowers. The curse kissed everything blue and took away nature's colorful originality.

It was eerily silent. Every snapped branch sent tingles down their spines. Stoltland was here, but where? Brehan's team paused after hours of non-stop riding. They all dismounted and stretched their legs. Brehan and Rielen checked the maps and their sundials.

Pinx rebraided her long black hair and stuffed it under her green neck scarf. She was scared. She knew this journey would cost them but trembled at what that price would be. Favien wrapped his arms around Pinx and let her lean back on him. He could see her fear and understood it.

"How are you feeling, love?" Favien gently asked Pinx.

"I believe after a week in the hot springs of Avondelle, I will be perfectly fine."

Favien chuckled. He liked her spunk. It was one of the many reasons he fell in love with her. He could not wait to marry her. "Make it two weeks, and I'll be your date."

"Look at Sakul. He looks so worried. I know Char is scared too, but he's putting on a brave face," Pinx whispered.

"It's what we all must do. This mission is bigger than all of us here. Being willing to sacrifice yourself for the future of others, for people you'll never meet, is exhilarating, but also it's terrifying."

Ashur and Norella joined Pinx and Favien, handing them jerky and water.

Favien nodded. "Thank you. Are you both doing well?"

Ashur lowered his scarf from his nose, revealing his still perfectly smooth, ebony skin and handsome smile. "I've dreamed about an adventure like this my whole life. I'm still flabbergasted. A quest to save all seven kingdoms with the most powerful monarchy is more than I could ever have hoped."

Norella leaned down to catch a closer glance at something moving on the snow. She saw tiny bouncing creatures. Hundreds of them came from the forest, looking very curious. They had giant ears for their small round heads and big, blue eyes that glowed. Their light blue tails were skinny with fuzzy white tips. "Look!" Norella pointed. "Do you see these adorable creatures?"

Brehan chuckled. "Those are Len Nove's *surzees. They are almost as light as feathers, so they don't sink in the snow. You're incredibly lucky to see them. Normally, they're scared to approach, but they must sense something good in you." Brehan felt his face go red. "I mean you all." He cleared his throat. "They must sense there's good in our group, not just you, Norella. I mean, you're good. Not that I know you're good, but I just…"

Char clapped Brehan on the back. "Easy there, burly man. Eating all those words is an unhealthy diet. If you're beauty struck by Norella, then just say so." Char wiggled his eyebrows at Norella, who was red as an apple.

Norella yelled. "Char! Stop that!"

Brehan shoved Char aside. "We're losing daylight. We need to keep moving." He mounted his horse quickly and gripped the reins tight, and yet he couldn't help but steal a quick glance at Norella. He could feel himself being pulled toward her, but was his heart completely healed from his loss? He wanted so badly to be free of grief, but if he wasn't, he could hurt Norella.

Max felt they were moving like frozen molasses. He hated snow in the treetops. He and Finn were ahead of the queen's convoy on opposite sides of the trail, slowly progressing through the trees. The Elysian treetop archers were the elites of the archery division. Max became their leader after Sealyn was crowned.

They had to be extra careful not to knock too much snow below; otherwise, enemies could spot them. He leapt again and felt his foot slip on an icy branch but caught himself with his underarm. Max paused to scan the area. He noticed movement to his right, then heard a twig snap.

His heart started pounding. Would this be animal or human? Would it be friendly or attack? He squinted and adjusted his position on the large tree. In the thickness of the forest, he saw a small group of dark-dressed men. He counted three. Immediately, he made the bird call, signaling the potential threat to Finn. It seemed like hours, but it only took minutes for Finn to join Max in his tree.

They used sign language, discussing their thoughts. Finn thought they were of Stoltland, but Max wanted to be sure. They quietly climbed down the tree, then etched their way toward the hooded figures. Max and Finn wore white fur cloaks with white scarves to cover their faces. They were camouflaged against the snow-covered ground. They neared the campsite and could hear voices and the crackling fire.

Something felt wrong. Max noticed a tiny surzee bounce next to him with its large blue eyes filled with tears. It shook its head and lowered its ears, then hopped away quickly. Max surveyed the campsite again. What were they missing? Then, he spotted it! He counted four tents but only three men. He looked at Finn, held up four fingers, and pointed to the tents, then all that Max felt was pain in his left shoulder blade.

Finn pushed Max forward, barely missing the swinging blade of the Stoltlander's sword. Max could feel the knife in his shoulder but could not reach it. He felt the warm blood spilling across his back. The pure white snow was now stained with Max's blood.

Finn quickly scurried up a low tree branch and shot his deadly arrow at the missing Stoltlander. The dark figure dropped with a thud. The metallic smell was undeniable; blood from Elysium and Stoltland had once again been spilled. The three other figures began running toward Max. Finn climbed higher to get better angles and began firing his arrows.

Max kept reaching his right arm behind himself, trying to bend in a way that would allow him to reach the bloody knife. Every strain felt like an ax was sawing him in half. Finn missed his first shot, but his next arrow hit the fastest runner in the neck, and down he went. Finn shot another arrow that landed in a Stoltlander's shoulder, but he kept running. He quickly reloaded and fired again, hitting the slowest runner in the thigh. He tumbled to the ground, moaning. Finn was trying to load his next arrow as fast as possible, but he slipped on the icy tree branch. Max was still straining to reach the knife. The black soldier was seconds away from Max.

Finn continued falling from the tree. Max's fingers finally slipped around the cold heel and flung the knife forward, ripping through his own skin. Max hurled the knife through the Stoltlander's neck with a powerful scream. The enemy soldier dropped to his knees, choking on the knife. Then there was silence. His eyes were open, and his face was covered in splatters of blood, but he was dead.

Finn landed hard and coughed, trying to regain his breathing. The two laid there composing themselves, then heard the groans from the last breathing soldier. They could tell he was trying to escape. This could not happen. Finn took in a deep breath and rose to his feet. He stumbled to help Max to his feet, and then they walked to the Stoltlander, who was dragging himself to the campsite. Finn stepped on the thigh with the arrow protruding through. The soldier let out a searing cry. Max lifted his sword to the soldier's chin, and Finn readied his bow and arrow. The soldier slumped in defeat and did not resist Finn roping his hands and feet together. They had no choice but to take him prisoner.

CHAPTER 14

PANTORIAN

The needle went through the open, oozing wound as Madilina patched up her husband. Tiny sobs were all she could manage. She hated seeing him in pain but knew he needed to see her strong. She clipped the end of the thread and hoped her sewing would be enough. Zuri made a thick, green paste that smelled like a horse stall and mint. Max flinched when Zuri painted the green substance on his wound. She wrapped a bandage around it, then stepped away to let Madilina dress Max.

Zuri joined the heated discussion between Sealyn and Finn.

"Explain it again, Finn. I really want to understand why you two left your positions," Sealyn said through gritted teeth.

Finn dropped his blue eyes. His head ached from the fall. "I'm sorry, majesty. Max wanted to make sure they were Stoltland soldiers before relaying information. The trees were too far apart for us to make a clear assessment without spying from the ground." He felt defeated.

Tilmond stood from the Stoltlanders' campfire. "This might be the worst thing that could have happened to us. How can we explain three deaths and a wounded soldier to Len Nove's king?"

"They did attack our men first," retorted Jace.

"But what proof do we have?" Tilmond questioned.

"Our royal word should be good enough, right?" Jace heatedly spoke.

The corner of Jem's red eyes crinkled, and he shook his head. He could not believe how easily Jace was thinking himself royal. He wondered if Jace knew the dead men or if he would try to free the prisoner. These were his people before he became royalty.

Sealyn stared at Ajorn and Stawyer, who were tending to the Stoltlander's wounds. She felt like needles were pressing into her skin. Again, Stoltland took blood from one of her men, one of her friends. She had to play this right. Stoltland had to be here to claim Len Nove's power. The Elysians called their power source the Heart of Elysium, but she was unsure what Len Nove would call it. This had to be their mission. Sealyn sipped her hot broth and spoke, "I believe we can use this to our advantage. We came in peace, but Stoltland came for war. We will offer the prisoner as an offering of good faith from us. Hopefully, Char and Sakul can do a good enough job of playing their roles."

"Well said, my queen!" Jem raised his cup to Sealyn. Jace's grey eyes narrowed at Jem. Something about the way he said "my queen" burned inside Jace. Anger boiled like a hot stew in his stomach. He glared at the fire. Tilmond saw Jace's anger and noticed—something strange. Something that lasted only half a second. Did he see fire reflected in Jace's eyes, or did his eye color change?

Ashur paused to take in the site of the ice city of Pantorian. This was the capital of Len Nove. It was in much better condition than the last city they passed. Tholgerton City looked like it was trapped in a dream state. They finally saw people there, but the people seemed not to notice them. The buildings had thin layers of bluish ice on them, while the people raked snow from the streets in a slow state. It looked like they were in a trance.

Pantorian looked alive. It was built on a wide, small mountain. Homes and shops were carved and coiled around the mountainside. The streets were stone and wide enough for two carts to move side by side effortlessly. The slope around the mountain was not steep but continued until a flat top that held the white stone palace, the military bastion, and other important economic buildings. Every shop and home was painted blue with white doors.

Brehan stopped his horse next to Ashur. "I've never seen Pantorian look this good. Normally, it's covered in snow."

Ashur's brows drew together. "What would cause such a drastic change?"

Brehan did not want to answer Ashur's question. He turned to address the caravan behind him. "This is where we dismount and split up."

Ashur felt uneasy. He knew there was a dark reason Brehan did not answer his question, but he wanted to stay optimistic. As a young boy, he dreamed about traveling the seven kingdoms and defending his Elysium. He worked tirelessly to become the best soldier for this very moment. He would not waste it.

Brehan untied the bag of clothing. Rielen handed everyone their blue cloaks, hoping this would help them to blend into Len Nove's society. Their eyes would be the problem. The only ones not to receive the blue cloaks were Char and Sakul. They were meant to stand out.

Favien put his hand on Char's shoulder. "Remember, Char, we will be walking nearby as you walk to the palace. We will mirror how the Len Novian people react to you, so it will be hard for you to spot us."

"Excellent. Now, where's our wine? I need the strong stuff for this quest," Char chuckled with a hint of uncertainty. Norella tossed Char a bottle, then tossed Sakul his bottle. He nodded to her. Char uncorked the bottle and took a long swig, and gasped slightly. He raised the bottle, "Here's to all my drinking days finally paying off," and with that, he and Sakul parted ways with their comrades.

Sakul drank the red liquid with panic flowing through his veins. Each step he took was heavy, like he was walking through mud. He looked at Char, who seemed to be enjoying his new endeavor. How could he be so calm? They walked the incline of Pantorian, noticing that the shops looked similar to the market shops in Avondelle. He was so confused. All the rumors they had heard about this place made it seem like Len Nove was one big ice block, but people were hustling and bustling, enjoying normal day pleasures here.

Char decided to really engage with his mission. Sip after sip, he twirled and spun young ladies around as he passed them. He would stop and buy bread and cheeses, then skip to the next person willing to dance. Char could not believe he was enjoying himself; it made the life-and-death mission disappear. He pictured the gruff Brehan glaring at him for having fun and chuckled to himself.

The delights of the wine took effect on Sakul, too. Sakul and Char linked arms and danced in circles, singing one of Elysium's favorite songs. Crowds started following them. They noticed others joining in their mischief and hoped this would benefit their cause, but their cause started disappearing from their thoughts. Eventually, Char, Sakul, and the crowd danced their way to the open flat area. Char could see guards surrounding the entire perimeter. Musicians, who seemed rusty, had joined the party, which just egged Char and Sakul on more. Downing the remains of their bottles, they danced and sang all the way to the front of the palace.

Horns blew loud over the crowd's noise. Silence fell, and the two barely could stand upright. They forgot this was Northern wine. They stared in awe at the two huge doors. The doors were covered in blue gems, sparkling with dark secrets. Their mouths gaped at the beauty, but then the doors opened. They expected the royal guard or the royal family, but who stood before them was the least of whom they expected.

Diary Entry

I hate Elysium. More than that, I hate that detestable Sealyn. She's toxic. Even Ryker and Graelynd are pompous irritations. They strut around, thinking they own the world. Well, they don't, and soon, I will! I will, I swear it!

I've kept up my practice of the dark magic, and I do say that I'm probably one of the best that history has ever seen. That green bird won't stand a chance the next time we face each other. He won't be able to handle me and my dragons; he's just one bird against a massive army.

Today's complaint: Phyre. Yes, my husband's mother. She constantly complains, so I've decided to lock her in a further away tower and forbid any family from seeing her. She needs to be taught a lesson. I'm the queen, not her. She must bow to my words now. Such a pest.

Until next time,
Queen Corentine

CHAPTER 15

THE ARKOOTHA BEAR

Char blinked as he stared into the dark abyss of Malum's black eyes. How was the commander of Stoltland's army here and in the palace? Why would he be the one to greet them? What were they supposed to do now? He looked at Sakul, whose mouth was open.

Malum's lip curved upward. Malum had silky black hair with light brown skin. He was tall with muscular, broad shoulders. He liked seeing Elysians in fear, especially Char. They had a history.

Char and Malum first met on Pax Island, near Shunal but between Elysium, Korpam, Stoltland, and Havas. The island was known for "underground" military competitions. They were ruthless and by invitation only. The Grandee ruled the island. Most commanders feared him, but he only wanted to remain ruler of Pax Island, nothing more.

Char and Malum competed against each other in almost every event. The wins were even until the last day of the competition. Char amazingly was the victor, but throughout the entire six months on the island, Malum bullied and harassed Char. The bad blood between them was high. Char worried about payback.

"Well, if it isn't the little bird who couldn't handle military orders," Malum jeered.

Sakul's face sunk into confusion. "Char, what does that mean?"

Malum stepped closer to them. "It means that Char might have won Pax Island honor, but he has no battlefield honor. He's a coward." Malum spat at Char's feet.

Char weighed his options. It was so hard for him to concentrate, with the Northern wine infecting his ability to focus. If he insulted Malum, then he would most likely be thrown in the dungeons. If he went along with what Malum said, then he would realize there was a game to play, and they'd end up in the dungeons. If he was honest about their plans, then dungeons. Either way, he could get some sleep.

"Oh, c'mon, Malum. I know you can't possibly be holding onto a childhood grudge. Let us sit down over a fresh bottle of ale and food to catch up."

Malum's black eyes narrowed. "What business do you have here, Char?"

This was it. Char had to think of something clever because now the tactic had changed. He could not give away that Sealyn was right behind them nor that they came to warn Len Nove about Stoltland. "Did the king not receive Queen Sealyn's Nicht? He should have arrived months ago."

Malum tilted his head. "No. What was the message?"

Char hesitated. He had to keep things just as they normally would be between kingdoms. "Malum, the message was between Elysian and Len Novian royalty. I'm not sure why you would ask for such details to be told to you."

Malum laughed an evil laugh. "Excellent deflection, little bird. Perhaps you Elysians haven't heard, but Len Nove needed us to help run their kingdom. I'm in charge now."

Char's mouth fell open. Sakul looked at Char with bulging eyes. Char's heart started beating rapidly. His fingers were numb, and he could smell fresh bread inside the palace. "Well, in that case, Malum, I would like to inform you that I am starting a diplomatic position for Queen Sealyn."

"Really? You?"

"Yes—me. Why is that so far-fetched?"

"I'm sure I don't have to answer that."

"Regardless, I'm here to keep the peace between our lands. Nothing more. Since you're now in charge, as you say, then why don't we discuss things? I'm most interested in your plans for Len Nove." Char shifted his stance, trying to keep his toes from freezing.

Malum slowly nodded his head, then smirked. "Join me. I'm eager to hear your diplomatic plans for Elysium and Len Nove." He motioned for them to come inside.

Brehan watched as Char and Sakul entered the ice palace. He was in shock that Stoltland had taken over. Where were the king and the rest of the royal family? Was Stoltland's queen here too? He needed to reconnect with his group. There would be no way they could win a fight against two armies, much less one.

The snow kept falling, making visibility incredibly difficult for Doebromir's team. He felt like vines were pulling his legs to the ground. Progress was not going well. Jashun plunged forward to catch up to Doebromir. He needed to have a private conversation with him.

"Doebromir," Jashun started. "I just wanted to make sure we're good. I don't want any bad feelings between us."

Doebromir pulled his wool scarf from his mouth. "Jashun, I'm not going to lie. Your story didn't add up. I feel like you're not telling the whole truth, which makes me question why. If you're having issues with en-"

Jashun stopped him. "Don't even say it. I'm not envious."

"I didn't say you were. I was going to say, if you were starting to struggle with it, there's no shame, Jashun. You simply just need to ask for help."

"You sound like you speak from experience."

Doebromir chuckled. "Because I do. It was before Sealyn was queen. I confided in her that I was starting to become jealous of Favien. She connected me with Commissioner Herb; ever since then, he's been my counselor to keep that curse at bay."

Jashun blinked. "I'm shocked, D. I had no idea."

"Well, as you can imagine, it's not something I yell from treetops," Doebromir laughed. "But I'm not ashamed to admit I needed help. We all need that from time to time, even big boys like me." He smacked Jashun on the shoulder. Jashun smiled.

Sorcha slipped and fell face-first into the snow. Sune quickly helped pick her up, then froze. He heard the growl. He knew that sound well. It was an *Arkootha bear. These bears are larger than most bears and solid white with blue underbellies. The outside of their front paws have long, sharp hooks that curved like a mammoth's tusk. Arkootha bears have a high-pitched growl that would scare off other predators. Sune yelled for the group to run.

Rivers tried to run, but it felt like running in a dream, telling the body to go but not listening. They shouldn't have left their dog sleds back at the campsite, but Ezen said this way would be easier to navigate. Everywhere they looked, there was white snow with a blue haze. Ice smacked them in their faces. Hearts pounded hearing the terrifying bear call. The beast was hungry.

"Hurry!" Doebromir echoed.

They could feel the vibrations of the bear running. How large was this creature to make the ground tremble? Sune readied his bow. They could barely feel their numb feet, and the cold air made breathing almost impossible while sprinting. Rivers could hear the heavy panting of the bear. She looked back and saw the ferrous blue, glowing eyes. She jerked her head forward, throwing herself off balance, and crashed into the snow. She tried to pick herself up, but the bear was on her in seconds. She let out a piercing scream as the bear sank its giant teeth into her leg.

Sune released his arrow, and the bear let out a roar. Rivers scrambled to get away, but the bear dug his tusk of a claw into her side. Again, Sune shot another arrow into the bear's body. He could see the bear weakening and the dark crimson blood pouring out around Rivers. Doebromir and Jashun came running down the paths they already made in the snow with their swords drawn. They plunged their swords into the side of the bear. The bear threw Rivers like a wet blanket.

The bear swung its claws at the soldiers, but its wounds caught up to the wild beast. It faltered, and Doebromir drove his sword into its neck, sending it to an icy grave. Sorcha screamed for Rivers, but Rivers made only small moans. She was bleeding badly. Sorcha immediately started applying pressure to the wounds, but there were too many.

"We have to find shelter if I'm to have a chance at saving her," Sorcha shouted.

Jashun looked around in a panic. He squinted past several blue trees and thought he saw a cave. Perhaps that was the bear's cave. He pointed. "Over there. Hurry." They lifted Rivers with care and tried to move as quickly as possible. Rivers moaned in agony. Sorcha tried to comfort her while they moved.

Jashun was right; it was a cave, but it was shallow. They noticed it had a round door inside the shallowness. Doebromir slammed his shoulder into the door, and the frozen wood broke. A gust of stale wind whirled past them. This was not the smell of an animal home. It smelled of death.

"Get inside quick," ordered Sorcha. "Hand me all the bandages in my pack." Sorcha cleaned the wounds as best as possible, but the blood kept pouring. Tears flowed from her green eyes, willing her friend to push through the pain. Sorcha replayed their memories in her head. Rivers celebrating with the Green Phoenixes winning Feydom. The girls laughing at Norella's new crush on Brehan. Another blistering scream from Rivers pulled Sorcha back to reality, and then Rivers started coughing blood.

"What's happening?" Sune asked frantically.

"Her lungs are filling with blood! I don't think I can stop this," Sorcha cried. "Rivers! Rivers!" Sorcha shook her friend as she went silent. "This isn't happening. This isn't happening," Sorcha kept repeating. She yelled Rivers' name one last time, and then there was nothing. No noise, no movement from Rivers. Only faint drips of water could be heard. They huddled around Rivers in sad disbelief, then heard a loud crack.

"What was that?" Jashun yelled.

Ice and dust started raining on their heads. They looked up and could see the cave cracking and shaking. Large stones fell in front of the door, and more kept falling. Flowstone and stalactite cracked above where the group was gathered around Rivers. "Move!" Sune screamed.

The group jumped, barely missing the massive cave-in. A sickening feeling ran through their bodies—Rivers was now buried underneath the rubble. Sune quickly pulled out and lit three torches from his pack. They were completely sealed in.

"What are we supposed to do now?" Ezen whispered.

"There has to be another way out," Doebromir said, also trying to convince himself.

"We can't just leave Rivers," Sorcha scolded.

Sune placed his hand on Sorcha's shoulder. "I'm sorry, my lady, but we can do nothing for her now. We must find a way out." Sorcha looked back at the flickering light on the rubble. How could she leave her friend like this? She was still covered in Rivers' blood. This wasn't right. She needed to bury her, not just leave her in the wilderness, but she knew the moment they tried to dig her out, the cave would collapse on them.

They felt defeated and started walking through the icy cavern. Their stomachs growled, and their feet ached. Jashun thought the worst had to be over, but he was fundamentally wrong. He thought he saw something odd in the walls, like shapes. He and Sune walked closer to a wall and screamed. There, they saw frozen bodies. This was no ordinary cavern; it was a catacomb.

CHAPTER 16

FAR FROM HOME

Max bit down hard on the small tree branch as Jem seared his wound with his hot knife. He couldn't scream for fear of other Stoltland spies. Tears pricked his eyes. Madilina couldn't watch; instead, she fed crumbs of bread to the group of surzees that kept following them. Sweet Madilina remembered her mother reading her stories about Len Nove's creatures. She hoped they would be able to see the three breeds of unicorns native to the ice lands: the *Ice Horn, *Diamond Horn, and *Blue Horn. The paintings of

these creatures were stunning. In her childhood dreams, she had them all as pets. She forced herself to think about the unicorns and not the smell of burning flesh.

Max's wound kept oozing, so they had no choice but to sear it shut. Jace wrapped his arm around Sealyn. He gently tucked several wisps of brown hair behind her ear. He liked seeing her dressed like a warrior. She was so fierce.

"Max is going to be ok, Sea," Jace comforted.

"Yes, but until then, he'll suffer. I hate hearing one of ours suffering. Max might be a great warrior, but he also has a gentle side. Did you know he once saved a turtle for his mother as a young boy? That turtle still lives with his family, almost like another brother."

Jace chuckled. "I had no idea. I thought it was Madilina who was the animal whisperer."

"Max too. That part of Max is the reason I'm sad. I don't want the fields of battle to harden his gentle nature."

"They won't. We'll make sure of that," Jace paused, not wanting to ask his next question. "Sealyn, what do you think Stoltland being here means?"

Sealyn fidgeted with her bow. "It means it was a smart tactic to go for our ally. Although Len Nove has been quiet for decades,

Stoltland didn't know the extent, but now they do. I wish our kingdom would have done more, but we were so focused on the battles in the south with Korpam. Do you think Corentine will be here?" She didn't want to use the title of mother for Jace. She felt like that might sting more.

Jace's grey eyes tensed. "My gut tells me no. She won't execute the plan if there's a big risk to herself. She will send someone else in her place. I fear whom she may have sent."

"Who would she send, Jace?"

"Commander Malum. He's the worst!" Jace said a little too loudly. His tone sparked the interest of the rest of the group. They joined their royals. Jace continued, "He tortured me when I was younger. He locked me in the dungeons for days, claiming I was an idiot who locked myself in, and then he would poison my food, not to the point of death, obviously, but just enough for me to be sick for weeks. He was, and still is, a bully. He would beat on me every chance he could. I could handle the physical torment, but I think his words were the worst. The harassment and belittling still echo in my dreams. Let's pray he's not the one who's here because if so, he will have dark tricks waiting for us."

Sealyn locked eyes with Tilmond. He understood. She was worried that she had just sent Malum a play toy: Char. They all knew about the bad blood between those two on Pax Island. This had now become a rescue mission.

Sweat beaded atop Sakul's brow. His anxiety was in overdrive. How could things be this bad? Stoltland now ruled for Len Nove, which meant his queen was walking into a trap. He tried not to make eye contact with Malum. He hated looking into those soulless black eyes.

Char chomped away on the bread and cheese the servants provided. He was shocked at how cozy the ice palace was. The floors, walls, and ceilings were solid ice; even the tables and chairs were ice. He was glad they at least provided blankets and pillows to sit on. He didn't see any of Stoltland's banners yet, which was a good sign, but it was clear Stoltland's presence affected the land. He didn't forget the infected lorkin.

Char and Sakul stood as the large rectangular banquet hall doors opened. They had been waiting for the royal family and Malum to join them. The royal family was massive in size. Each one was at least six and a half feet tall with extremely pale, white skin. Their extremely long hair was also white with blue streaks. Princess Drifa's beauty enchanted Char.

"My apologies for keeping you waiting," Malum said. "I had to inform the royal family of your arrival since they were unaware." Malum took the head seat where the king would have normally sat. The two Len Novian siblings exchanged glances. This did not go unnoticed by Char and Sakul.

Char lifted his silver goblet. "No need to apologize. We are excited and pleased to see you all."

King Egil cleared his throat and spoke hoarsely. "What news of Elysium?" His voice sounded raw.

Char stilled. He had to choose his words carefully.

Malum slid his ice chair back and propped his feet on the ice table. "Yes, Char, do tell us all the Elysian news." He gave a wicked grin and winked at the young royals.

Sakul saw Char's hesitation. He wanted to help. Why would Sealyn have chosen him to come with Char? She always had a backup plan embedded in her primary plan. Was he the backup? All he knew was parties, and right now, he was missing a huge one back at home. He knew the diplomats would be coming for Perdonair—he froze, and the hairs on his neck rose. Perdonair— that was it!

"Perdonair, your majesty." Sakul managed to squeak out.

Malum squinted. "Say again?"

"Perdonair. We came to invite the royal family for our annual Perdonair festivities, especially to come to watch Feydom."

Char beamed at his friend. "Yes. Sakul is right. This wine has my memory spinning. We wanted to see if you would care to join us this year?"

The royals exchanged sharp glances. It was like they were trying to communicate with their blue eyes. They were all playing a dangerous chess game with Malum. An awkward silence fell over the room. No one knew who would speak next.

Malum chuckled and dropped his feet, then leaned his elbows on the table. "The royals aren't traveling right now. The winter snow has already set in, as you can see."

Char saw the hope die in Princess Drifa's eyes. Her pale pink lip started to quiver. Prince Dag reached over and clasped his sister's hand gently. What had happened to these twins? Char knew Malum had to have done something.

"Well, in that case, we won't keep you from your duties. We'll be off, back to Elysium." Char stood from the table, along with Sakul.

"Sit down, boy," Malum said with disdain. "You green-eyed pests aren't going anywhere." Char and Sakul slowly sat down, barely breathing. "Char, you know, your cousin has one major weakness."

"Is that so?"

"Yes, when it comes to you, she's never far behind."

Char shot up again and threw his knife at Malum. The game was up. Char realized Malum was going to use them as bait for Sealyn. Malum dodged the knife by an inch. Char and Sakul raced across the icy floor as best as they could, only to be met by dark Stoltland soldiers.

"Take Lord Char and Lord Sakul to the dungeons. They will be our guests until our little bird queen decides to show up for her cowardly family, and throw the royals back in their cages, too."

The black armored soldiers grabbed the royals from behind. Princess Drifa screamed in protest. King Egil begged for mercy with a raspy plea. Prince Dag tried to fight off the soldier to protect his sister, but he was too weak from malnourishment. The soldiers dragged their captives down thousands of stairs until they reached the cold dungeons. They were each thrown into separate cells, only separated by bars. Clasping the iced iron bars, Char yelled after the soldiers, who strolled away laughing.

Sakul watched across from him as the two siblings reached for each other through the bars, crying. The defeated king slowly shuffled to his locked door and leaned his head on the iced-over bars. The king looked across to Char, who was still screaming and shaking the door, and raised his fragile hand. Sakul walked to the bars connecting his cell and Char's and forcefully told Char to stop. Once Char calmed his breathing, he looked at the aged king. Egil's blue eyes had tears flowing. The king spoke quietly. "We have much to discuss."

Char had never felt so far from home.

By order of Commander Malum of Stoltland:

Search and find Queen Sealyn of Elysium. She will be close to Pantorian. Kill any who resist you, but do not kill Sealyn. I want her alive, along with her grey-eyed king.

Approved by King Egil of Len Nove

CHAPTER 17
THE RESCUE PARTY

Avondelle was bustling with news of the diplomats' arrivals. The market was covered in Perdonair decorations. The beautiful autumn colors danced across the new stone buildings with flowers and vines. Festive wreaths were hung on each door, proudly anticipating Feydom. Children skipped around wearing their favorite players'

jerseys with their favorite teams' colors painted on their faces.

Sipping hot apple cider and eating Jam Pies, Siany and Novaly sat outside *Nijeel's Choice,* soaking in the day's beauty. Siany was so surprised at how much the city rallied behind the festivities. Avondelle felt the absence of Lord Sakul's talent in planning, but the Vinurs of the Court stepped up to help aid the royal family.

"Now that you've met each suitor, who do you like the most?" Novaly asked.

"I don't know the answer to that question."

"Yes, but it's fun to fantasize, so if you had to choose today, who would you choose?" Novaly loved romance, so Siany often found herself playing hypothetical games like this with her. Novaly was always sneaking the palace's romance novels.

"Well, if I had no choice but to choose today and only based on the brief meetings I've had," Siany paused and closed her eyes. "I would choose Lord Saemeon."

Novaly squealed and kicked her feet up and down like a child being tickled. "I knew it! I just knew there was something there. I saw how he looked at you, and, oh my, the way I saw you smile. That's a love smile, that was. I just knew it. Oh, and just think about it. Hill Chimes. You would have a mansion in Hill Chimes. What a magical place! Can you imagine all the romantic strolls to take in the meadows? The hills would sing love songs to you while you dance under the stars." Novaly sat back in her chair and gazed up, looking lost in the clouds.

Siany shook her head. Novaly was the dreamer about book romances. It was quite entertaining. "I don't know if it's a love match, Novaly, but it will be interesting to see how this goes. He has all the credentials needed for a good husband."

"Credentials? Really? Siany, please tell me those credentials include how handsome he is?"

"He's not bad looking."

"Not bad? Not bad?! Have you lost your mind? That man is gorgeous!"

"Who? Me?" Nijeel came to their table just in time to hear Novaly's compliment. The girls giggled, and he poured them more cider.

"Oh, Nijeel, don't you feel love in the air?" Novaly asked dreamily.

Nijeel laughed. "I don't know about love, but the crisp autumn air is finally here. Before you know it, the Trundata Ball will be here."

Siany forgot about the ball. The Trundata Ball was the social highlight of the winter season for Elysium. She would be expected to pick a theme but also be expected to pick a date to the ball from the diplomats' sons. Picking a date showed who was in the top running for her hand in marriage. She felt sick.

"Did I say something wrong, your majesty? Or perhaps the cider is not to your liking?"

Siany shook her head. "No. No, Nijeel. I'm just feeling the pressures of court. The cider is delightful."

"Excellent, majesty."

Siany tilted her head. "Nijeel, you hear all sorts of gossip, don't you?" Nijeel nodded his head hesitantly. "I thought so. Have you heard any news about the night everyone was poisoned? Any names come up to who's responsible?"

"I've heard several mentions of Stoltland, of course, but Elysian names, no, majesty."

Siany dropped her head. "It was a long shot to ask."

Nijeel leaned in and pushed his spectacles up his nose. "If I can offer some wisdom, though?" Siany nodded. "I would step back and see who would have the motivation to poison Avondelle. What would push a person to do that? Hatred? Vengeance, perhaps?"

"Vengeance," Novaly repeated in a scared tone.

"Vengeance is a powerful motivator, but if it is vengeance, who then would have the same vengeful heart not to harm Elysium, just to teach a lesson?'"

Siany's body went cold, and she felt nauseous. She started wobbling. Nijeel braced Siany.

"Siany, are you all right?" Novaly whispered.

"Yes and no. I need to get to the palace at once." Nijeel summoned Siany's guard for their horses. Siany and Novaly mounted their horses quickly.

"Thank you, Sir Nijeel. As always, your wisdom has proved to help protect Elysium."

"Always here to serve, majesty." Nijeel bowed.

Siany, Novaly, and the palace guard galloped back toward the palace. The cool air blew Novaly's autumn flower crown from her red hair. Siany was on a mission. Once the horses stopped in front of the palace steps, they dismounted breathlessly.

"Siany, wait. What's this all about? Do you know who poisoned everyone?"

"I have a feeling, and I hope I'm wrong, but for now, I need to write a letter to Port Rowlin."

Stawyer and Ajorn squatted at the tree line, staring at Pantorian. They had finally reached the capital of Len Nove. They knew Behan's group would already be in the city, blending. It was now their turn. The prisoner and Max's injury slowed them down considerably. Scratching his dark brown beard, which had grown thick on the journey, Stawyer contemplated how they were going to rescue Char and Sakul. The two made their way back to the group.

"All clear, your majesty," Ajorn said.

Sealyn shook her head. "Something doesn't seem right."

"No, it's true, Queen Sealyn. We didn't see any soldiers in our path," Stawyer said.

"That's the problem."

Twigs snapped. Everyone froze. The surzees scattered. Hearts pounded. With a thud, Finn landed in the middle of the group from his tree hiding spot. "Duck," he yelled.

Everyone dropped to their knees. Axes whizzed by them, landing in the trees nearby. Appearing from the blue haze, a large group of black armored Stoltland soldiers surrounded them. Jace and Jem stepped closer to Sealyn. They all drew their swords and prepared to fight. Sealyn felt her hands grow hot. She didn't want Stoltland to know what she could do, but she needed to be ready for the worst.

"Surrender now, and we take you to the palace peacefully."

"We come in peace," Tilmond said.

The dark soldier chuckled. "As evidenced by the wounded prisoner. Like I said, surrender."

"He attacked us!" Max yelled. "You want your comrade. Then let us walk ourselves peacefully to the palace."

The Stoltland leader turned his head and nodded to a group behind him. Three arrows fired. The Elysians dodged the arrows, but the arrows still hit their target—the prisoner. All three landed in his chest, and his body went still with death.

"What is this madness?" Sealyn exclaimed.

"This is the last time I ask nicely. Surrender or else." More and more soldiers joined the Stoltlanders. Sealyn's group was completely outnumbered. It would be a slaughter if they chose to fight.

Jace grabbed Sealyn's hand and nodded. Was this it? Were they really about to be captives to Stoltland? The dark leader grew tired of waiting and lunged forward. He grabbed Stawyer, catching him off guard. The Stoltlander held his sword to Stawyer's throat.

"Now, Queen Sealyn. Do I have your surrender?"

"Stop! Yes." She dropped her sword. "Let him go."

"Order the rest of your group to drop their swords." Sealyn nodded for them to obey. Each dropped their weapons with bitterness.

"Let him go."

The dark soldier nodded and dropped his sword. Stawyer walked back to his friends, reaching for Ajorn, but the Stoltlander's sword plunged through his chest. Sealyn screamed. Ajorn caught Stawyer as the Stoltlander drew his bloody sword from Stawyer's chest. Stawyer coughed blood. The rest of the soldiers seized the Elysians. With force, they jerked Ajorn away from Stawyer's dying body. They protested in screams and begged to help their comrade, but all they could do was watch their friend lay open-eyed on the ground, choking helplessly. There, in the crimson snow, their comrade died.

The catacombs were eerily quiet. Doebromir remembered Zuri telling the war council about the Len Novian catacombs. Seeing them up close was surreal. As the Elysians passed by the frozen bodies, they could see that each person held a square rock in their hands. From what they could tell, the rock had the name of the person carved in it. They couldn't read the names due to the ice, but it felt odd. Why would they seal people in ice and label them? The bodies looked like they could walk out of the icy walls at any moment.

Sune's red hair glowed in the torchlight. He hated confined spaces and tried to keep his heart rate calm. He hoped Ezen could find a way out quickly. He handed Sorcha a piece of jerky, hoping the food would help stop her tears. He couldn't imagine what she must be feeling. To lose a friend so violently leaves a mark on a person's soul.

"How are you handling it all, Lady Sorcha?" Sune asked.

Sorcha shook her head. "I can't even begin to process what I just witnessed. I failed. I failed my friend when she needed me most."

"You didn't fail, Sorcha. You tried your best. None of that was your fault."

"I know. It's just perhaps, maybe, if I had listened to—" She stopped talking and folded her arms, shaking her head. She didn't want to think about that possibility.

"What were you about to say? Listened to who?"

"My father. He wanted me to pursue the magical arts of herbs, but my mother told me not to. She feared mixing magic with herbs, so I stayed away. Apparently, my grandmother is a magical alchemist in the herbal arts, but I've never met her. I don't even know what she looks like."

"Why?"

"She and my mother argued about that subject, so they stayed away from each other. Now, I'm wondering, if I had had a relationship with her, would I have been able to conjure something that could have saved Rivers?"

"You can't think like that, Sorcha. I don't think even the wisest alchemist could have saved her." Sune wrapped his arm around Sorcha's shoulders. She looked up into his jade-colored eyes and noticed how his freckles flaked across his nose. When she focused on his face, she noticed for the first time how handsome Sune was. He had such a gentle face, and then she remembered Sakul. What was she doing?

Jashun looked back at Sune's arm around Sorcha. He glared. He missed his step and slipped sideways into the icy barrier. His hands smacked the wall, and then loud whispers sang out from all angles.

"You hear that, right?" whispered Jashun.

Doebromir nodded. "I can't figure out what they're saying."

"It sounds like a different language," Jashun shivered.

Sakul leaned his bald, shiny head on the icy stone wall. He sat with his legs stretched out. He was one horror story away from losing his mind. King Egil finally finished recapping to Char and Sakul what happened, which made Sakul nauseous.

"Let me get this straight," Sakul interjected. "Stoltland's army took your capital by way of their Tor, which is apparently an old magic passageway between kingdoms. They have ships arriving each week with Nicht slaves and departing with barrels of ice to take back with them. Stoltland also has a mission to find Len Nove's source of magic, which the old text refers to as

PaloMae, and Malum has been torturing you three for its whereabouts. Did I miss anything?"

King Egil nodded. "I fear you both may be next to torture."

"Why do you say that?" Sakul asked with panic.

The king dropped his head and then looked at his children, who were still latched to each other. "Because he makes me watch." A lump caught in his throat, and he shook his head. Egil took a big gasp of air, choking on his next words. "He makes me watch what he does to my beautiful children." Char cursed Malum's birth.

"I hate that for you all, but why do you think we're next?"

"He's growing tired of my resistance. You two showing up just opened another game for him."

Sakul's green eyes watered. He did not want to be tortured. "Don't lose hope! We have people here. They will come for us."

A loud clang echoed through the dungeons. The twins jumped and clasped each other tighter. Scuffling could be heard, along with loud voices. Stoltland soldiers had more blue-cloaked prisoners and shoved them into the two cells that belonged to Sakul and Char. Once the blue-cloaked prisoners stood and removed their hoods, Char gasped.

Prince Dag released his sister and walked to the front of the cage, grasping the ice bars. "Who are you, and why did they arrest you?"

Char shook his head. "They are our rescue party. Allow me to introduce Commander Brehan, and this scruffy one is Lord Favien." Char pulled back Norella's sleeve and kissed her hand. "This gorgeous minx is Lady Norella, and over in Sakul's cell is Lord Ashur, Lady Pinx, and finally, Lord Rielen, the queen's cousin."

"Some rescue party," Dag huffed. "What hope do we have now?"

Char placed his hand on Brehan's shoulder. "My fellow Elysians, these chipper people are the royal family of Len Nove: King Egil, Prince Dag, and Princess Drifa. I don't know if I even want to know how you all were caught."

Favien held Pinx's hand through the bars. "At least our queen isn't here."

"Yet," spat Dag.

Brehan grabbed the bars. "Why don't you back off, child?"

"Easy, Brehan," Char said. "The prince and princess have both been through terrors; we don't need to speak out loud."

Sakul leaned to Rielen. "Any news on Sorcha?"

"Doebromir didn't make his checkpoint. We're not sure where they are."

Sakul felt sick. At least they weren't locked up; that meant there was still hope for Doebromir's team and his amazing Sorcha to be safe.

CHAPTER 18
LIBERO MEUS ANIMUS

The sled cages were bumpy and cold. Snow, ice, and feces flung into the Elysians' faces as the sled dogs took them around the city of Pantorian. Zuri was so grateful for her beaver leather clothes. Months before the quest for Len Nove was to take place, Sealyn had ordered the beaver leathers for her military and the Vinurs of the Court. That decision was paying off. Zuri knew something wasn't right. The soldiers weren't taking them to the palace.

They weren't even taking them into the city.

When the sleds rounded the base of the mountain city, a giant, elliptical amphitheater made completely out of ice came into view. Zuri was in a cage with Finn and Madilina, and she looked at Finn with fear. What did this mean?

This amphitheater was legendary. Hundreds of years ago, Len Nove built it for events. They wanted to have similar games like Elysium with Feydom, but each king failed to complete the large structure. Why would Stoltland soldiers take them to this place? And why would Stoltland worry about restoring old ruins?

Malum stood in the large doorway of the amphitheater. Jace's heart dropped. Sealyn immediately grabbed Jace's hand. This was not good. Sealyn's mind swirled. It was hard to know what a psychotic enemy would do next.

Malum stretched his arms out wide. "Greetings, Elysians. Welcome to my masterpiece."

Blue-eyed Len Novians were chiseling and sculpting the structure. Sealyn saw their chains. Malum had enslaved hundreds of Len Novians to build this structure. She glared at him.

"Oh, come now, Queen Sealyn. Don't be smug. We're just sprucing up the greatest structure this kingdom has ever seen!"

Malum turned and walked inside. The soldiers pushed the Elysians forward.

They led them up a narrow staircase that curved. Their legs ached as they climbed and climbed. Finally, they appeared on a flat opening that was a centered overhang. Clearly, this section was for royals to sit in during the events. The original stone was still standing, but Malum used ice for any missing or broken parts of the arena. It was extraordinarily massive.

"Have a seat, your majesties," Malum motioned for Jace and Sealyn to sit at the centered blue and silver chairs. A blue canopy covered their seating, preventing any snow from falling on them. Jace locked eyes with Malum. Jace felt something stronger than pride tug at his heart as he took his seat. His fists made his knuckles turn white.

"So?" Malum asked.

"So what?" snapped Sealyn.

"What do you think of my restoration? Isn't it marvelous?"

"You seriously want me to compliment you after your men just murdered one of mine?"

Malum's black eyes narrowed. "From what I hear, your men killed a few of mine first. Seems fair." He shrugged.

"They attacked us first!" Max yelled, then received a punch to the gut from a soldier.

Sealyn stood. "That's enough. We're leaving, so uncuff us."

A wicked smile spread across Malum's light, brown face. "But you would miss the games."

"What games?" asked Jem

"I'm glad you asked, you red-eyed fox," Malum winked at Jem. Jem glared. "Feydom." Malum patted Finn on the shoulder.

"Feydom?" Sealyn questioned.

"Oh yes, Feydom." Malum locked eyes with Jace. "We know all about Feydom. Don't we, Jammy Jace."

"Shut it, Malum," Jace said.

Malum laughed, then clapped twice. "Bring in the contestants."

Sealyn walked to the edge and gripped the icy banister, her hands still in chains. Her heart froze. Time stopped. Her friends joined her at the edge. Madilina gasped. Out walked every prisoner from Len Nove's dungeons. Sealyn felt her hands turn hot. She could kill Malum right here, right now, but she could lose more of her friends and family. What was she supposed to do?

Malum stood close behind Sealyn and whispered into her ear. "How does it feel to be powerless? You will watch them compete and die, and you will be powerless."

Tears of anger filled Sealyn's eyes. Her memory flashed back to her father and grandfather teaching her how to outmaneuver the opponent. She could almost hear her father's words, "You must let them think they're winning at all costs. Give them the ego they need to be their own undoing. Find out as much of their plan as possible, then make the least expected decision that will save the most lives."

Sealyn swallowed hard. "Fine, Malum. You want a game, then let's play. What are your rules?"

"Simple rules. Your Elysians and 'want-to-be' Elysians," he eyed Zuri, Finn, and Jem, "will play for your freedom. Same rules as Feydom. Day one: Clod: all fourteen flags first, you win. Day two: Clod continues, if not all fourteen flags are gathered, and Vision starts. Shoot all ten pipscots, and you win. Day three: Clod and Vision continue if none of those goals are met, and Wings starts. Just be ready for this day. If, and I mean if, your people survive all three days, then the group with the most wins, wins." Malum clasped his hands behind his back and rocked on his feet. He was proud of this game.

Sealyn needed more information. "You want to split us into teams so that we would play against each other?"

"Not exactly. There won't be seven teams like you Elysians play. Let's honor the reason why Len Nove is cursed." Zuri and Finn flinched. "It will be two teams. Just like that gruesome day: the Len Novians versus the Mammoths." Malum laughed.

"How dare you!" Zuri yelled. A soldier raised his hand to smack her, but Finn stepped in front and took the hit.

Finn wiped blood from his lip. "Don't forget the role Stoltland played that day."

"Oh, no need to fear, Finn-a-ginns. The Elysians will all be Roamers, but Stoltland will be the Tacklers. You know, to represent the instigators we were." Malum wiggled his eyebrows at Zuri. She lunged for him but was swung backward by the guard jerking her chains.

Sealyn was trying hard to find the loopholes in his rules. They would literally be battling anything Stoltland had to throw at them for three days. She looked at Pinx and Norella. They had only had self-defense training, not battleground training. How were they going to survive? She could not watch them die. Sealyn shook her head. "What's the catch, Malum?"

"Catch? I would have thought you knew that the entire game is a catch. Well, one more thing: if your team doesn't win any part of Feydom, then everyone dies!" Malum threw his hands up excitedly.

Think. Think. Think. Sealyn pushed her mind. She had to think of something.

Jace shook his head fiercely. "No, Malum. No! Those are completely unfair terms."

"Easy, Jammy Jace. Good news for you is that you're team captain for the Mammoths."

Jace blinked. "Crown royals don't play Feydom."

Malum stepped nose to nose with Jace. "In what world would I ever consider you a crowned royal? You will always be the grey-eyed freak that nobody cared about or wanted. You are an embarrassment to Stoltland. Remember how embarrassed you were covered in jam?" Jace's eyes narrowed. "Exactly, Jace. That's how embarrassed we are of you. Besides, if you die, then Queen Sealyn will need a new husband."

Jace lunged, but Malum stepped back and drew his sword. He held it to Jace's neck. Sealyn stepped in front of Jace, carefully pushing the sword down. Sealyn knew they only had one trick up their sleeve that Stoltland didn't know about. She recalled her father's voice, "When it's your turn to make terms of the deal, make sure they're the fools, not you."

Sealyn had to have faith in her people. Blind faith. Isn't that what Lizz had said? She had to trust her instincts about Stoltland's curse: pride. Sealyn nodded. "I will agree to your terms, Malum." Her comrades gasped. Malum grinned. "On one condition." Malum folded his arms. "If we continue to day three for Wings, I ask that one player play for both sides. In the history of Feydom, barely any team has ever scored a point for Wings. It's almost impossible. If this player, scores all seven points, then we all win our freedom."

"What?" exclaimed Malum. "No. No way. That's too easy."

Sealyn smirked. "Almost impossible is too easy? A Wings team usually has five players."

"Almost, Sealyn. Almost."

"Well, what about completely impossible? Instead of using Nomosevs, use Caelidons," Sealyn said convincingly. She saw him thinking through the decision to use the all-feathered, winged horse rather than the nomosevs. She needed one more addition to the terms to seal the deal. "I'll add one more stipulation: you get to pick the player."

Jace's eyes bulged. What was she thinking? Malum scratched his chin. He looked around the group on the upper level, then scanned the prisoners.

Sealyn's heart pounded. She prayed she was right about his ego.

Malum extended his hand to Sealyn. "Deal."

Sealyn shook Malum's hand. "Who do you choose as our Wings' player?"

He walked past Sealyn and pushed Max to the side, then grabbed the exact person Sealyn prayed he would choose. "I choose her."

"Lady Madilina?" Sealyn tried to say in a shocked and disappointed voice. "You're more of a monster than I thought, Malum." Malum beamed at his choice.

Sealyn knew the pressure she just placed on Madilina, but she also had a different feeling about her, and she had to trust it. The deal she made was either the worst she could have done, or it will go down in history as one of Stoltland's greatest ego moments. Malum took one look at Madilina, saw her tiny size, and thought she was nothing. Perhaps the least likely is the most valuable.

Tiny Ella sat at Queen Mother Graelynd's feet, waiting for her to drop more pumpkin. The little exiguum loved eating pumpkin and all the other autumn fruits and vegetables. King Father Ryker watched his caring wife drop another piece of pumpkin for Ella. He chuckled to himself. He loved how much his wife loved animals. Her pure heart still made his head forget time existed.

Ryker looked around the seasonally decorated dining room. He was thankful for his family attending Perdonair's celebration along with the diplomats. Watching his daughter, he knew Siany was uncomfortable with all the suitors but hoped she could find happiness with one of them. Like Siany, he was anxiously waiting for the investigation results.

Siany sent out the palace's best investigators to Port Rowlin for her hunch. They could think of nothing else. Feydom was quite the entertaining game, but even as exciting as each day had been, their minds were completely engulfed in what the investigators would find because if Siany's hunch was true, then she would face imprisoning Sealyn's friend.

Novaly leaned to Siany. "This turkey is delicious! I can't wait for dessert." She tried to keep Siany's thoughts happy. Novaly was always a positive spirit.

"I agree. I'm really looking forward to the pecan pie. Grand Queen Karis told me she was in the kitchens helping make the pies," Siany said.

"Then, I know the pies will be extra special this year!" Novaly gobbled up another piece of turkey.

Captain Graegory burst through the dining room doors. He ran to Siany and Ryker and knelt behind their chairs.

Ryker whispered. "Is the report here?" Graegory nodded.

"Is it what we feared?" Siany questioned. Graegory nodded again. Siany dropped her head. Heart heavy, she knew she had to gather the war council. Her anticipation of pecan pie was now ruined. The war council had already been placed on high alert, so when she rose from the table and made the head nod to the members, they all left the banquet to converse in the war room.

Siany felt sick as she read the report. She kept rereading the last word, "Confirmed," over and over. This was not happening. How could she face the council with this information? The report held the identity of the person responsible for the poisoning. Elysium would want justice. She wished Sealyn were here to deal with this, but it would be twice as hard for Sealyn to face this because the criminal was her friend.

"All right, Siany, we're waiting for you to tell us what the report says," Prince Adomin huffed. Adomin never feared getting to the point with his niece. His arm had healed nicely, but it still ached from the arrow wound, which made him a little grouchy at times like this.

Siany nodded and set the paper down. "Of course. I'm sorry. This is very hard to process."

"Would you like me to read it?" Ryker offered.

"Actually, yes. I believe that will help."

Ryker held the report and read aloud.

Majesty,

We have the proof and witnesses of the poisoning, which led to our king and queen's kidnapping and disappearance, along with the death of Lord Temm. We have found that this culprit is the traitor Lord Drystan's wife, Lady Pyry."

The room gasped. Ryker continued.

We searched her house and found hidden correspondence between Pyry and Queen Corentine. We also found spell books and empty bottles with the residue of the exact same poison that was missing from Lady Zuri's apothecary shop. Her servants came forward and confessed to helping carry out Pyry's plan. Her father paid large sums to a small army of men to transport all of those who went missing. I'm afraid the evidence is irrefutable. Lady Pyry and her father are being held at Port Rowin's prison until further notice. It is my professional opinion that the person ultimately responsible is Lady Pyry. This is confirmed.

Awaiting instructions.

Inspector Caelimont, Head Palace Inspector

"I knew that family wasn't done after Jace killed Drystan," Prince Royce said.

"So what happens now?" Captain Graegory asked.

"A trial. I just can't believe Pyry would do this. Sealyn loved her like a sister! This is madness," Siany said.

Ryker placed his hand on Siany's. He leaned in and whispered. "Sweetie, you know our law: death for death."

"I know, father. Someone must die."

Death crept around every corner and every wall. The icy catacombs were an unending maze of discomfort, a constant reminder of their loss. The food rationing was becoming unbearable. There was no way of knowing how far they had traveled, either. Days ran together since they had no sun to guide them.

They were miserable. To make matters worse, Ezen had developed a fever. They dragged themselves through the tunnels, hoping the next turn would lead to a door, any door at this point. Doebromir held up his hand, and the group paused.

"Did you hear that?" he whispered. The group shook their heads. An odd sound came echoing down their tunnel. "There! That. Did you hear that?"

"What kind of noise is it?" Jashun questioned.

"Sounds like moving chains? Or the scraping of chains?" Sorcha said.

They walked quietly, scared of what they would find. They took another turn and saw a faint light coming from the end of a long tunnel. The frozen bodies glistened on each side of the tunnel. Doebromir snuffed out his torch, and Sune did the same. They did not want to attract any unwanted attention.

Sune grabbed Doebromir's shoulder. "Let me go investigate. We don't need to risk everyone's footsteps. I'm light on my feet." Doebromir nodded.

Sune glanced at Sorcha, then quietly tip-toed to the end of the tunnel. He could hear himself breathing and heard the raspy catch. They would all be sick soon if they didn't find a way out. He paused at the corner and slowly peered down the tunnel.

He saw two Stoltland soldiers standing with spears, watching two Len Novian men lift a woman into an empty space in the ice wall. Sune's mouth dropped at the sight of what happened next. The ice opened a hole for the dead body, but wait—the body wasn't dead! He saw shallow breaths. These men were sending people to icy graves before they were dead! Like paddles pushing through icy waters, the ice opening made the "chain-dragging" sounds.

Sune stilled himself. He wanted to run and save this poor woman, but he risked his friends' lives. Had it really come to this, choosing who lives between people you know versus people you didn't? He watched helplessly as they placed the woman's body in the hole, and the ice closed around her, sealing her in.

"That's the last one," a Len Novian said.

"Finally, let's head back to Zykoan," a Stoltlander said. The group pulled the large sled that had carried the bodies in and rounded a corner. Sune watched them leave his sight and then heard what sounded like a door close.

He sprang forward and ran down the tunnel, hoping he could somehow open the ice back up. The group saw Sune leave, and they took off after him. Doebromir quickly relit their torches to see through the darkness. Sune slid in front of the young woman. She looked like she was sleeping. He banged his fists on the ice. Loud whispers echoed from the walls. The same words they had been trying to figure out.

"Stop, Sune!" Sorcha yelled.

"I can't. She's still alive."

Loud whispers rang through the catacombs. Sune banged harder.

"Sune, you have to stop. The ice isn't moving," Doebromir ordered.

Sune paused, breathing heavily. "The ice just swallowed her, but I saw her breathing before they placed her in the wall."

Jashun slid away from the wall. "Swallowed her? What kind of death trap are we in?"

"I don't know," Sune said. "But I have to try to save her." He drew his sword and banged the hilt into the ice. A small crack formed, then a burst of energy through all of them against the other wall. Loud whispers that felt like wind filled the tunnel.

Sorcha rubbed her head and coughed. "Did I hear 'libero meus?'"

"And I think 'animus,'" Sune croaked.

Jashun tilted his head. "Libero meus ani-"

"Don't!" cried Sorcha.

"What?"

"Don't say all those words together. They're from the old magic. It could be the curse calling."

"But Sorcha, we're not of the Len Novian curse, so that curse can't affect us," Sune said.

"We don't know what can affect us with Stoltland at play."

Ezen stood rubbing his back. "Do you know what those words even mean?"

"I think 'libero' means 'release,' right?" Doebromir asked.

Sune nodded. "And 'animus' means spirit or purpose or soul. I can't remember which." Sorcha made an inquisitive face. Sune raised his hands. "What? You think you're the only smart one here?"

Sorcha smiled. She had forgotten how to smile. "So all three together translates 'release my spirit?'"

Jashun shook his head violently. "No. No. No. Don't repeat any more of that. I don't want any dead spirits being released. We have got to get out of here!"

Sune jumped to his feet. "That reminds me—there's a door around that corner."

"Then why are we still inhabiting this death chamber?" Doebromir asked.

The group charged toward Sune's directions, and there at the end of the tunnel was a wooden door. Doebromir slid the iron latch, then pushed. Along with sunlight, a gust of salty sea wind blew past each one. They blinked against the light, and when the eyes finally adjusted, they saw in the distance large ships and a bustling town.

"Sune, where are we?" Sorcha asked.

"My lady, we are at the port of Zykoan."

"How far away are we from Pantorian?" Jashun asked.

Sune looked at Doebromir. "Miles and miles north, which means we can't help our queen."

Commander Malum,

I'm growing tired of no progress. Obviously, the old king is not worth trying to break, so finish playing with your toys and find me the source.

The season to attack Avondelle is almost here. We're sending a test now to see how the dragons will manage.

I expect you to break Sealyn, but don't kill Jace. I mean it, Malum. He could be worth something.

Magnanimously,
Queen Corentine, Queen of Stoltland & all seven kingdoms

CHAPTER 19
NOT JUST ANY CLAW

Malum was not king of Len Nove, but he was king of mind games. A month had gone by, and he had kept everyone prisoner. He kept Sealyn and Jace in separate royal chambers and the rest he locked in the servants' chambers. At least they were all warm and well-fed. Sealyn knew Malum had an agenda, though.

For the past two weeks, servants had been in and out of her room, taking her measurements and bringing in strips of fabric. What was Malum up to? She hated being apart from Jace. She needed to see him. She wondered if he was being treated the same way. No one ever spoke to her. It was the same routine each day. Breakfast arrived early, then an hour later, the trays were cleaned, and Sealyn would do her exercises. She wanted to stay fit for whatever plot Malum had. The servants served hot tea, then lunch, then cleaned, then more fittings, teas, more fittings, dinner, then silence.

Sealyn's solace was that she found an old rotten trunk hidden in the wall of her room when she first arrived. She had felt uncomfortable snooping around the dead queen's chamber, but what else was she to do? The walls were a deep royal blue, adorned with tiny white stars, and white curtains trimmed the windows. The bed was made of white marble and covered with deep blue blankets and white furs. Several white armoires and bookcases lined the walls, and a beautiful white marble fireplace was in the center.

Sealyn discovered the secret door as she paced by an armoire opposite the large bed. A tiny keyhole appeared. She thought she had imagined it, but she retraced her steps and walked by again, and the keyhole reappeared. Crouching beside it, she ran her fingers over the silver metal and then heard a click as it unlocked itself. Sealyn pressed on the wall, and a small section opened, revealing the trunk. The small room was filled with cobwebs and a damp smell. The trunk's inscription read, "Quid Vos Desiderium."

Sealyn knew that was the old magic language but decided to disregard caution; besides, the inscription meant "what you desire." When she opened the trunk, there was only one item: a book called *The History of Len Nove*. Sealyn figured the old magic had worn off because this was not what she had desired. By day three, she had finished reading the book and decided to put it back, but when she opened the trunk, there was another book: *A Mammoth's Tale*.

This continued. Once she finished reading one book, a new one would appear in the trunk. She realized this was what she desired. The trunk was revealing the hidden secrets about Len Nove. The old magic wanted to help her.

After a month of being Malum's captive, Sealyn had just settled into her bed to continue reading *The Mammoths' Last Battle* when a servant unlocked her door. Sealyn quickly hid the book under her pillow. The blue-eyed servant curtsied and handed her a note, then left.

My Dearest Queen Sealyn,

Your presence is requested for dinner tomorrow night. It will be the party of a lifetime.

Affectionately,

Commander Malum

Sealyn gagged. Going to a party was the last thing she wanted to do, then a sickening feeling came over her. What if Malum was celebrating some sort of victory? Had he found Len Nove's source of magic? She pulled out the book and began reading as fast as possible. She needed all the answers she could have. Knowledge would be the weapon that killed Malum.

Before the servants had arrived to dress Sealyn, she managed to read one more tiny book. Odd that the trunk chose this book for her to read before dinner. It was a children's book called *The Necklace.* The book was only a few pages long with faded pictures.

Page one: picture of Len Nove's past king and the words, "The King"

Page two: picture of a large mammoth and the words, "The Mammoth King."

Page three: picture of the king and the mammoth smiling, and the words, "They became friends."

Page four: picture of the king with his hand on the mammoth's tusk and the words, "Magic bond."

Page five: picture of a blue gemmed crown and necklace, and the words, "The Medeis."

Page six: only a picture of the king wearing the blue gemmed crown and the mammoth wearing the blue gemmed necklace.

That was it. Six pages of a children's book, and somehow the trunk thought this was important. The servants dressed Sealyn in royal blue fabric. It was incredibly heavy. The dress was an off-the-shoulder with a deep V-neckline. Tiny blue diamonds covered every inch of the dress, which is why it was so heavy. Sealyn hated that she loved how gorgeous the blue ball gown was on her, fitted at the waist with a large flare of sparkles.

Instead of dwelling on the beauty of the gown, she focused on the story. The trunk was trying to tell her something. Yet, her mind drifted to Jace. She wondered if he would be attending the ball. How would he look at her wearing blue? If her people were attending, would they think she betrayed them by wearing this gown? This had to be another Malum trick.

She shook away those thoughts and rested on page five and pictured the words "The Medeis." Why would this page be the only page written in the old magic language? She tried to focus as the servants combed and pinned her hair. She had been warned long ago to be careful of the old magic language, but every time she encountered it, it seemed to help her. The servants painted her eyes and lips, enhancing her stunning beauty.

What was she missing? Stoltland was here for the source of Len Nove's magic. She also needed to find that source and claim it to break Len Nove's curse. A servant gently placed a large, blue gemmed necklace around Sealyn's neck and said, "Done." Sealyn blinked. She ran her fingers down the gaudy jewelry. It reminded her of the picture in the book.

"The Medeis."

She gasped, making the servants jump. She now knew what the source was, but where to find it would be the next problem to solve.

Lord Saemeon spun Princess Siany around the dance floor. The diplomat's son from Hill Chimes had dark wavy hair and dark green eyes that watched only Siany's face. Siany blushed innocently. The Trundatta ball was coming to an end, and she wanted nothing more than for this night to continue forever. The yellow fire flowers made the room seem like the sun was inside, dancing with them. Siany chose the theme "sunshine" for the ball. The costumes people wore were astonishing. From golden headpieces to ombre sunset gowns, the ballroom glowed with brightness. This had been her goal. She wanted her people to feel bright, like the sun's rays.

Siany had enjoyed her time most with Lord Saemeon from Hill Chimes and Lord Edvard from Blissendelle. The two men were each other's opposites. Saemeon had darker features while Edvard had golden hair with bright green eyes--even their interests were opposites. How would she make this decision? She thought about setting up a series of challenges to see which one would win, but she tossed that idea out when Novaly called it "barbaric." She was glad her father told her she could take her time. Time was what she needed because time would bring back Sealyn.

The final song finished, and the bells chimed, signaling the final speech of the evening. Siany stepped to the center of the ballroom. "Thank you, my wonderful guests. Tonight has been one of the best nights of my life, and I have all of you to thank for that. I applaud everyone's costumes and dancing skills." She paused and looked at Lord Edvard. He was the better dancer. "I wish you safe travels back home and look forward to next year."

Everyone clapped and made their way to their carriages. Novaly locked arms with Siany, and both walked into the garden library. Siany's parents, grandparents, aunts, uncles, and cousins were all sitting around, drinking tea and eating Puffin Pies.

"Well, Siany, Lord Saemeon looked very happy after that last dance," Anadelvia teased. Siany blushed, not knowing what to say. Anadelvia's tight-fitted golden gown sparkled against the fireflowers. Her gown made it obvious why she was the crown's stylist, even though she was Siany's cousin.

"I agree," said Prince Adomin, Anadelvia's father. "Didn't I count five dances with him tonight?" Siany rolled her eyes. She knew where this was going.

"Five with Saemeon and four with Edvard, to be exact," Lord Menry added. Menry, the second eldest brother to King Father Ryker, was particularly good at paying attention to details. Every story he told always had extra details that didn't aid his stories.

Lady Ebbalee squeezed her elderly hand with Siany's. "Does that mean Grandma will have great-grandchildren soon?" Ebbalee liked to refer to herself in the third person when talking with her grandchildren. She looked at her son, King Father Ryker, and winked.

Siany dropped her head. Her family could be quite overwhelming when they wanted to be. "I think I would like to court the lords first before having children." She regretted saying those words the moment they were out.

"Lords!" exclaimed Lady Tintallina, aunt to Siany. "My, my. Dating more than one at a time seems scandalous, Siany." Tintallina's sweet face turned pink like it always did when she was embarrassed. Her son, Jdru, nudged her and wiggled his eyebrows. In that moment, Tintallina's eyes watered. Jdru's mannerisms reminded her of her other son, Char.

Novaly shook her head, laughing at Siany. "I told you not to say anything."

Siany groaned. "I know. It just slipped out."

Prince Royce stood looking out the window intently. "Majesties, hurry. Come look at this. Dun is walking funny."

Some of the royals raced to the windows while the rest of the family pushed each other for a glimpse into the remaining open space. Dun had a limp, and blood covered his green wings. Siany's heart dropped. She pushed past her family and ran to the outdoor patio, descending all the steps at lightning speed, even in her golden costume. She reached the giant phoenix and froze.

"Dun! Oh, no. Dun! Tell me that's not your blood."

Dun's yellow eyes were sad and bloodshot. The rest of the family caught up with Siany and stood beside her in shock. Dun turned to show them his other side, where blood was pouring out of a wound in the upper part of his leg. King Father Ryker saw the object lodged into Dun's skin.

Ryker grabbed it and looked at Dun. "This will hurt." Dun nodded, and Ryker yanked it free. Dun made no sound. Lord Menry quickly applied his coat to the wound and wrapped his long scarf around the large leg. Half of the family helped escort Dun inside the palace to help tend to his wound and comfort him. The rest remained fixated on the object in Ryker's bloody hands.

"Is that a claw?" Lord Jdru asked. He swallowed hard and scratched his reddish-blonde beard with nervousness.

Ryker nodded. "Not just any claw—a dragon's claw."

Ezen's fever finally broke after weeks of battling a touch sickness. They felt relief because no one wanted to report to Sealyn that her cousin died on their watch. Jashun thought they were fortunate to run into an Elysian sympathizer on their first day in Zykoan. Sir Verraeter, a frail old man, was more than happy to have the entire group stay in his small home. His wife died a few years ago, so the place was a mess, but Sorcha saw that as her calling. She cleaned and made herself helpful wherever she could. Verraeter let the group stay in his one-room home, which became cramped very fast. They gave Ezen the bed, then constructed mattresses out of blankets and hay for the rest. The hay had been imported from Korpam, oddly enough.

Verraeter explained that Stoltland landed many months ago and helped resurrect their port city. Between fire Nichts and fire salts, the city became a functioning port again. Word even spread to several other kingdoms. Selling ice and fish was their trade. Hundreds of barrels of ice and fish were sent on ships to every kingdom except Elysium. Ice Nichts maintained the ice until they were docked and transported. Some kingdoms were desperate for water, so the barrels of ice fetched a high price at the big markets.

Sune and Doebromir helped fish and cook for the group. Jashun fixed all things broken in Verraeter's home. They were settling into a comforting routine after staying with Verraeter for a month. Sune and Doebromir returned from their day of fishing with news from the port. The group sat around the shabby wooden table while the pot bubbled over the fire. They could smell the delicious potatoes, carrots, and beans Verraeter bought at the port market.

"We saw a new flag at the port today," Doebromir said. "Orange with two crossed, black swords, and a black tiger head at the top." He plopped the fish on the table and began descaling.

Verraeter froze. He was a scruffy old man with a large scar across his left eye. He slouched and had missing fingers, lost to frostbite.

"I'm not familiar with that flag," Sorcha said, still gazing into the stew. She was trying not to look at Sune's handsome, freckled face. She kept wanting to run her fingers through his red curly hair, so she forced herself to look at the soup and concentrate on Sakul's features.

"You should count your blessings," Verraeter said with his scratchy voice. "That's not a flag I would wish to tangle with, so let's avoid it."

"But what makes it so bad?"

Verraeter huffed. "Because I said it was, woman! That should be reason enough."

"Hey," yelled Sune. "You can't speak to her like that. She's a lady."

"Keep telling me how to run my house, boy, and the next time a Stoltland soldier comes by for an inspection, I'll let him find ya."

The Elysians found it odd that Stoltland soldiers would come by three times each week, checking to make sure Verraeter was keeping up with his household chores and his trade job at the docks. They initially thought Verraeter was part of a rehabilitation program, but they saw the soldiers checking on every home in the city. They also noticed Verraeter was lazier on the days the soldiers weren't scheduled to come by.

Sorcha decided that this had to be part of breaking Len Nove's curse. If Len Nove's curse was idleness, then part of undoing it must be accountability, but this form of accountability came with an agenda and was more like dictating.

Verraeter slammed the door, leaving the group stunned at his outburst. Sorcha shook her head, shaking her black springy curls, and whispered, "I just wanted to know what the flag meant. Nothing more."

"Ignore the ol' bitter ice cube," Doebromir jeered.

Sune helped gut one of the fish. "Pirates."

Sorcha jerked her head toward Sune. "What?"

"The flag. It means that ship is full of pirates, and not just any pirates: Korpam pirates."

Sorcha's eyes bulged. "Because of the orange and tiger head?" Sune nodded.

Jashun threw a spoon. "Great! Just great. We're stuck here at a port governed by Stoltland, and now there are foul Korpam pirates too." His brown cheeks turned red with anger.

"Why are Korpam pirates so bad?" Sorcha asked.

"Pirates, in general, are awful. They have no rules. Some even kill for sport," Sune paused and stared at the next fish, almost in a trance, then he looked at Sorcha. "But Korpam? The one thing Korpam hates more than anything in this world is *green eyes*."

The emerald queen descended the white marble stairs into the large, vast ballroom. The walls were still iced over and decorated with elongated blue banners, each one featuring a sparkling silver mammoth in the middle. Blue fire flowers glowed underneath in white pots. The room's décor felt cold; beautiful, but cold. She marveled at the ceilings. Ice chandeliers and silver mountain paintings dazzled every inch. The floor was royal blue with sparkles that twinkled under the light.

She locked eyes with the one man that made her weak, Jace. He was dressed in all black. Of course, Malum would make Jace wear black. His brown hair was pulled back, and his beard had thickened. He looked older with a dark beard. The rest of the Elysian prisoners were dressed in green and looked well fed, but then she noticed everyone's chains. Escaping tonight would be hard to manage.

Jace saw his bride walking slowly down the staircase. His breath caught. For a moment, he thought he was dreaming. Sealyn radiated power and confidence, even under these circumstances. He was so proud of her. How could Malum dress Elysium's queen in blue? Everything was a game to Malum. People were just pawns to him. Jace needed to speak to Sealyn about how to get her home alive.

Malum, matching his hair, dressed in all black and met Sealyn at the bottom of the stairs, and instead of extending his hand for an escort, he held up a set of arm chains for her.

"Really, Malum? Are you that scared, and you think those chains will protect you?"

Malum snorted. "No, majesty. It's merely a precaution. This way, you know your escape will be that much more difficult—as well as your people's escape."

Sealyn knew she could pick the locks easily. She had been trained for this at Fort Kippen. Survival training had been the worst training a person could go through, but she had surpassed the expectations. Now, Malum was tempting her: save yourself and leave behind your people. She held up her wrists willingly and smiled. "Clasp me in irons all you want, but it's really you who is clothed in chains."

Malum snorted and grabbed the center of the chain, pulling Sealyn behind him. He smiled an evil smile at the group. "Greetings, guests. Tonight's ball will be the last fun night for you. For tomorrow, Feydom begins." Malum dropped Sealyn's chain and clapped his hands. Music began to play, and servants filled the empty tables with food. Malum extended his hand to Sealyn. "May I have the first dance?"

Sealyn glared. She brushed past him and ran to Jace. They tried to embrace, but the chains prevented it; instead, they walked to the dance floor and held onto each other, swaying with the music. The rest of the Elysians followed their leaders and paired off with dance partners. Char was tempted to drown himself in wine but resisted. He knew tomorrow would not be the day for hangovers. Malum grabbed Len Nove's princess for his dance partner. Tears flowed from her blue eyes.

Jace cupped Sealyn's face. "You have no idea how much I've missed you. I thought I would go mad if I went one more day without seeing you."

"I felt the same, but something extraordinary happened in my room," Sealyn explained the magical trunk, the books, and her theory of the source.

"That is extraordinary! What are we to do with that information?"

"I don't believe you can do much. Tomorrow is Feydom. I need you to stay alive."

"Sealyn, if I need to sacrifice myself…"

"Don't! Don't finish that sentence."

"I'm serious, Sea. If my death can aid the annihilation of Stoltland's rule here, then I'm willing, but more than that, I want my death to protect you. I only wish I was immortal so I could die a thousand times saving you."

Tears slid from Sealyn's emerald eyes. "I can't," she gasped. "I can't breathe in this world without your heart beating."

"How about I agree not to die, and you agree not to do anything reckless?"

Sealyn chuckled softly and wiped her nose. "Counteroffer, Just Jace. You don't die, and I agree only to be reckless if it's well thought out."

"How could I expect anything less?" He leaned in and whispered in her ear, "By the way, you look ravishing in blue." He kissed her neck, and tingling sensations went down her entire body. Sealyn missed his touch, his kisses. She craved him, but they would have to put aside their wants and desires. Tonight was about tactics.

They decided to go to one of the food tables to talk with Char and Tilmond. Tilmond towered over Char, but Char didn't mind. He gladly ate a piece of perfectly cooked meat. Malum had only provided leftovers for the past month. Char and Tilmond both bowed when Sealyn and Jace stood beside them. Sealyn was about to divulge what she had discovered but stopped when Malum showed up.

"Please eat. You will need your strength for tomorrow," Malum glared at Char, then looked to Elysium's queen. "Sealyn, why don't we leave these deplorable men to their appetites, and you and I have a dance? I've been anxious to have my hands around your gem-covered waist." Malum glanced at Jace, daring him to advance.

Sealyn could feel her rash behavior wanting to take over. She grabbed an ice plate and fork, intending to place shaved beef on her plate. She tried to ignore him.

"Ah, Sealyn. Don't worry about eating now. I'll make sure my room is filled with food for us afterward." Malum winked at Jace.

His wicked grin was asking for it, so Sealyn answered. She advanced quickly and stabbed her fork through his hand. She dropped the plate, and ice shattered across the floor. The music stopped once Malum screamed. Everyone on the dance floor stood in shock. Blood trickled down Malum's black sleeve as he held his forearm.

"You stabbed me with a fork!"

"You bet I forking did!" Sealyn glared.

Char laughed.

"You think this is funny, Char?"

Char nodded. "Oh, it's forking funny."

Guards ran to Malum, while the others held swords to Sealyn's neck. She didn't flinch. The guards shoved Sealyn beside Jace, and a palace doctor aided Malum's wound.

Jace whispered to Sealyn. "That was reckless."

"But clearly well thought out."

Malum screamed again when the fork was yanked out. A servant wrapped his hand, blood soaking through. "That's it! The ball is over! You've all had your last laughs. Tomorrow will be justice. Take them away."

Sealyn grabbed Jace's hands, then was quickly ripped away from him. Everyone shouted their goodbyes, and voices cracked over the heavy three words "I love you." No one knew what Malum had in store for them. Sealyn's heart crumbled, knowing she enraged him even more, but one thing was for sure, Malum's sword-fighting hand was damaged.

CHAPTER 20
NOT THE ONLY LUXEN

The air was crisp and freezing cold. Sealyn thought it probably felt like Malum's heart. She sat in her Elysian beaver leathers, covered in fur blankets. King Egil, Prince Dag, and Princess Drifa also sat with her on the platform. The Len Novian royals looked miserable. A new addition to the platform at the arena was a cage off to the side of them.

The center of the arena was covered in tall ice trees and random ice boulders. Everything was arranged to create a confusing maze. Snow covered the arena floor. Malum arrived at the royal platform, followed by guards and Norella, Pinx, and Zuri. Malum shoved the ladies inside the cage. They were dressed in their kingdom's battle leathers as well.

Sealyn stood. "What is the meaning of this?"

"I'm no monster, Sealyn. And because I'm not a monster, I'm keeping the lovely ladies out of the game, except for Madilina. She's locked up below and out of sight."

Sealyn saw the ladies shivering. She ran to them and quickly pushed a blanket through the bars before the guard grabbed her. Her heart ached to see her friends in a cage. She mouthed "I'm sorry" to them. They all smiled, trying to be brave. Pinx had tears in her almond-shaped eyes. Pinx knew Favien was a Roamer, so that meant he would be in the arena the longest; all Roamers would.

Horns sounded, and the stadium seats started filling up. Blue- and black-eyed people stared at the royal platform. Malum greeted them and put on his best performance for entertainment. Another horn sounded, and a side gate in the arena opened. Guards spilled in, and then Jace, Brehan, Char, Finn, Favien,

Rielen, and Ajorn walked in front of the platform. They strained their necks to see Malum. Malum motioned for the guards to bring Sealyn forward. She grasped the ice banister and looked at Jace. Her heart ached.

These men would be fighting for their lives for the next twenty-four hours. Malum's rules were cruel. No one would be coming for the injured. If you sustained a wound of any kind, you stayed on the arena floor, and your teammates had to tend to you. They were provided with swords, shields, and knives. Nothing else.

"Are you ready?" Malum yelled. The stadium erupted. This would be one of the longest days of Sealyn's life.

A final horn blew, and Feydom commenced. A gate at the far end of the oval opened. Young Len Novian soldiers ran to their positions to guard the flags. They scurried through the maze with ease. It was obvious they had practiced. After the Len Novian soldiers, large Stoltland warriors ran through the ice forest, preparing to battle the Elysians. Some had wolves with them, and others had lorkins. Blood was going to paint the snow red, or maybe black.

The crowd cheered as the Elysians made their way through the twisting turns. Brehan could see his breath as he slowly exhaled. His sandy blonde hair had crystals of ice on the ends. This weather was brutal. He rounded another corner, expecting a soldier, but instead, it was a wolf. The white wolf looked sick but also enraged. Its eyes were black, and a black stripe ran down its back. Stoltland's poison again.

The wolf charged. Brehan dodged, and Jace jumped from behind the corner, surprising the wolf. Jace lunged, stabbing the wolf's side. It howled, and the crowd cheered. Favien, who had been behind Jace, didn't hesitate and sliced the wolf's throat. Black blood spilled over the pure white snow. Jace stared at the black blood dripping from his sword. He couldn't let Drystan's memory haunt him now.

Char peered around Favien and saw the dead wolf. He wanted to panic, but he dug into his mind for his training on that horrific island. He could do this. They had to beat Malum at his twisted game.

Finn and Ajorn were fighting a lorkin on the adjacent side of the maze, while Rielen defended himself from a Stoltland soldier. Finn flipped over the lorkin to attack from behind. His blue eyes were fierce. Ajorn held the creature's attention, making loud noises and waving his sword in the air. The large jaws snapped at Ajorn, missing him by inches. Finn jumped on top of the lorkin, and the lorkin thrashed its tail and rolled, pinning Finn to the snow. Ajorn saw his opportunity. He sliced the lorkin from neck to tail. Black blood and entrails gushed out. Ajorn let out a deep breath and wiped black blood from his ebony cheek. Rielen slipped on the blood, and the Stoltland soldier's sword cut Rielen's arm. Rielen's yell made Ajorn jerk his head in that direction, and without hesitation, Ajorn yelled, "Down!" and Rielen flattened himself on the cold ground. Ajorn threw his knife into the Stoltlander's throat.

Finn scrambled free, covered with the insides of the lorkin.

"You're disgusting," Ajorn said.

"What, this? No, it's Malum's latest fashion trend. I'm sure the ladies will love it."

Rielen had Ajorn wrap his arm, hoping the blood wouldn't drip. Rielen noticed something around the lorkin's leg. Strapped in white rope was a white flag. This was going to be harder than they thought. Not only did they have monsters and soldiers to fight, but the flags were also camouflaged and moved. His brown hair was covered in snow, and his clothes were now bloody, but Rielen made sure to grab the flag. No fireworks burst. Another rule Malum instilled. All flags would be counted at the end of twenty-four hours. No one would know the total until then, but they now feared that the game's point was more just killing the Elysians rather than flag counting.

The fighting went on and on. The young Len Novian soldiers were no match for the well-trained Elysians. It was like Malum knowingly sent them to their death. The Len Novians didn't go for flags; they were obviously ordered only to kill them. More lorkins and wolves kept being released into the arena. Sealyn screamed for her cousin, Rielen, to look out, but the lorkin was too fast. It sank its teeth into Rielen's leg. Sealyn's hands went hot. Rielen was family, her blood. Ajorn stabbed the underbelly five quick times. Releasing Rielen, the lorkin moaned and gave in to death.

Rielen screamed in pain. Finn tried to hush him so the enemy wouldn't know where to find them. Finn helped prop Rielen against an icy boulder. Finn and Ajorn scanned the area, ensuring no other enemies were nearby. Rielen needed a moment to catch his breath. The area under his leg began to spread red. The snow was now soaked with blood.

"We have to take him back to base camp," Ajorn said.

"How do we signal to the others?" Finn asked.

"I have no idea, but we can't wait." The two lifted Rielen.

Rielen yelled out. "Don't forget the flag. I earned that one." He said through gritted teeth. Finn yanked the flag from the lorkin's lifeless leg, and the three hurried back to the base camp, which was located directly below the royal platform with a covered tent. Finn dove into his memories of last year's Feydom, when he pulled one of the flags and watched the green fireworks burst into the sky. He had felt such joy in that moment. He promised himself to hang onto that joy to get him through Malum's games.

As the sky darkened, Malum stood and stretched his arms. "Well, I'm tired." He nodded to his guards. The guards grabbed Sealyn and started pulling her toward the stairs. Sealyn kicked and screamed. Malum huffed. "My dear Sealyn, you need your rest."

Sealyn did not want to leave her people here, especially Jace, but she knew Malum would have all his men drag her away no matter what. "Fine, Malum. I'll go without a fight if you allow my ladies to stay with me each night of Feydom." Malum nodded.

Inside Sealyn's bedroom, the ladies hugged each other once the servants took their chains off. They held onto each other for long moments, crying. Knowing they had little time, Sealyn motioned the ladies to help slide the heavy desk in front of the door, hoping to keep Malum out. Sealyn rushed to the secret door and opened the trunk. The ladies stood in shock at the secret door. To Sealyn's delight, it had four books waiting on her. How did it know? She didn't care but whispered a soft "thank you" anyway. Sealyn grabbed the books, hurried to her oversized bed, and motioned for the ladies to join her.

They sat on the bed listening to Sealyn explain the trunk, the books, and the source theory. Pinx still had tears in her eyes. How could they just leave the men out there like that? "I didn't want to leave," she quietly said.

Sealyn tilted her head. "What?"

"I didn't want to leave the platform."

"Pinx, Malum would have left you all there. You would have frozen to death. I couldn't let that happen."

"Better that than abandoning the ones we love!"

Norella placed her hand on Pinx's. "Easy, Pinx. Favien needs you alive. How can you help him if you're frozen?"

"I just—I just," Pinx sniffed. "I just didn't want Favien to be alone."

Zuri piped in. "He's not alone. He's surrounded by some of the best warriors of Elysium." Pinx nodded as tears streamed down her face. Norella brushed Pinx's long black hair and braided it into a thick side braid, and then she did the same for her own long blonde hair. They needed those fleeting girlish moments to hold onto their sanity.

The ladies settled into silence as they read. Pinx's words echoed in Sealyn's mind, "abandoning the ones we love." Did she do that? Were Pinx's words deeper than that? Was she wanting her to use her Luxen powers? Sealyn didn't even know if that was possible. Her biggest concern was Rielen's injury. She saw how much her cousin was bleeding. How could she help him?

"This is interesting," Norella said. "Listen. 'Len Nove's palace has many secrets, but one of the most delightful secrets is the underground tunnels. Some tunnels reach even as far as Port Zykoan, but most of those were made into catacombs.'"

Zuri shivered. "I know those catacombs. I got lost in them."

"When?" gasped Norella.

"I was very young. Please, I don't want to talk about it."

Sealyn's eyes stared out the window. Why would the books tell them about the tunnels? How would this help her save her cousin? She felt like the only way to save him is through the old magic, but using it always illuminates something green. Her power would expose her. Then an idea formed, "Norella, does the book say where the entrances to the tunnels are?"

Norella read and skimmed the pages, flipping through more. "Ah, yes! Here it is! There are several. One is almost below us. Oh, wait. Never mind, that's a sewage tunnel."

"Where does the sewage tunnel lead?" Sealyn asked.

Norella held the book open so they all could see. She traced her finger on the page. "It leads to the arena."

Sealyn bounced off the bed and pushed open her window. The cold air rushed inside and stirred the flames of the fire. Her room was so high up that jumping would be deadly. She saw the grate from the drawing below. If her plan worked, then this would open the door to the old magic like she never dreamed. "Zuri, hand me one of those tiny sewing needles and the thick thread."

Zuri handed the small items to Sealyn. "What's going on, Sealyn?"

"I refuse to sit idle." She set the items on the windowsill, then whispered the words, "Akousay mei."

Zuri screeched. "Sealyn! No! What are you doing?"

"Hush, Zuri. I don't believe the old magic is evil. I think someone wanted us to think that. Now, trust me." Sealyn repeated the words: "Akousay mei." Her palms turned green, and swirls of gold flickered in between her palms. Sealyn said, "Involvo." Instantly, a small green encasement formed around the items, protecting them. The green ball hung in the air like a floating bubble. Sealyn closed her eyes, imagined the grate, and said, "Cedo." With the command of "go," the ball floated down the tall palace wall and through the grate's bars.

Sealyn's eyes remained closed, and she concentrated. She silently gave thoughts to the magic, willing it also to be her eyes so she could see where it was going. She kept telling it to find Elysian blood, and the faster the ball went. The open window allowed the ladies to hear the screams of the arena. They all prayed for their Elysians.

Sealyn became the magic. She darted around corners with ease. It was like she could feel her target. Her mind saw visions of cells, and in those cells were the other Elysians. She almost faltered but knew she had to stay focused. Her cousin's life depended on her. Finally, she came to the gate her people had walked through earlier that day. The ball slid through the locked bars easily. The guards on either side had fallen asleep.

She saw the base camp and could hear muffling and moaning. She had to hurry. The entire Elysian group was gathered around Rielen.

"If we can't stop the bleeding, he won't make it," Brehan said, breathing hard.

"There are too many wounds. We need to stitch them," Favien panicked.

Ajorn huffed. "Sure. Let's do that, and where do you suppose we go shopping for needles?"

Sealyn wasted no time. She guided the ball above Rielen. The group stood frozen in shock. Sealyn spoke, "Shairya," and two green hands formed, holding the needle and thread. The group gasped. Rielen remained still. Sealyn spoke, "Solzo." The hands began stitching Rielen's wounds perfectly.

Jace knew. His Sealyn was saving her family. She was risking exposing herself, but here she was, performing magical surgery. How miraculous! Once the hands finished, they set the items down, then cupped Jace's face. They almost felt real. Sealyn spoke, "Praepes," and then the green power turned into a tiny bird and flew back through the bars.

Sealyn stopped the bird in front of Madilina's cell. Madilina heard the wings and felt her back grow hot. She rose from her cot, saw the tiny green bird, and felt the connection. Somehow she knew this was the old magic, Sealyn's magic. Madilina's back grew hotter. What was happening to her? The bird smiled and nodded, then dissipated.

Sealyn opened her eyes and fell into her ladies' arms. Her nose was dripping blood, and her face was pale. The ladies helped Sealyn to the middle of the large bed. They brought her water and made her drink it. Norella sliced the lemons the servants left for their tea and shoved a slice in Sealyn's mouth.

Sealyn quickly squirmed and came back to full consciousness. "What was that for?" Sealyn protested.

"Your mother said she used to do that to you and Siany when you were children."

Sealyn gave a slight chuckle, and propped herself up. "It worked." She still felt weak.

Zuri poured the tea and brought biscuits to the bed. "What worked? That evil magic overpowering you?"

Sealyn rolled her eyes. "No, the magic helped save Rielen's life. I was able to see and hear the boys and stitch his wounds." Pinx choked on her tea, and liquid trickled out of her nose.

Norella laughed. "That's not ladylike, Pinx."

"You saw them? Are they all right?" Pinx squeaked while wiping her nose.

Sealyn nodded. "Yes. They all look worn out with some bruises and scrapes, but they're safe."

"So what does this old magic mean?" Zuri asked reluctantly.

"It means the old magic is no longer to be feared, but embraced. We'll be able to access it through the old language."

Norella tilted her head. "Everyone, or just Luxens?

"I'm not sure," Sealyn said. "But I'm not the only Luxen here."

Diary Entry,

I don't care about the curses. I only care about having my name live forever. Ruling all seven kingdoms will ensure that. Once I have all the kingdoms, I know my son, Jace, will come back to me. He'll see what a weak queen Sealyn really is. Everyone will finally see me as I want to be seen: powerful and almighty. My commands will be the law for all lands. I can do this. I just need those beastly dragons trained, but Haedon is too much like his incompetent father to get things done the right way. I swear, if he fails me, I'll kill the woman he loves and make him watch. He must learn the consequences of failing me.

Ending my entry now. I must practice my dark powers on the old queen. She hates being tortured, but it helps me grow stronger.

Until next time,
Queen Corentine, Queen of all Queens

CHAPTER 21
MADAM BIP

Maekel could hardly believe herself. Nexgen was finally here! She could feel the tiny flutter inside her belly. In a few months, she would be a mother. She would fly around thinking of which powers her child would possess. She truly didn't care. She just wanted a healthy baby. Her tiny fingers rubbed her small stomach, and she whispered, "I can't waits to meets you."

Miola, Siany's personal Nicht, fluttered

into Sealyn's bed chamber. "I figureds I would finds you in heres." Miola had inherited her mother's blue hair but had her father's deep perception of knowing a Nicht's heart.

"I comes in heres to talks to the baby and to Queen Sealyn's memory."

"Memory?" Miola questioned sternly. "Queen Sealyn is nots dead!"

"I knows! I didn't means any harms. I guesses I just thinks out my thoughts like I'm talkings to her."

Miola nodded. "I understands. I cames to fetches you. It's time!"

The two enchanting Nichts fluttered to the open field near Lady Raquel's house. White emangaton flowers stood ready to receive the tiny embryos. All the Nichts of Avondelle came for this moment. It was a private ceremony. No humans attended. They would only attend the blooming of Nexgen.

Maekel found her flower, and it opened to her touch. The flower was three sizes larger than she was. She and Trit flew inside the flower. The petals provided privacy for the couple. Healing Nichts and Long-Distance Nichts waited patiently on the snow at the base of the flower with a cot. Maekel was brave, and after a lot of effort, she and Trit placed their embryo onto the sticky, sponge-like tentacles. The pink and red petals inside wrapped the embryo securely. That was it. They had done all they could. Now came the waiting.

Trit called for the Healing and Long-Distance Nichts for Maekel. They laid her gently on the cot while the Healing Nicht ensured she was well enough to travel. Once the pink-headed Nicht gave her blessing for travel, the Long-Distance Nichts flew Maekel to Princess Siany's bed chamber. Siany had given strict instructions for Maekel to recover in her room. Miola and Trit would look after her, along with several others.

Queen Mother Graelynd was perched in Siany's sitting room, sipping tea. She was so happy for Maekel and Trit. Maekel never stopped talking about how excited she was to be a mother. Graelynd chuckled to herself. "Siany, my dear, I think it's wonderful how you're taking care of Maekel here."

"Thank you, Mother. She saved my life. I owe her, but it's also an honor to do so."

"Saved your life?"

Miola froze mid-flight. She and Siany locked eyes. This was supposed to be a secret between the hidden library crew. No others knew Maekel was a Limpid Nicht.

"I only mean she had quick ideas during the palace skirmishes. Without those quick suggestions, we would have been lost."

"Ah, I see," Graelynd wasn't convinced that was the truth. "Maekel is certainly special." Graelynd took another bite of her Jam Pie. "Mhmm, these are certainly delicious."

"Seriously, mother? You think you can avoid the subject of why you're really here?"

"Why in all seven kingdoms would you think I'm here for any other reason than to see my sweet daughter?"

Miola coughed and giggled.

"Just go ahead and ask what you're wanting to ask."

"Well, while I'm here, I wanted to know if you had chosen anyone to attend the spring Nexgen with you?"

"Mother, you're joking. A dragon claw shows up lodged in Dun's leg, and you want to know if I have a date to the spring Nexgen festival?"

"I guess so," Graelynd smirked and sipped her tea. A daughter always thinks she knows more than her mother. How wrong Siany was about to be.

"Mother, I don't have time to think about dates. I must figure out how to block Stoltland from sending any more dragons through their Tor."

A knock sounded at Siany's door. Graelynd smiled. "Miola, that should be Madam Bip. Please show her in."

"Madam Bip?"

"Why, yes. Didn't I mention that?"

"No, mother. You didn't," Siany said flatly.

Madam Bip entered the room, bursting with energy. "My glorious majesties!" She kissed Graelynd and Siany on their cheeks, then handed them each a bottle with her famous, sparkling purple PurFizz. "You both look remarkable but troubled. Have some sips. Like I always say, find your purpose with PurFizz."

Siany looked at her mother like she had lost her mind. "Would you care to elaborate on this particular meeting?"

"Siany, darling, you remember Madam Bip?"

"Of course."

"She might be famous for her PurFizz, but what you didn't know is that she's one of the most powerful, magical alchemists our world has ever known."

"What?" Siany exclaimed.

"'Tis true, your majesty. My family has been practicing the old magic for generations. Now dat the old magic is unlocked, my abilities have grown."

"Grown in what way?" Siany's eyes narrowed.

"I tink you know," Bip winked. "But perhaps a demonstration will convince the interim queen?" Siany nodded. Bip stood and walked to one of Siany's orchids. Bip picked two petals and grasped one in each fist. Bip closed her eyes and inhaled deeply, then when she opened them, her green eyes glowed, and the plants in the room began to grow taller. Vines wrapped around the room, growing larger.

Siany's mouth dropped. "You're a… you're a…"

"Yes, majesty. I'm a Luxen. A Ligatum Luxen to be exact."

Siany shook her head. "A what um?"

Bip laughed her deep belly laugh. "Oh heavens, you are funny. My apologies. Dat's the old tongue. Ligatum means 'tethered.'"

"I'm still lost."

"I'm not sure how. You do know 'bout the three types of Luxens, right?"

Siany scowled. She hated not knowing all the answers. "Let's say I do, but need a refresher. Explain them to me like I'm a child." Graelynd laughed. She knew what her daughter was up to.

"My pleasure, majesty. I won't use the old tongue. The three types of Luxens are Tethered," she pointed to herself and smiled. "Transference, and the most powerful is Cognition. Would you like me to elaborate?" Siany nodded. "Well, for me, I must hold an object to channel the magic. Usually, the channel can only happen with that object's elements. Like with the orchids, I was able to tap into all the plants in the room and bend them to my will. For those with Transference, they have a creature connection. They can touch an animal, and its special abilities can be transferred. Very difficult to perfect."

"So I could touch my cat, and what? I would grow a tail?"

Madam Bip laughed hard again. "Oh, majesty, I should be paying for a comedy show. No, there's nothing special about the tail, but a cat's jumping, or perhaps night vision, would be what the Transference needs."

"Sure. Sure," Siany's head was spinning. "What about the Cognition Luxen?"

"Ah, yes. The most powerful one. These are rare. Most are either Tethered or Transference. A Cognition comes once every few thousand years."

"Why?"

"Why? Because that's normally too much power for one person to have. Usually, they go mad or turn so evil that someone kills them."

"But what can they do?"

"They need no elements nor creatures. They can control magic with only their mind."

Char ached everywhere. The morning break was almost over. Surprisingly enough, Malum's men had given them a break. He wanted to crawl into a hole and never come out. The Stoltland soldiers made several sneak attacks on them through the night. Luckily, those soldiers hadn't witnessed the magical stitching. Rielen still had a fever, though. They had managed to keep the fires lit through the night and stay alive.

Favien sat beside Char. "Char, you've done great. I'm still shocked by your skills."

"Like Sealyn says, 'Being predictable is boring.'"

"Jace surprised me, too. He's oddly agile."

"How many flags did we get?"

"Five."

Char hung his head. That was a very low number for their first day. Rielen was completely out, Finn was limping, and Brehan's eye was swollen. They all had cuts and bruises. How would horses affect their day? Char wondered if that meant larger beasts to fight.

Day two of Feydom went by in a complete blur. The Elysian horsemen came out with vengeance. Tilmond led his men just like he would into battle. They started smashing the ice trees when they could but most were too thick to attempt. White pipscots would burst, making it harder to see everything. They would camouflage the flags that much more.

Stoltland soldiers brought in terrifying bears. Sakul was thrown from his horse, completely knocked out. They laid him beside Rielen. Ashur's horse died from an insane bear attack, but he was still able to play the game. Max tried his best, but his injury made it impossible for him to use his shield. He sustained another arrow to his shoulder. Finn decided his ankle was too weak to be in the heat of the battle, so he chose to stay and guard the wounded at base camp. Tilmond was the last to go down.

An arrow sunk into the side of Tilmond's leg. He couldn't continue. They were failing. By the end of the day, the remaining players were covered in their own blood along with their enemies'. They could barely lift their swords. They opted not to play through the night. Rest was more important. They had to keep a lookout, though.

Jace stared into the fire. His throat was raw and swollen. He could feel a sickness starting to take root. He had no idea if they would last through the night, much less day three. They had only gained four more flags, a total of nine. The horsemen didn't do much better with three pipscots. Negative thoughts kept circling around him, but then tiny green balls landed in front of each person. Sealyn brought them exactly what they needed: echinacea tea, turmeric tea, willow bark tea, and peppermint tea, along with biscuits and jerky.

How had she managed this? She must be gaining strength. He was so grateful to her. His throat felt instantly better after making and drinking the peppermint tea. They all sat silent, trying not to let the guards know how happy their surprises had made them. Could this small amount of hope help them? Perhaps, but tomorrow depended solely on Lady Madilina. She had to win, or else they would all die.

CHAPTER 22
HOPE WAS LOST

Madilina woke to clanging and her locks being opened. She had barely slept. Her stomach was in knots. Today rested on her shoulders. She was terrified. How could Sealyn have this much faith in her? The soldier grabbed her and escorted her down the hallway. Her heart pounded with each step. Her bright blonde hair was tightly braided, ready to face the winds of flying.

Would these Caelidons like her, or would they resist? The day was full of too many questions but only one outcome. She had to save Max, her sweet husband, and all her people. She had been so protected from violence, but now, she would face all the evil Malum had to offer.

When Madilina entered the arena, Sealyn stiffened. She was still feeling a little weak from the effort of channeling so much magic last night. The ladies had faked illnesses to gain all the teas needed to help treat the Elysian players. Sealyn sent all the tea bags and food she could before passing out. She tried to eat a large breakfast. She had no appetite, yet she forced the food down, knowing that today, she would need all her strength.

Madilina looked at Max, then at the giant floating ice bowls above the arena. She didn't see any of Malum's men on flying horses. Could none of them ride the creatures? She looked back at Max. He shook his head. Something wasn't right. Max's eyes shifted to the perimeter of the amphitheater. Tall platforms extended well past the stadium seats until they were parallel with the floating ice bowls. There were two on each side, and each one had a large Stoltland archer. Madilina was going to be Malum's moving target.

Madilina looked back at Max. She tried to run to him, but the guard caught her and kept her away from the group. She cried and yelled for her husband. She didn't want to do this. She couldn't do this. She looked up to the royal platform and saw Sealyn looking down. Sealyn's eyes looked like they were glowing green. Something was different. Madilina's back burned again. She felt like the grapes at the vineyard, being squished and stomped.

The horn for Wings sounded. Four Caelidons took off in flight, and Madilina climbed on the fifth. She could tell he accepted her. At least, that was a good start, and then she was soaring high above the amphitheater. She looked at the players on the arena ground. The Horsemen and Roamers trudged forward, giving their best. She would do the same. An arrow zipped past her face. The Caelidon dove. He was spooked. Madilina hung on, trying to direct him.

They flew to the floating platform with the weighted ice balls. She grabbed one, and then they were off to their first target. The Caelidon was fast. Faster than the arrows that flew by them. Madilina managed to toss in a ball in the first bowl gently, but the Caelidon had to stay in one spot flapping its wings so the ice would not break. This made the Caelidon an easier target. The Caelidon saw the arrow and jerked. Madilina slipped, falling toward her death. Another Caelidon flew under her and scooped her on her back.

Sealyn cheered. Six more to go. She had faith in her friend. Malum was angry. He realized Sealyn had played him. He had no idea the tiniest Elysian could ride the Caelidon. In his thoughts for choosing her, he had convinced himself that this all-feathered creature would surely fly so fast that she would be dead within the first five minutes, but what he was watching now alarmed him.

Madilina tried to place the second ice ball, but an arrow skimmed her arm. She dropped the ball below, crushing a wolf on the arena floor. Blood flowed from her wound, splattering onto the pure white feathers of the Caelidon. Madilina picked up another ball to make a pass.

Max was tired of watching these men try to kill his wife. He hobbled behind an ice tree near where one of the platform archers was. Madilina was making another pass to drop the ball. Max aimed and said a small prayer. The Caelidon hovered by the bowl. The Stoltland archer readied his bow. Max released his arrow; it found its target's neck. Down the archer went. Madilina scored another point for Wings. Max sank to his knees, feeling his wounds. He didn't have much left to give.

Finn saw what Max was doing, so he joined his teammate and readied his bow. Madilina found confidence after the second point. She easily made bowls three and four since they were near the empty archer platform. She felt like just maybe she could win. Her Caelidon started breathing heavily. It was tired. Madilina squeezed her legs, signaling which direction for the Caelidon to go. She guided it to another Caelidon. Madilina jumped to the next one.

Her adrenaline was surging. The fresh Caelidon flew with speed. She was going to need it. The other bowls were near the other archers. Securing themselves behind an ice boulder near another raised platform, Max and Finn tried to shoot another archer, but he fired back at them, making it difficult for them to return fire. They were at least distracting him. Madilina made a pass for a bowl, but an arrow landed in her Caelidon's side. It let out a horrifying cry, and down they both went. Another Caelidon flew near Madilina, and she jumped again, landing safely, but watched as her other Caelidon crashed to its death. Her heart broke, and she screamed.

Anger flooded her. She hated Malum. How could he do this to such majestic creatures? They were innocent! She looked at the royal platform as they flew past it. Malum was laughing— laughing. What a vile monster! She searched frantically for the tired Caelidon. Had Malum taken it away because it landed on the ground? His rules were ridiculous.

She was left with only three Caelidons to win this twisted game. The odds were low for Madilina to win. Sealyn wished she could help Madilina, but she had to play the game fair. If she interfered and Madilina won, then Malum would kill them all for cheating. She had her backup plan ready but did not want this day to come to that. She had already freed herself from her chains by making a key with her powers. Next, she needed to unlock the cage for her friends.

The crowd erupted with chants, which helped fuel Sealyn's plan. Sealyn walked away from the banister, acting like she needed a moment to compose herself. She had the blanket covering her hands to hide the unlocked chains. Malum laughed and called her weak. No one paid her any attention. Sealyn seized her opportunity. Her magic elevated the cage's keys from the soldier's belt quietly. The crowd's cheers provided all the coverage she needed. She spoke the words needed to unlock the cage, then slipped the keys back. She nodded to the ladies, who had been watching with breaths held, and then Sealyn returned to the front of the platform to watch.

Finn's arrow landed in the side of the archer, and he fell into the stadium. Madilina made a pass for the bowl near the dead archer and scored another point. She just needed two more points, and they could all go home.

Home. That word seemed so foreign now. She forgot what her bed felt like. She ached for Puffin Pies and coffee at *Nijeel's Choice*, but, more than anything, she wanted her husband's arms wrapped around her. Wanting his embrace would ignite the fire in her that she needed to win.

The Caelidon was tired, so she hopped to another. She saw the tired Caelidon be escorted out of the arena. Malum was trying to make this harder than necessary. Only two Caelidons remained, and two points were needed to win. They dove for the bowl. An arrow whizzed past them; some even shaved the tips of the Caelidon's wings, but he didn't flinch. He was just as focused as Madilina. She gently tossed the ball in. Another point! Arrows came flying at them.

The Caelidon dove deep into the arena area. He tried to dodge the trees, but one of his legs hit an ice branch, sending them both spinning. The other Caelidon nipped at Madilina's back leathers and held onto her with its teeth. Up they went.

Madilina hated seeing the other Caelidon crash into the icy forest. She prayed he would heal.

Malum turned to Sealyn as she took her position next to him. They both stood at the edge of the banister.

"If you concede now, I'll make sure they all have quick deaths," Malum teased. He smoothed back his thick black hair.

"Sounds like fear, Malum."

He grunted and turned back to the arena. Elysium had to lose. He would make sure of that.

Madilina's arm throbbed from the multiple arrow scraps. She felt bad for bleeding on the feathers of the last Caelidon. She was probably the fastest of all five. They would need this speed. They rounded with the ice in hand, ready to make a final drop.

Malum yelled a command for all arena players to release arrows to the sky. This was illegal, but of course, Malum would cheat to win. With a final stab to a poisoned wolf, Jem saw what the players were doing. He yelled to his teammates for action. He stabbed another Stoltlander and charged after the arena archers. His horse took out two players before he had to jump off. Jem wanted blood. His red eyes echoed vengeance.

Jace and Ajorn were bloody and tired from fighting more lorkins than they could count, yet they took their swords to the archers, but more lorkins came at them. Where were they all coming from? Favien dodged an arrow, slid under a Len Novian soldier, and shoved his sword up. The Len Novian coughed blood and dropped. They had to take out as many soldiers who had arrows as possible. Madilina needed them. Favien felt bad for killing the Len Novians. He felt like they were just as much imprisoned as they were, but if he had to choose between his life or theirs, then he chose his, so he could protect his kingdom and his Pinx.

Madilina neared the bowl, but the Caelidon bucked to miss an arrow. The blood around her arms made it impossible to hold onto the balls of ice. It slipped from her fingers. They had to go back to the platform for another.

Madilina was growing tired. She had exhausted herself. How much more could she take? Her arms felt frozen from holding onto the ice balls, and she kept losing blood. The day started to grow darker. She wouldn't be able to see the arrows at night. What was she to do? She had to make this final drop count.

She looked down and could see the men fighting for her. She saw Max dragging himself to another target. He was killing himself to protect her. No, Max would not die today, nor anytime soon. She grabbed the heavy ice, and they were off again. This time she would make it. This ball of ice would be the winning point.

The Caelidon flew faster than she had all day. It's like she knew this had to be it too. The Caelidon's wings made an abrupt stop at the bowl. She stayed hovering. As Madilina leaned to place the last ball of ice in the bowl, two arrows hit the Caelidon, and she faltered, causing Madilina to drop the ice ball. The Caelidon let out an agonizing cry. Madilina screamed, "No!"

Jace watched the two arrows sink into the Caelidon. He felt sick. He hated watching anything horrible happen to animals, but now, all their hope was lost. There were no more Caelidons for Madilina to fly on. They had failed Sealyn and failed to help Madilina. Jace did not want to watch Madilina fall to her death, but how were they to help? He looked to Sealyn and mouthed, "I love you." She had to keep living, no matter what happened in the arena.

Max stopped breathing. His love was falling to her death. This wasn't happening. This had to be a bad dream. Any minute he would wake up; any minute. Why wasn't he waking up from the nightmare? He screamed, "Madilina! Please! No, Madilina!" He tried to run, but his body was breaking down from blood loss.

He needed to hold her one last time, even if it was both of their last breaths.

343

Prince Haedon,

You are becoming more worthless by the minute. Get the juveniles under control, or we'll have no choice but to send every adult dragon we have.

I want Avondelle completely destroyed!

I've enclosed another book for you to read: <u>Dragons. Can they be trained?</u> Your entire reputation depends on this battle.

Powerfully,

Queen Corentine of Stoltland and the seven kingdoms

CHAPTER 23
ONCE AGAIN

Sealyn gripped the ice banister. It was time. Sealyn yelled, "Exsuscito!" She allowed her palms to grow hot. She sent a wave of green under the falling Caelidon. The magic formed a large blanket that carefully cradled the dying Caelidon and her friend. Sealyn gently set the Caelidon and Madilina on the ground. Malum was in shock at what he was seeing. He tried to make a sound but couldn't.

Madilina cried. She failed. She tried to comfort the Caelidon. Sealyn repeated the word "Exsuscito" over and over. Madilina kept hearing the word "awaken" on repeat in her head. Was she losing her mind? She felt her back grow so hot that the leather started to burn away. What was happening? Madilina looked at the Caelidon and stroked her feathers. The innocent creature nodded her head toward her wings. What was she signaling her to do? "You want me to stroke your wings?" The Caelidon nodded one last time. Madilina touched the wing, and with its last breath, the Caelidon transferred to Madilina exactly what she needed.

Madilina's back burst into green flames, then feathered, green wings that looked exactly like the Caelidon's wings emerged from her skin. The wings flapped at her command. It was like a part of her that had been missing was finally home. She knew these wings, and they knew her. She looked one last time at the still Caelidon and petted her. "Thank you for your sacrifice," Madilina said before she flew high above the amphitheater. She wanted to fly away but had to return to reality. Sealyn had just exposed herself, and it was up to her to win this final play.

Malum drew his sword and held it to Sealyn's chest. His sword wobbled with his injury. "You're a Luxen!" Malum grabbed the blanket from Sealyn, thinking this was the source of her channeling to form a blanket under the Caelidon. Sealyn, of course, did not know the knowledge about channeling objects, but did she really need to? Removing the blanket revealed her unlocked chains. "How? How is that possible?" Malum questioned.

Madilina swooped down to the final bowl with the last ball of ice. Her arms felt cold and sore from carrying the ice all day. She was ready for this horrendous game to be over. All she wanted was Max. Her heart raced. She could only think about freeing her people. The green wings guided her to the target, where she gently laid the ice. It was over! She did it. She won Feydom with Wings! She chuckled to herself, "Literally, with wings."

The arrows stopped flying at her, so she saw her opportunity to fly to Max, who was propped up beside an ice boulder. He was bleeding badly. The ice magic cleared the maze of forests and rocks. Max almost fell backward, but Madilina's wing reached him first. She curved her wings around him, then cradled his cheeks with her bloody hands and kissed him. She pressed so hard into him that he let out a yelp of pain. He needed a doctor. Madilina looked to the royal platform, hoping Sealyn would help, but gasped as she saw Malum's sword at Sealyn's chest.

Sealyn tilted her head at Malum's reactions. She cut her eyes to the cage with her friends. They knew to be ready.

"The game is over, Malum. Free everyone now."

Malum whistled. "I'll show you what freedom an Elysian should have." More of Malum's army entered the arena. Some held spears above the wounded Elysians, and others drew swords against the active players. Five soldiers surrounded Jace with arrows, ready to release at any second.

"What is the meaning of this? Have you no honor in your word?"

"Honor? You dare speak to me about honor!" Malum spat. "You Elysians think you're so far above everyone else, but you're just like the rest of us. Cursed!"

Sealyn sneered. "Actually, not true. Our curse is broken. What do you think unlocked the old magic?" She tried not to waver, but she felt the toll the magic had taken on her.

Malum's mouth gaped. His anger began to overflow. "Lock them away!" he yelled to his troops.

Sealyn saw her people below too tired to fight back, too wounded even to try. Snow began to fall. What was she supposed to do? The soldiers marched all the prisoners out of the arena except for Jace. He remained surrounded. She could use her power for a sword, but then Jace would be killed. All she had left was mind games.

"Have you found the source yet?"

Malum's eyebrows lifted. "Source? And how do you know about that?"

"Because I'm not as stupid as you look."

"Insults? That's what you've resorted to," Malum chuckled. "I like a rowdy girl." He looked at the young queen and licked his lips. "If you know about the source, then you must know what it is."

Sealyn froze. She was a step ahead of him. Malum didn't know the source was the necklace. She couldn't reveal that she knew it. "Of course not, Malum. A kingdom's source is confidential from all other kingdoms, and ours is even hidden from the royals. I don't even know what our source is."

Malum dropped his sword. "I don't have time for this. Surrender peacefully, and I'll take you back to your room, but if you give even a slither of a struggle, then I'll have them release five arrows on your grey-eyed freak and then send you to the ice fields for hard labor."

Sealyn paused. She knew what the source was, but she had yet to learn its whereabouts. The trunk. She needed more time with the trunk. With her heart aching, Sealyn looked at her love before speaking. "I'll surrender, Malum, but my people must be cared for. No harm can come to them—that also goes for my husband."

Once again, Sealyn found herself a prisoner of Malum. This time, though, she knew her plans. The servants left Sealyn with a tray of food, and Sealyn bolted for the hidden door. She flung the trunk open and coughed on the dust that came from the extremely old scrolls in front of her. Gently, she unrolled the scrolls on the floor. The faded ink showed battle plans, but not just any battle plans: these were the actual plans of King Zephnon, the king who betrayed the mammoths all those thousands of years ago.

Sealyn slid her fingers over the mammoths' position, and then her hand went to her mouth when she saw the strategic groupings of Len Nove's army alongside Stoltland's. This was just like what Zuri had told her.

Why would the trunk provide her with these battle plans, especially knowing she wanted to know where the necklace was? Was the necklace lost on the battlefield? What if it was buried under layers of snow? Where was this battlefield?

She turned the scroll to see if any landmarks stood out to her. Nothing seemed familiar. Of course, Len Nove's landscape had changed so much these past thousands of years, so how was she supposed to recognize anything? Her heart sank with disappointment.

She left the scrolls on the floor and opened the trunk, thinking it would have another book to guide her, but it was empty. What did that mean? Did the magic run out? Perhaps the scrolls were its final message to her. If so, the answer to the battlefield's whereabouts would be on the parchment.

Squinting, she looked over the faded ink in the corners. Recognizing the symbol of the valley, she gasped. That was it! The map wasn't pointing to the battlefield. It was pointing her to the retreat location. Surely the mammoths would have protected the necklace in a place they felt safe. She looked closer and then ran to the window, holding the map up, trying to make out the differences in landscapes. If that symbol revealed Len Nove's famous mammoth valley and where it was positioned on the scroll, then it was completely unreachable, or was it?

CHAPTER 24
WASN'T EXPECTING THAT

Char ached with cuts and bruises. He made every vow he could think of that Malum would die the most painful death. Once the healers left, they all felt an eeriness grow inside the dungeons, which smelled like old urine. They could hear water droplets falling and light echoes of cries from cells in other rooms. Char looked around his cage. They would not be

able to make the journey home in the conditions they were all in. He saw Madilina clutching Max. Char was still in shock that Madilina was also a Luxen. Her wings were gone now, but he wondered what sick game Malum would have in store for her.

They heard the shuffling of footsteps. Everyone froze and clung to each other. Four Stoltland guards entered. The Len Novian royal twins gripped each other tighter as fear took hold of them. A soldier opened the princess's door first. She screamed and tried to press herself against the ice wall. Her brother held onto her. Another soldier opened the prince's door and yanked the siblings apart. The princess's guard yanked her long white hair, dragging her to the opening. She kicked and screamed.

Char yelled for the guards to leave them alone, but the soldiers laughed. The princess tried to claw the soldiers' faces, but two soldiers managed to carry her away while the other two chained the brother, forcing him to come with them.

"Malum's in a particularly angry mood tonight, little prince," a soldier warned. "If you want your sister to survive, then you better talk her through it." He shoved the prince forward.

The doors closed and echoed through the icy dungeon. Len Nove's king fell to the ground weeping. Favien winced and held Pinx tight. "We have to do something," Favien said.

"And what do you suppose we do?" Jem remarked. "Don't you think we want to fight our way out?" Jem kicked the straw on the floor.

Servants scurried down the dungeon's stairs, carrying food and water. They quickly gave the food and left, but two Stoltland soldiers went to the cell where Jace was confined alone. They both had buckets of jam with them. Jace sat on the cold, damp stone floor with his head held low. His arms were over his knees. The soldiers scooped the jam from their buckets and threw it at Jace. The Elysians yelled for them to stop, but they continued. They mocked him as they threw the jam. "Jammy Jace. Jammy Jace. Come and get us, Jammy Jace."

Finally, the buckets were empty, and the two soldiers left laughing. During the jam throwing, Jace had huddled himself against the back ice wall, trying to shield his face. He felt shame. He couldn't face looking at the Elysians. His mind reverted to him being a child covered in jam from Malum and all the children of the palace laughing. He felt small. Once again, he was the grey-eyed outcast. His stomach turned. Tears pricked his eyes. He wanted to kill Malum.

Pinx knelt beside the bars connecting their cell to Jace's. "Jace?" He said nothing. Pinx persisted. "King Jace, are you all right?" Jace barely made a movement.

Favien pressed his face close to the icy bars. He hated seeing his friend this way. Malum was playing games with his king! "King Jace, there's no shame for you. Malum is a twisted goat, and we'll kill him. Don't you worry about that."

"I second that, Jace," Char added. "We've all encountered bullies, but you and I have a history with Malum. There's no shame here."

Jace felt something land next to him. Brehan stood shirtless and freezing. "My king, please use my shirt to help clean off the jam." Favien, Char, Finn, Ajorn, Ashur, and Jem quickly took off their shirts and tossed them to Jace too. The others were too wounded and needed to stay warm. With their shirts gone, their bare chests and backs revealed the cuts and bruises from the game. They all had lost size too, due to the lack of food.

Tears fell from Jace's eyes, but he still hid his face from his friends. He took the clothes and wiped his head and face first, then cleaned off the rest. He stood and faced his subjects. How were they managing this well? He loved each one of them. Jace handed the shirts back to his friends. Char licked the jam on his shirt. "This tastes delicious. I bet it will pair nicely with this stale bread."

Jace made a slight chuckle. "Thank you, my friends. How are Tilmond, Rielen, Max and Sakul?"

Zuri knelt beside Rielen, the queen's cousin, checking his temperature. "The next few nights will be the hardest for them," she said. "As long as Malum keeps providing care, then they have a chance."

Jace smacked the bars and walked in circles. "We can't be at his mercy. Eventually, he will grow tired of being his version of kind."

"So what do we do?" Norella asked quietly. She looked deep into Brehan's unwounded eye. She wanted him to tell the group everything was going to be all right, and she would believe him. Her anxiety was rising and needed assurances.

Brehan's head shook slowly. "Malum is unlike any commander we've faced. He outsmarts us at every corner. He even outmaneuvered Queen Sealyn's Luxen powers."

"But did he?" Pinx questioned. All eyes glued to the intelligent Pinx. Her nose was pink from the cold, and her almond-shaped eyes had excitement in them. She stood and began to pace. "Think about it. Sealyn never does anything without a backup plan. No offense, King Jace, but she could have fought and won, sacrificing the other monarch--you. Elysium's crown would have been protected, and we could be warm by the fires of Len Nove's palace."

"So you're saying this is my fault?" Jace growled through his teeth.

"No, no, majesty. I'm pointing out that Sealyn protects her kingdom at all costs, which means she chose not to take that route tonight."

Jace shook his head. "She did not choose me over her kingdom!"

"Easy, Jace," Favien tried to intervene. "Let Pinx finish her theory."

"I'm sorry, Jace. I know this isn't easy," Pinx said. "Sealyn wanted to be back in her room. There's a hidden door with a magical trunk inside." Hearing about the hidden door and trunk, the Len Novian king rose from the ground and walked to the bars to listen. "The trunk has been providing details and secrets about Len Nove. We read everything from history books to port trade entries."

"Wait," Jace interrupted. "Sealyn mentioned this to me at the ball. I had almost forgotten about the magical trunk. Did she ever find the source's whereabouts?"

Pinx smiled. "No, but we know it's the mammoth's necklace, or at least that's what the children's book signified."

The king huffed.

"Something to add over there?" Char said incredulously.

"The necklace is a myth," King Egil horsely spoke. "It's a legend. A children's tale."

Zuri stood with tears in her eyes. Finn put his hand on her shoulder. She found the courage to speak to her king. "Lies. You know the old tales are true. The old advisors hid the truth in children's books so that it wouldn't be lost."

"Traitor!" King Egil yelled, then coughed.

Char cursed at the king. "How dare you speak to Lady Zuri like that! She's one of the bravest ones here."

"She abandoned her kingdom along with that young man." He pointed at Finn, who lowered his head.

Tears flowed from Zuri's azure eyes. How could he think that? Why would her king be this angry? Did he not know what she risked?

Char stepped closer to the cell's bars. "Listen, Egil. Zuri fled your kingdom to find a way to break Len Nove's curse. She and Sealyn worked tirelessly on that project," Char patted Finn's back. "Finn too. You should be proud of their efforts to save their kingdom, your kingdom."

"Please, your majesty," Pinx said. "Is the necklace the source?"

The king backed away from the bars and crossed his arms. He fought day and night not to reveal this information. He watched his children be violated and tortured for months and never broke. Should he risk everything with these Elysians? He slowly lifted his head and locked eyes with Jace, then nodded.

Pinx gasped and jumped. "The part we didn't know was where to find it. This is my theory. Sealyn needed one more chance to find out where the necklace is, so she saw an opportunity to save Jace, give us time to heal, and find the location of the necklace."

"That sounds like, Sealyn," Char said.

King Egil cleared his throat and coughed. "She won't find it. She can't. Thousands of years of snow and ice block anyone from having that power."

"Then you know where it is," Norella stood and crossed her arms. "I think it's time you start helping us." Brehan's lips curled. He liked seeing Norella be bold toward a king.

"Even if I told you where it was, you couldn't get to it, nor could we get a message to Queen Sealyn," Egil grabbed the icy bars. "Face it. Your fate is in her ability to interpret what the trunk gives her."

Weeks went by. The dungeons began to play mind tricks on the prisoners. The Elysians started fighting more and more with each other. However, the wounds were almost healed, and Rielen recovered fully from his fever. Malum's torment was a perfectly timed schedule. It's like he wanted them to expect his torture— to anticipate it with gloom.

Soldiers would take the twins every other day, sometimes with the king. Every two days, the soldiers brought Jace fresh black clothes, then would toss jam on him. Lastly, every third day would be twenty-four hours of wolves walking the hallways. They had long chains around their necks so the guards could control them when they wanted to take them away. The wolves would paw inside the bars, clawing at the prisoners. They would snarl and snap all day and night, hoping that one human would weaken and become food.

One early afternoon, Jace finished wiping jam off his new black clothes. He hated jam and was tired of this torment. The morale of the dungeons was low. He heard the princess and prince arguing quietly. What could those two argue about?

"Tomorrow I will," Princess Drifa said. "The wolves come tomorrow, and so does my freedom. I can't take this anymore." Her eyes had dark purple circles under them.

"You can't leave me here," Dag begged. "His entire appetite will be on me then." He paused. "I know that sounds selfish, but I wouldn't be able to handle it."

"Let's die together, then."

"Together?"

"Yes, we'll both give our wrists to the wolves, and it will just be painful for a few minutes, then we're gone from this horrible world."

Jace walked to the bars. "You can't give up. I know it's awful right now, but trust that Sealyn will find a way."

Dag scowled at Jace. "Stay out of this, Stoltlander! How can you even say that when you're covered in sticky jam and wearing the color of our enemy? The color that takes advantage of my sister and me. Your eyes are evil, and I hate you!"

"Stop that, child!" Char scolded. "You can't speak to our king like that."

"King? Stoltland doesn't even recognize him as your king. Why should I?"

"If you want to agree with Malum, then be my guest," Char spat.

Jace swallowed. "Easy, friends. Look, Dag, I know what Malum has done to you is unspeakable, and he will pay, but don't let him win. If you both end your lives, then he's one step closer to controlling Len Nove," Jace sighed. "I told Sealyn at the ball that if my death can aid in helping break the curse and ridding Len Nove of Stoltland's rule, then so be it." Dag blinked in shock that a Stoltlander would be willing to give his life for strangers. Jace continued. "I'm not saying we'll be free today or this year, but I'm asking that you hang on for as long as your heart will allow. Sometimes blind faith is all we have."

A small rustling sound startled them.

Norella stood quickly. "Hush. Did you all hear that?"

The rustling sounded again and louder.

Norella's eyes grew wide. "There. Did you hear that?"

The prisoners walked to their bars facing each other and peered down the hallway as much as they could. Thousands of tiny feet were running down the stairs. Into the space between the cells, surzees poured around the prisoners. Pinx squeaked, but Norella shushed her. They watched the tiny creatures climbing the bars and gnawing on the locks. When the gnawing didn't work, the tiniest of them used its claws to unlock the doors.

The prisoners pushed open the doors. They were in shock. The surzees scattered, except one. The largest had a small scroll strapped to its back. Jace bent down and undid the scroll. The large surzee scurried off, then Jace read aloud.

"My fellow Elysians and allies,

If you're reading this, then my new friends have freed you. They have cleared a path for you into the palace. Grab the weapons you see along the way. I found a way out, and I'm going after the source. Take the palace back! You can do this. I love you all so much.

My Loyalty,

Queen Sealyn Araelien

Also, Princess Drifa, Malum takes his tea in his bed chamber at this time. Make it slow."

As soon as Jace finished reading, the twins sprinted up the stairs, their frail father following behind. Brehan grabbed Norella's hand and pulled her up the stairs. The rest of the group joined willingly. They saw the path Sealyn mentioned in her note. Guards were lying all around the hallways and staircases, their necks bleeding out onto the blue rugs. The surzees obviously wanted their kingdom back. The freed prisoners quickly grabbed as many weapons as they could.

They knew not all the guards were dead. Being swift and stealthy would be their only tactic. Jace followed behind the twins. He wanted to make sure they were safe during their vengeance on Malum. Tilmond, Favien, and Jem went with Jace. Tilmond ordered Ajorn to take Pinx, Norella, Zuri, and Rielen to the kitchens so that they could pack provisions for their journey home. Madilina, Max, Brehan, and Ashur went to secure the front gate. Madilina wished she could have her wings again, but she wasn't sure how to unlock the magic.

Char looked behind him and saw Sakul bent over, hands on his knees. He was breathing hard. "Seriously, Sakul?"

"I hate stairs, Char. We climbed them so fast," he said as he gasped for air. "That was the fastest I've ever climbed."

"Congratulations on your record, but we've got to go," Char paused and walked to the window. He saw Sealyn fending off two guards at the stables. He looked around, panicking. Everyone had left, and no one was going to the stables. Char grabbed an iced-over vase and threw it, breaking the window.

"Char! What are you doing?"

Char broke the rest of the glass with his sword. "Time to go, Sakul. Our Sealyn has gotten herself in a bind at the stables," he motioned for Sakul to follow. "Out the window."

They both hurried out the window, feeling the bitter cold air against their ratty clothes. His body was weak, but Char ran full speed into the Stoltlander. The Stoltlander rammed his head into a beam, knocking himself out. Sealyn spun and sliced the other soldier's neck.

"Thanks for the assist, Char."

"Well, I figured I owed you since you sent an army of rats to free us."

"Good to see you, Sakul. Still out of shape?"
Sakul panted and nodded.

Sealyn untied the massive snow horses and handed reins to Char and Sakul. "Well, I guess it's us again. Let's go."

Char sighed dramatically. "Really, Sealyn. Can't we just save the pretty royal and go inside for a snack?"

"Saddle up, Char," Sealyn mounted her horse. Char and Sakul grabbed the two soldiers' coats and mounted their horses. Sealyn kicked her horse, and they sped away, passing the arena and heading toward a large mountain. Char looked at Sakul with a questionable expression. Sakul shrugged and hoped Sealyn knew what she was doing.

Ice and snow blurred their vision along with the blue haze. The horses panted hard. They were so close to the mountain that Sealyn needed to get to, but fear struck. She could see something large coming toward them, and then she heard a loud-pitched cry. An Arkootha bear was coming for them. "Dismount!" Sealyn yelled. Char and Sakul flung themselves into the snow.

Sakul felt the air go from his lungs. He hated his life right now. He tried to press up, but his body begged for help. Char scrambled to his feet. He saw Sealyn charging at the bear. What in all creation was his cousin doing? He saw her jump in the air, yelling a word he couldn't pronounce, and then she landed hard on the ground, pounding her fist into the snow.

Snap.

Pop.

Crack.

The bear came to a sliding halt and started sniffing the ground in a panic. The earth began to shake, and a huge crack forced its way to the bear, splitting the snow and ground. The bear trembled and wasn't sure which way to run. The crack split far enough for the bear to fall deep into its abyss. Char and Sakul ran to catch up to Sealyn.

"Sealyn, you can split the ground?" Char asked.

"I guess so."

They watched as the crack continued to the mountain, then they saw the horror. The mountain began to fall. An avalanche was heading straight for them.

Char's mouth fell open. "Tell me that was a part of the plan. Sealyn?" Char looked at Sealyn with wide eyes. "Tell me that's part of your plan!"

"Um, no. Wasn't expecting that."

"What do we do?" panicked Sakul.

"Run!"

The three tried to escape the avalanche, but the ground kept splitting longer and deeper. They couldn't outrun the forces of nature that were taking over. Sealyn felt herself leaning backward. She was falling into the cavern she created. She screamed for help, but Char and Sakul were falling with her. All she could see was blue darkness. They slid for miles, it seemed. The avalanche covered the crack at the base of the mountain, but a large ice tunnel formed, allowing them to slide further away from safety.

Finally, the three slid into a wall of ice. They smacked into it hard. They moaned loudly. Everything ached. The air was frigid cold. Slowly turning upright, they sat with their backs against the ice wall and stared into the long ice-covered tunnel. They were trapped in a deep ice cave that no one could get to.

"What are we supposed to do now?" Char groaned.

Tears slid down Sakul's cheeks. "I just wanted the chance to see Sorcha one more time." His nose was bloody, and his lip was busted.

"Stop that, Sakul," Char said. "I'm sure Sealyn can figure something out." Char felt the dripping of blood going down his head. He reached up and touched the wound; it would need stitches. He could tell his shoulder was injured, too.

Sealyn slipped in and out of consciousness. Using that much power to split the earth drained her. Her body had thinned from the magic. Cuts and bruises covered her skin. She didn't know how long it would take for her to recover. Sleep called to her, but then she heard a sound that felt ancient. Ancient? How could a sound feel ancient? Her head ached and throbbed. She leaned her head back and tried to shake the sound off, but again, a low grumble was heard. She lifted her head and looked at Char and Sakul. They heard it too. She was not mistaken; a deep growling was coming from behind the ice wall.

Prince Haedon,

Commander Malum has gone dark. He's not returning letters to me. We need to move now. Ready the dragons for transport, even the pregnant females. We have one shot at this, Haedon.

You better deliver me a victory.

Magnanimously,
Queen Corentine of Stoltland
and the seven kingdoms

CHAPTER 25

DUN SHOOK HIS HEAD

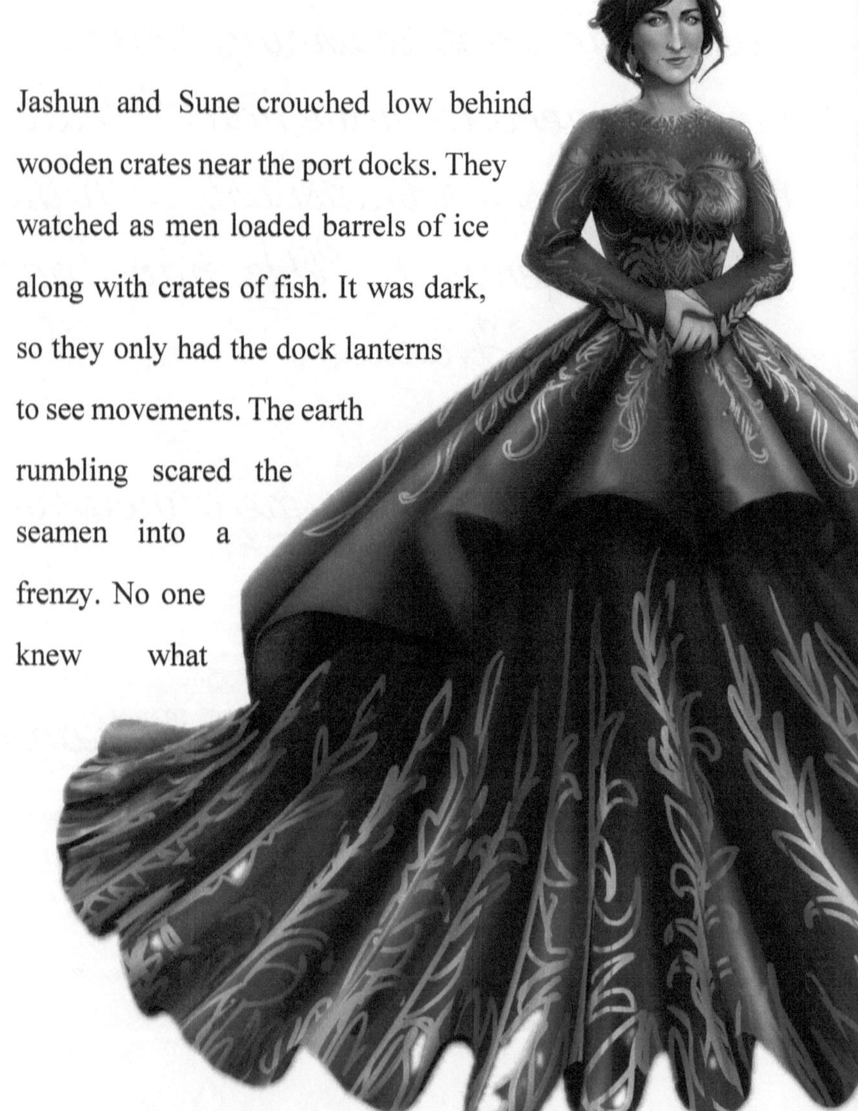

Jashun and Sune crouched low behind wooden crates near the port docks. They watched as men loaded barrels of ice along with crates of fish. It was dark, so they only had the dock lanterns to see movements. The earth rumbling scared the seamen into a frenzy. No one knew what happened, but it sent fear into the port city.

Squinting through the crate slats, Sune saw Stoltland soldiers and the Korpam pirates pushing each other. They stumbled out of the local tavern with swaying steps. Brawls were a nightly occurrence. Sune secretly hoped to catch a glance at the nefarious pirate captain, but so far, he made no appearance.

Doebromir quietly joined Jashun and Sune. The moonlight bounced off his bald head. "Anything new to report tonight, gents?" he asked.

"Another brawl, but it does seem like the Stoltlanders and the pirates are loading their boats to leave," Jashun said. He wrapped his scarf tighter around his light brown neck. The air was frosty.

Sune signaled for them to hush and pointed toward the docks. Doebromir's eyes grew wide. He was in disbelief. "It can't be. Is that our caretaker shaking hands with a Stoltland captain?"

Jashun's stomach dropped. Shaking hands with a captain only meant one thing—a deal had been struck, but what kind of deal? Would Sir Verraeter betray them? If so, where would they go? Whom could they trust? Jashun whispered frantically, "Should we go back to the house and get Sorcha and Ezen?"

Anger burned in Doebromir. It was clouding his judgment. He scratched his burly beard. "I want to get closer. We need to hear what they're saying."

Sune shook his head, and his red curls danced in the moonlight. "Doebromir, we can't. Someone might see our eyes."

Doebromir pulled his hood low, casting a shadow down his face. He stepped quietly and tried to stick to the shadows. Jashun and Sune followed. Sounds from the tavern and the loading of boats kept them from hearing Verraeter's conversation. The Stoltland captain nodded to several soldiers, who then mounted their horses and sped away. Ice prickled down Doebromir's back.

The darkness felt evil. Something was wrong. Jashun grabbed Doebromir's shoulder. "We should go back. I have a bad feeling."

They turned to walk home but ran into a broad figure with flames in his eyes. Doebromir sucked in his breath. He recognized the steel-cut, tiger head helmet; this was the pirate captain. Two other pirates drew their swords. The Elysians grew still. They could not make trouble.

The captain wore a burnt orange sash over his thick grey fur coat and a necklace made of shark teeth with a large metal tiger's head at the center. He pulled off his helmet, exposing a face that seemed oddly familiar to them. "Well, well, well. What have we here, boys?" The pirate captain grinned an intimidating smile. "Looks to me that we've struck emerald treasure tonight."

Doebromir dropped his head. "Apologies, Captain. We meant no harm. Just passing by."

The captain chuckled and adjusted his stance. "Elysians don't just pass by, especially here in Len Nove." He stepped forward. "What are you doing here, boy?"

Silence.

A dark-skinned pirate with orange eyes stepped into the light. He had a gold front tooth and rib bones for a necklace. "The cap'tin' asked ya a question. Ya best speak up."

Jashun's mouth was dry, and he was sweating. Korpam hated them, but how much did pirates hate them? Would this be their last moment? How much truth could they tell without betraying their queen? Jashun looked to Sune for guidance.

"We mean no disrespect. We humbly ask to part with no issues," Sune said.

"I'll tell you what," the captain replied. "I'll make a deal with you three. We won't kill you where you stand *if* you tell us information about your Elysian monarchy that I may find helpful.

If the details you give are worthless, this world will have three fewer pairs of Elysian green eyes."

Doebromir discerned this was a trick. There was nothing they could give these men. "Captain, surely you know as much as we do on the details of the monarchy."

The pirates laughed. The captain patted the shoulder of the dark-skinned pirate. "We've been at sea for over a year now, and as you can imagine, the Stoltlanders are tight-lipped when it comes to sharing information about Elysium."

"Would you know the news that Queen Sealyn is our queen now?" Doebromir asked hesitantly.

The captain cut his flaming eyes to his comrades. They advanced their swords and held the blades to Jashun and Sune's necks. Doebromir held his hands up. "Wait. Wait! Why was that bad? It was just a question."

"Because, you fool. Everyone knows about Sealyn, the third-generation bloodline, taking the throne. Even the deepest sea creatures speak about this," the captain placed his helmet back on his head. His fiery orange eyes glowed through the tiger's mouth. "Your words are meaningless, as is your life to me." He drew his sword.

"What about our new king?" Jashun yelped.

The captain froze. "New king? What new king?"

Doebromir glared at Jashun, but Jashun spoke without hesitation. "He's a Stoltlander."

"A Stoltlander?"

"Yes, his name is Jace, Queen Corentine's illegitimate son."

Slowly, the captain dropped his sword, and his comrades did the same. He looked past Jashun like he was staring into a distant memory. Instead of killing them, the pirates brushed past the Elysians, then the captain paused and turned his head to the side. "The grey-eyed child, correct?"

"Correct, Captain," Jashun said.

The captain nodded and walked away with his comrades to the tavern. Doebromir grabbed Jashun and shoved him behind crates. "What did you just do?"

"I have no idea. How was that bad to give information that the world already knows?"

"I don't know, but this could turn out bad for Elysium," Doebromir said. He looked toward the dock where the Stoltland captain stood with Verraeter. Verraeter looked nervous. He scratched at his arm, irritating a new boil on his rubbery skin, then the horsemen returned with prisoners.

Sune's heart sank. He recognized her clothes. Ripping off the hoods, the Stoltland captain laughed at the sight of Sorcha and Ezen. Their hands were bound behind them. The captain tossed a small sack to Verraeter, who delightedly shook the bag. Swiftly, the Stoltland captain pulled a knife and stabbed Verraeter in the heart. Sorcha screamed. Sune jumped from behind the crates. Doebromir tried to grab him, but he was too quick. Sprinting to the dock, Sune slipped on a patch of black ice and tumbled, allowing Stoltland soldiers time to capture him.

More soldiers came from the tavern and tackled Doebromir and Jashun. They were completely outnumbered, so they had to face the hard truth: they were prisoners of Stoltland now. Doebromir yelled in frustration. How could their time in Len Nove come to this? They survived the Arkootha bear attack and the catacomb maze and stayed unnoticed for over a month. Why now? He struggled as the soldiers clasped iron chains around his wrists and ankles.

"Take them on board. I'm sure Queen Corentine will be most pleased when we bring her these fools."

Sorcha fainted. The anxiety was too much. In chains, Sune caught Sorcha. He would always catch her. She was more than beauty; she was a warrior. He would ensure she made it out alive, even if it cost him his life. Sune glanced at the tavern, where the pirates raised their pints to him. Sick snakes. They could save them, but those pirates willingly chose not to. A Stoltland soldier took Sorcha from Sune and carried her on board.

Tears flowed from Jashun's green eyes. He never felt betrayal so deeply. He didn't want to see Corentine. What would she do to him? He never answered her letter. Would she remember that? As he walked across the boards to the ship, he looked back and shivered at Verraeter's outstretched arm inches away from the small sack of spilled silver coins, now covered in his blood. Justice? Jashun thought so.

Queen Mother Graelynd sat in her chair in the garden. A warm breeze gently swayed her wisps of dark brown hair. Spring was approaching. The massive green phoenix was lying before the queen mother, unintentionally becoming her muse. Capturing the golden sunshine beaming off Dun's back, Graelynd carefully glided her brush, as not to use too much yellow. She loved watching Dun take his afternoon naps. It was peaceful. He did so much for them, so she felt like she could watch over him for a few resting hours.

Suddenly, Dun jerked his head up, and his eyes dilated. Graelynd felt the color drain from her ivory face. Dun sniffed the air. He looked at Graelynd with intensity. Graelynd stood, fearing what she would ask. "Can you defend?"

Dun shook his head.

"Can you find help?"

One nod is all he gave. Green flames engulfed him, and the flames flew high in the sky, then out of sight. A terrible thought invaded Graelynd's mind; if Dun could not defend what was coming, could they defend? What was this force that a mythical creature could not overpower?

Running down the garden pathway, Ryker caught his breath. "My love, was that Dun's green flames?"

"Yes. He sensed danger," she said. "But then I asked him if he could defend, and he shook his head, so I asked if he could find help, and he disappeared into flames. Oh, Ryker! I fear what is to come."

Ryker quickly held his wife in his arms, trying to comfort her. "We have faced many battles before, love. We can defeat what is coming, but we must prepare. I trust Dun will find us aid.

He's frequently seen in the Lost Forest of the Hill Chimes territory. Perhaps there's someone or something in the forest that can help?"

"I better warn Madam Bip."

"And I will gather the War Council. We will also need to evacuate the frail and weakest."

"I agree. I will ensure the Vinurs of Sealyn and Siany start the first phase of the evacuation process immediately."

Ryker cupped Graelynd's cheeks and kissed her nose. "My love, you are everything to me. I am not Ryker without you. I promise you that I will do whatever it takes to keep you safe."

"Us safe, my darling. For I cannot stand to live without you either. We fight for Elysium, but we also fight for each other."

"Agreed."

CHAPTER 26

AN ARMY OF DRAGONS

Siany paced in the war room. She wore her green and brown battle leathers with her hair braided back, ready to fight. Trying to silence the bickering of the war council, who sat around the stone table, Siany concentrated on every place Elysium could be weak for an attack. She had tripled the guard around Stoltland's Tor. The magical portal between their lands could not be their undoing. When Ryker, her father, told her about Dun's response, she immediately ordered for the on-call reinforcements to be stationed at every port city.

Stoltland would want to make a show of their attack. A port city would give them that. She felt a tinge of guilt and sadness when bidding the diplomats farewell, but they needed to lead their territories. One day, she would ask them back, hopefully. However, Siany felt like something was missing. Vital information about what was coming was hidden from them.

The palace felt uncomfortable with the extra soldiers and guards at every turn, but it was necessary. Fort Kippen sent their fastest soldiers to help defend; they felt the border of Len Nove would not be where Stoltland attacked. Siany agreed with their advice. She felt like the Tor would be the major attack point.

Eldest brother to Queen Mother Graelynd, Prince Adomin, stood with frustration. His chair smacked the floor with a loud clash. "It's been days. We can't just sit here and wait to be attacked!"

"Stay calm, Adomin," King Father Ryker said. "We don't have any idea where to attack. The good news is that Dun gave us the alarm to be prepared, which we are."

Adomin grumbled. "So we think."

"That's enough, uncle," Siany said. "We have done all we can to prepare, and the evacuations to Fort Kippen are running smoothly." Siany shook her head and folded her arms. "I feel like we're missing something, though. Why would Corentine attack again? She failed with the element of surprise last time, so what would give her the confidence to attack a second time?"

King Ryker leaned back in his chair, lost in distant memories. He recalled only once in his lifetime that Stoltland made a bold move. They had held off their forces but were unprepared for the dragons. He shivered at the memory of that black dragon. Prince Royce, second eldest brother to Graelynd, had to invent long-range crossbows within minutes. Avondelle would have burned to the ground without achieving this invention. Could this be what gave Stoltland their confidence? Was an army of dragons coming for Elysium?

With that terrible thought, Ryker made eye contact with Prince Royce. Royce did not like the seriousness in Ryker's eyes. He long feared that look. He started nodding his head. "I will go at once with Captain Graegory and ready the towers with the dragon slayers."

Graegory's almond-shaped eyes went wide. "Dragon slayers? What is happening?"

"Years ago, Stoltland combined with Korpam and attacked with a great army at Calenburg," Ryker started. Siany wished Favien was here. This was his favorite war story. Her father sometimes liked to embellish this story, but today, he would tell the hard truth. "We were outnumbered, but the reinforcements from Blissendelle finally arrived right when we thought we could fight no more. We rallied our energy and drove the enemy back."

Ryker stopped and leaned forward, resting his elbows on the stone table. The rest of the story would scare the younger generation. He did not want to awaken the creatures that thrived in nightmares. He cleared his throat. "Then came the *Org dragons. There were four. These dragons looked like the lower half of their bodies were dipped in white paint, while their tops were black as night. Orgs spit balls of fire that explode upon impact. We had no idea how to fight such beasts."

"Why are you telling this story again?" Lord Jdru asked. He had heard his Uncle Ryker tell this story a hundred times, but he thought he told it more for fun. He thought the dragons were Ryker's imagination.

"Because the Org dragons are real, Jdru. I didn't make them up. Other dragons exist as well. I think there are around twelve types, if I'm not mistaken, but not all are dangerous."

Prince Royce nodded. "Ryker speaks the truth. One of the worst dragons spits lightning, while another type spews bubbles."

"Bubbles?" Jdru questioned. "All right, someone has to be joking, and I'm not sure why, especially at a time such as this."

Ryker leaned over and squeezed Jdru's shoulder. "No one is joking, my lad. We didn't teach nor talk about dragons here because we thought they were gone, or at least dormant. We lost so many soldiers that day. We had finally narrowed it down to one dragon, but it left the battle site and flew for Avondelle. It tortured us as we made our way back to the capitol. We were its game. The speed Nichts had taken word to the palace where Prince Royce was. He busied himself on a new device that would be able to launch a heavy spear into the beast. Long story short, after several attempts, his device killed the last dragon."

"And that's what you think is heading for us?" Graegory asked. His palms began to sweat. He thought of his sister, Pinx. He hoped he would see her again, but now, facing a dragon, he doubted it.

"Yes."

"But if you killed four Org dragons before without a magical green phoenix, then why would Dun flee for help?" Jrue asked.

Ryker paused. He wasn't sure if he needed to be the one to answer that question. He instead turned to his daughter, Siany. She hesitated but stepped forward.

"Because it's not just four Orgs coming. It's an army of dragons; perhaps the curse awoke the *Toxicon and *Noxhorn, too," Siany paused and saw her father's confused and suspicious expression. "Yes, Father, I read all the documents in the martyr's coffin, even the pages about dragons," Siany walked to her uncle. "Prince Royce, how many dragon slayers are in our inventory?"

"Only thirty."

"Then ready the closest thirty towers to Avondelle. We must move fast!"

All rose and left except Ryker. He sat in a nightmare state. His mind replayed the Battle of Calenburg. He could smell the burnt flesh of the soldiers. He closed his eyes and saw the scorched skeletons and men in flames running for help. The screams. He could still hear them. The heat was so intense that he had to check to see if he was on fire. His eyes kept burning, but the worst part was the ashes landing on him; he knew the ashes were all that remained of fallen comrades.

Ryker felt a gentle touch on his leg, then a peaceful whisper. "Come back, my love. You're safe here with me." Ryker opened his watery eyes and saw his beloved wife kneeling beside him. Graelynd gave him a sweet smile. That was all Ryker needed.

She grounded him. More than beauty, she was the essence of Elysium and his backbone.

Jace jogged to the banquet hall with Finn. He tried to shake the memory of watching Princess Drifa and Prince Dag stabbing Malum over and over. Malum didn't look human by the end of it. Malum definitely earned his consequences. Thinking about the twins, Jace figured it would take a lifetime of counseling for them to recover from what Malum had done to them. He prayed they would heal.

Once inside the banquet hall, the Elysians realized they had taken back the palace from the Stoltlanders. The surzees took out many of the soldiers, and the Elysians finished the rest. It seemed easy—too easy. The ground trembling seemed to have stirred a fight within the Len Novian citizens, because once they saw the Elysians taking back the palace, they started rebelling against the Stoltlanders. Jace sighed in relief, seeing all his friends free and with minimal wounds. He gazed around the room and didn't see Sealyn. How was she not back yet? They had been fighting for hours, or at least it seemed like hours.

"Did anyone see Queen Sealyn during the fights?" he asked.

Favien shook his head. "No, I don't think anyone did. She said she was going somewhere, right?"

"Yes, but shouldn't she be back by now?"

Pinx gasped. "Wait, I don't see Char or Sakul here either. Did they fall in battle?"

Panic went through everyone's veins. Tilmond stepped up to lead. "Stay calm. Let's not think the worst. Here's what we're going to do. We split up and look for Char and Sakul. We need to take an account of the castle anyway. Norella, Pinx, and Madilina, I want to commission you three to gain the king's trust. Perhaps you can even convince him to prepare food for us once we've returned?"

Lady Zuri grabbed Finn and shoved a set of keys into his hands. "We must free them," she nodded to the Len Novian servants. Finn agreed, and together, they began to free their people from the bondage of Stoltland. Zuri paused in front of a window. It was clear. No ice was on the window. She tried to focus on unlocking a short, scraggly girl's chains, but something else caught her eye. The blue haze wasn't as thick as it was before when they first arrived. What was happening, and what was the cause?

The ship creaked and rocked. It smelled damp, like unwashed feet. The cage bars were cold, but Sorcha leaned against them anyway. She pulled the blue cloak tighter around her. A tear slid from her green eye down her sweet ebony cheek. She felt defeated. How would they be able to escape? They were captives aboard a Stoltland ship. She feared everything around them. She feared the diseases lurking, the red eyes in the corner that kept staring, and, above all, she feared the water. One of her greatest regrets was never learning how to swim, and now she was surrounded by big swells of water. She closed her eyes, begging herself not to think about the ocean.

They could hear the captain shouting commands. Some were to avoid icebergs, and others seemed like chants to ward off the magical sea creatures. Either way, Doebromir was sick. He felt nauseous. Every movement was torture for him. He leaned his bald head between the bars, hoping the cold would help, but it didn't. Any minute and the vomit could come.

"Do you all want to play a game?" Jashun asked hopefully.

"A game? Seriously, Jashun?" Ezen scoffed. Ezen hated being away from home. This was the longest time he'd ever been away from his family. He feared he'd never see them again.

"Why not? We need to keep our morale up."

Sune crossed his arms and pulled his knees to his chest. "I'm not sure I want to play a game with a traitor."

"What?" Jashun and Sorcha both said together.

"Exactly as I said. Jashun betrayed our queen. He leaked valuable information to the pirate captain."

Sorcha's hand covered her mouth. "Jashun, you didn't!"

"No, I didn't! Sune is overexaggerating."

"Am I? Then why did the pirate captain leave us alone after what you told him? We should be dead."

"You should be thanking me that we're not! I gave him information that everyone knew."

Sorcha sat up straight. "What did you say, Jashun?"

"Only that Jace was king. Who doesn't know that?"

"Obviously, he didn't!" Sune leaned forward and crossed his legs. "Something about what you said gave him reason to spare us."

Doebromir puked and gave a loud moan. The stench made everyone queasy. Something could be heard scurrying in the corner of the ship. A creature the size of a large dog, yet looking like a frog with a jagged mouth, appeared. The red eyes belonged to this creature, a *Rana frog. It immediately began lapping up Doebromir's vomit. "Oh, gross. I think I will be sick again watching this creature eat that." These frogs were known to enjoy the foulness of foods, so sea crews would have several aboard their ships to keep them somewhat clean.

With closed eyes, Sorcha said, "Well, at least the vomit is being cleaned; otherwise, we'd have to smell it for days."

Jashun stared at Sune. He couldn't believe that Sune was still upset with him. "Sune, really? We need to move past this."

"Perhaps if you took what you did more seriously, then I could."

"Fine. Then educate me, oh wise red-haired wizard."

Sune huffed. "The pirate captain and his crew have never stepped on Elysian territory. Now, he knows there's a Stoltland king on the throne and sees Stoltland overthrowing Len Nove. He just might have the courage to attack ports because he may feel that Elysium has lost control of its kingdom."

Doebromir puked again, and the Rana frog was delighted.

"The last thing I wanted to do was cause harm for Elysium. I only wanted to save our lives."

Sune nodded. "It's noble to want to save lives, but it's honorable to sacrifice your own for the safety of others."

Diary entry,

I received word today from one of my ship captains that the pirate king was at Len Nove's Zykoan port. I must admit, I've never felt such anger. The darkness rose all around me, and I lost control. The mist turned to shards of glass and went everywhere. The glass ended up killing my dog and injuring my husband.

I blame the Pirate King. He will die, as will Sealyn. What was he doing at that port? He could easily mess up my plans.

On brighter news, my captain said he will be sending me special prizes. I can't wait.

Until next time,
Queen Corentine, Queen of all Queens

CHAPTER 27
TORN IN TWO

Sealyn watched the backs of her eyelids open and then close. She tried to regain her focus, but her head ached. Muffled noises were all she heard. After she realized someone was gently shaking her, she opened her eyes again. Her vision was blurry, but she finally could make out the face of a panicked Char. The fear in his eyes made her feel sick. She looked behind him and saw Sakul frozen still. What was he staring at?

"I need help standing." Char and Sakul wrapped Sealyn's arms around their shoulders and helped her to her feet.

They slowly turned her to face the ice wall. Sealyn gasped. "This can't be real."

Frozen in mid-stride, the king of the mammoths and his army stood encased in the giant ice mountain. She heard the grumble again. Was this sound coming from the mammoths? Were they still alive? Sealyn dropped her arms from Char and Sakul and steadied herself. She cautiously walked to the ice wall. Observing deep within the thick ice, Sealyn caught a glimmer around the Mammoth King's neck. It was the necklace; the source of Len Nove's power was mere feet from her.

Excitedly, she placed her hand on the ice, then felt vibrations. She heard whispers echoing around the ice. What were they saying? Her head throbbed, and she felt dizzy.

"Do you hear what the voices are saying?" Sealyn asked.

Char shook his head, but Sakul nodded. "Sealyn, I don't trust this. That language. It's… It's the—"

"Old magic. Yes, I know, Sakul. I can trust it. It helped save you during Malum's Feydom."

"Really? That's how you saved us?"

"Yes, but my head is spinning, and I can't make out all the words. Can you?"

Sakul hesitated. "Libero meus." He shook his head and swallowed. "Animus."

Sealyn's brows furrowed. "Release my spirit." She looked into the eyes of the Mammoth King. She felt him calling to her, but how was that possible? She was not Len Novian; only Len Novians could hear the mammoths. Her heart trembled. She took a few steps back and linked arms with Char and Sakul. "I need you both to know that if I release these mammoths, the ice wall could come down on us, or at the very least, an army of mythical mammoths would trample us."

A few tense moments passed, but then the words needed to move forward came. "To die with you would be an honor, my queen," Sakul said with a tear flowing down his dark cheek.

Sealyn looked to Char, her best friend. Char shook his head. "I always said you'd be the death of me. I used to think I was facetiously joking, but apparently, you're going to make me a prophet. I wish I could say it's been a pleasure, but it's literally been a pain in my neck. My neck hurts something awful."

The three chuckled, then embraced in a group hug. These could be their final moments, and they wanted to soak them in. Sealyn quietly said goodbye to her family, her friends, her kingdom, and then her Jace. How it pained her to say a farewell to her love that he would never hear. She feared what the world would do to him if she wasn't there to stand by him. She had to trust that her family would protect him.

They stepped back from each other, wiping their noses and eyes. Sealyn nodded to them, then turned to face the ice wall once again. Even with her thinning body, she felt confident this spell would work. Sealyn cleared her throat. The ice wall in front of her sparkled, inviting her to unleash what lay beyond. She made sure she annunciated the words perfectly. "Libero meus animus!"

Right after she said the words, Sealyn felt silly. Nothing happened, but only for a few seconds, then a loud popping sounded. The three Elysians held onto each other and braced themselves. A large crack started crawling its way down the ice wall. Flakes of snow and ice fell on top of their heads.

Sealyn could feel the energy being drained from her. Dropping to her knee, Sealyn wiped the blood from her eyes and nose. This spell had taken a lot from her, maybe everything. Char and Sakul crouched low and wrapped their arms around Sealyn, accepting their fate. Sealyn looked up to see the blue haze also being split by the crack, or was she that dizzy? She saw it as the curse was a blue veil, and now, the evil was finally being destroyed. "It's beautiful, is it not?"

"What is?" Char asked.

"Witnessing the veil being torn in two." Then, the world went black.

Favien raced into the dining hall, where everyone was eating like animals. They were starving and in need of nourishment. Favien tried to steady his breath before speaking, but it came out a few octaves higher than normal. "Stoltland soldiers are coming and in massive numbers!"

"I knew it couldn't be that easy," Tilmond huffed. They ran to the windows and saw the rest of Malum's army coming toward the palace. They didn't have an army. How would they survive? Tilmond looked to Max. "Max, take Finn, Ajorn, and Rielen to the towers and guide them in archery. "Brehan and Favien, you both will be with me at the front gate. Jem and Ashur, you will take King Jace, Madilina, Zuri, Norella, and Pinx to the king's chambers and guard the royal lines. Ladies, you're the last hope to protect Len Nove's princess. Understood?" Everyone nodded.

Once everyone left, Favien paled. "Is that what I think it is?"

Brehan squinted. "Hostages! Those cursed Stoltlanders have Len Novian hostages."

Len Nove was weak from the treatment of the Stoltlanders' cruelty and their curse. They needed an army, but who would fight for them? The Elysians watched in horror as the Stoltland soldiers made the hostages kneel with swords at their throats. How could they be this wicked?

"What are we to do?" Favien asked frantically.

Brehan stretched his shoulders and cracked his neck from side to side. "We have to fight as long as we can."

"Fight? Fight until when?" Favien was not convinced this plan was right. He didn't want to die in vain. He wanted to live and have a wonderful life with Pinx. He dreamed of a family one day. How could he let a moment of fear take those dreams away? "Could our arrows take them out?"

Tilmond shook his head. "There's too many of them. They would immediately become the main targets and break down the doors."

"There has to be another way!"

Brehan grabbed Favien's shoulder. "Favien, get a hold of yourself. You're asking for a miracle, and those don't exist."

Anger built up inside Favien. Miracles did exist. The green phoenix was proof of that. Sealyn's and Madilina's magic was a miracle, too. Brehan was wrong! They needed to give Sealyn enough time to complete her quest. He didn't realize it, but he had been holding animosity toward Sealyn for allowing Pinx to come on this journey. He blamed her for their predicament and for Stawyer's death. Forgiving Sealyn was the first step to believing in his queen again.

"You're wrong, Brehan. All we must do is have faith in our Queen Sealyn, and she'll break the curse. Then you'll have that miracle you're so reluctant to believe in."

They all heard a loud pop. Everyone froze, including the Stoltlanders. Heads looked around, trying to figure out what happened to make such a sound, then the ground began to shake. The people stood in disbelief as they saw the haze splitting open, like a curtain drawing back to reveal a theater's stage.

"What is happening?" Tilmond asked.

Favien's smile showed all his teeth. "That, my friend, would be our queen breaking curses! Hoorah!"

Brehan's face was pure astonishment. "So what do we do?"

A loud rumbling started, then screams. They saw the Stoltlanders drop the hostages and run. What were they running from? Suddenly, an army of Len Novians ran after the black soldiers. At the front of the massive blue army was a fierce female warrior. She commanded the troops as if she knew them. Where did they come from, and where had they been?

The warrior leader pounded on the palace door. Brehan cautiously opened the door and stepped back. The leader was tall, like the king with piercing blue eyes. Her white hair, streaked with blue highlights, dragged on the floor behind her. She looked almost familiar.

"Mother!" screamed Princess Drifa. The princess ran into her mother's arms. The two fell to the floor, embracing. Prince Dag quickly joined the bundle on the floor. Jace escorted the king to his wife. They had witnessed the massive army and instantaneously left the king's chambers.

Zuri kneeled in front of the king's family. "You said mother, so does this mean you're Queen Fraeya?"

The queen nodded, unsure of what to make of all the green eyes staring at her. Her family stood, and, finally, she embraced her husband. He was quite a few years older than her, but she didn't care. She loved him in her own special way.

"How? How is this possible? I thought you died," Zuri said.

Queen Fraeya cleared her throat. She had almost forgotten how to speak. "The magic that bound us in the ice broke. Our instinct was to come here." Fraeya froze once her gaze met Jace's. She quickly drew her spear and held it to Jace's throat. All Elysians drew their weapons. Jace raised his hands.

King Egil hobbled before Jace, guiding the spear down with his hand. "Easy, my love. This one is not what he seems."

"He's a half-breed. We don't allow that kind here."

Jace gritted his teeth. He was so tired of people calling him names. Malum's month-long mind games had pushed him over the edge. "Watch your mouth, witch!"

The Elysians gasped. They had never heard Jace say something like that before. Fraeya started lifting her spear again. She tilted her head and gave a wicked smile. "I've killed for less, boy. Name your grey-eyed kingdoms."

Jace felt the pressure against him. If he named Stoltland, then she'd think he was the enemy. He didn't know his father's kingdom or who his father was, so he had no other kingdom to help calm the tension. Bullying. That's all this was. Another tactic for someone to bully him, but not today. Not when they came to rescue them. "I am Jace from Stoltland, son of Queen

Corentine of Stoltland and a father whom I know nothing about, but I am k—"

"Rotten filth! Kill him and be done with it!"

The Elysians stepped in front of Jace with their weapons drawn. The king pleaded with Fraeya, and the Elysians tried to tell her who Jace was, but she thought it was a lie, and her army only heard her voice. They held their swords, ready to fight the Elysians.

"Your filth dies today, boy. You will die alone with no one, as no one."

CHAPTER 28

THE SADDEST DAY IN ELYSIUM'S HISTORY

There are moments in a person's life that are never be forgotten. Perhaps the moment was so joyous that she forever forms a smile remembering that moment, but other moments are remembered because they are seared into your mind forcefully, and this day was literally burned forever in Siany's mind, heart, and soul.

Madam Bip's potions were

breaking down. Stoltland's Tor was a massive black tree with silver leaves. It looked sick and smelled of rotten apples. A dark, wide hole was at the center of a trunk that swirled with colors of black and green. The Avondelle army stood fearfully as they watched dragon after dragon try to break through the protection spell of the Tor.

The first round of dragons sent were the *Noxhorns. They breathed blue flames and were the smallest of the fire-breathing dragons. The Stoltlanders were smart for sending them first. Their electric blue scales aren't as hard as other dragon scales, but they fight like nothing could kill them. The protection spell took a beating from the blue flames, but Madam Bip had an effect thrown into the potion: poison gas. Every time a Noxhorn used its flames, poison gas shot back, choking it.

Madam Bip held tight to her bag, which had several herbs and roots in it. She was transferring the magical properties to the protection spell. Sweat was pouring down her brow. Holding the bag tensely, she could feel the herbs and roots starting to turn to dust. The elements were almost out.

A tiny hole started to form in the spell. Stoltland sent the *Blackclaw dragon next, solid black everything, even its teeth. This dragon was the fastest of them all. Some of the orange flames started pouring through the hole. Archers fired their arrows as the Ice Nichts tried to cast their magic to protect anyone near the flames.

Madam Bip looked at Captain Graegory. Blood was slowly dripping from her ears. "Captain, I can do no more. I'm sorry. I will fall back to the palace with the Nichts and do what I can there to protect the royal line. Elysium forever."

"Elysium forever. Thank you, Bip."

This was it. Graegory knew they would send the big dragons next. The Orgs were coming. Graegory shivered at the thought. The first fireball burst inside the spell, creating a controlled ball of fire, but it melted the spell barrier. The black tree never caught fire. Evil glared through the dark hole, and the Blackclaw dragon confidently emerged and released its war on Elysium. Its fireball burst in front of five Elysian soldiers, melting their skin. The dragon roared with victory. Graegory gasped. He was not prepared for this. More dragons poured out of the hole. How could such massive beasts escape from a hole smaller than their size? The Tor must have an enchantment encoded in the spell.

Graegory pulled one of his men to safety behind a large boulder. He frantically patted the soldier's boots from the flames, then a shadow with wings soared above him. He swallowed and looked up. The Org dragon was free. The treetops were instantly in flames, and smoke started to cloud Graegory's vision.

The Blackclaws and Noxhorns joined the Orgs in the sky, gushing their vengeance on the thick Elysian forest. The towers shot their giant crossbows and luckily managed to kill several dragons. They would crash to the ground, flattening several trees and monuments. However, the towers soon became the target of the dragons. One by one, the towers began to fall. A Noxhorn dragon's blue fire exploded a tower near Graegory, but he dodged the blazing stones. How hot were those flames for stones to catch fire? He helplessly watched as more stones fell, crushing his comrades. He lifted himself up and ran toward one of the new recruits. A massive stone was heading straight for him. Graegory dove and pushed the new recruit from being smashed.

"Thank you, Captain," he said, barely able to breathe.

"Don't thank, soldier. Just do your duty and keep a lookout—everywhere!"

The Elysian soldiers found that the younger dragons were easier to kill; they were less trained, and their armor had not fully developed. Treetop archers made their way to the ground, avoiding being trapped in the burning trees. Graegory motioned for the archers to aim for the juveniles' wings, as that was their weakest spot. A year-one recruit fired his arrow, striking the wing of a vicious Blackclaw juvenile. It screamed, which caught the attention of what was assumed to be its mother. She bolted toward the year-one recruit. He scrambled to get another arrow ready, but the mother dragon let out her rage on him. She opened her mouth and devoured him. The other adult dragons dominated the battle along with her.

Graegory threw himself on the ground as a Noxhorn dragon flew right above him, his clamping jaws missing him by inches. He felt the heat of the dragon. His luck would eventually run out. How were they to protect their land from this? He prayed for help. Avondelle would soon fall, then all of Elysium. Tears pricked his eyes. They needed a miracle, and then he heard a familiar sound echoing through the forest. Dragons paused mid-flight, trying to organize their wings.

Graegory breathed slowly. He smelled the burnt trees and flesh mixed with the metallic scent of blood. He coughed and felt nauseous. The forest fire was becoming too much to take. He covered his nose and mouth with a cloth. Orange flames were everywhere, but what was that sound that made the dragons still? Slowly hiding behind a boulder, Graegory peeked his head above the rock and tried to hear the sound again, but he went rigid still when he saw part of an arm in front of him. He couldn't hold it in any longer. He leaned over and vomited.

The screech came again. Graegory's head snapped up, and he wiped the vomit from his mouth. He knew that sound. His mind went flooding back to him on top of the palace tower, face-to-face with two Stoltland soldiers who held swords at him, then Dun's screech knocked them off. This was Dun's call. He was back! And apparently, not alone.

The dragons roared, hearing the piercing screeches of the giant phoenix, but one call wasn't strong enough for all the dragons. Dun flew with his own army of giant green phoenixes. It was now the battle of wings. Feathers and scales collided. Claws and teeth scraped against each other. Soldiers had to dodge falling dragons engaged with fighting phoenixes. Dun's screech made an Org choke on its own fireball, then it exploded, raining dragon parts on the soldiers. The entrails were so boiling hot that steam emanated from the soldiers' skin.

Without warning, Stoltland soldiers burst from the black Tor. Graegory's troops were terribly wounded and weak from the dragon attack. This battle was vastly becoming a war they could not win. Stoltlanders took off for the palace. Graegory and his men fought the entire way, giving ground as more of his troops fell. Graegory took another stab to the arm. He could barely lift either arm now. His strength and willpower were giving out. He thought of Pinx. He had to fight for a better world for his sister.

Nearing the castle, he heard the call for the Elysian palace archers to release their arrows. The troops scrambled for cover and watched as all the Stoltlanders close to the palace caught arrows in their bodies. Graegory yelled for his men to join the palace soldiers. They did not need to go back into the forest and face being burned or eaten.

More Stoltland soldiers arrived, this time ready with their shields. Several made it through the archers' defense. Now, the battle was at the front gate of the palace. Out came a large number of palace soldiers, including Lord Aerrick, Sir Cian, and Sir Colt. Cian and Colt were so big that some of the Stoltlanders shivered at the sight of the cousins-in-law to Sealyn. The Stoltlanders didn't realize the palace would have this many soldiers, yet they chose to fight anyway.

Graegory found new strength to keep fighting, but he almost faltered when he looked out and saw what was coming toward the palace. Three Blackclaw dragons were moving at high speeds, and the blood-red-haired Queen Corentine was riding the middle one. He squinted and noticed her dragon didn't look quite right. Panic rose inside him. It was the dark magic. She created a dragon to ride with the dark magic. How were they to face the dark magic when the only Luxen Graegory knew of was Queen Sealyn, and she was in another kingdom?

Jdru pulled back hard on the crossbow in the palace tower and released the arrow. It sank into the forehead of the dragon on Corentine's left. Corentine hissed, and the other dragon roared. Jdru saw the dragon coming for them. He and the others ran down the steps as fast as they could. The Blackclaw's fire engulfed the top of the tower. Jdru felt the flames chasing them down.

Dun was in a tangle with a large Org. The Org was slightly bigger than Dun and was trying to use that extra weight as much as possible. Dun ripped a scale from the Org with his claw, sending the dragon into an uproar. The Org shot a fireball at Dun, but he dodged it. Dun was faster than the fireballs; his only worry was the dragon claws. Dun yelled a loud screech and watched the blood flow from the dragon's ears. Taking advantage of the disillusioned Org, Dun clawed another scale from the dragon, this time giving him the opening to the dragon's heart. Dun plunged his other claws into the dragon's heart, ripping it out.

Siany watched from the window and saw Corentine form a bridge with steps right to the palace's front door. Arrows couldn't penetrate the mist. She was not going to allow that witch into this castle again. Siany raced to the front door, ignoring the yells from family and guards. She drew her sword, readied her shield, and opened the doors right as Corentine stepped down the final step.

"Well, now, I would say that was perfect timing, you fake little queen."

Siany lunged and met Corentine's black sword. Corentine pushed Siany back, and Siany sliced again but missed. Then Corentine swung, but Siany blocked it with her shield. Again and again, the two swung their swords. Neither was willing to concede. Siany jabbed, finally striking Corentine's arm. Black blood dripped from the wound. Siany couldn't believe Corentine's blood was black. She really had given herself to the curse. She even looked like a curse would look if it could be in human form. Corentine wore pants and a shirt covered in black dragon scales, but luckily not every inch of her body was protected.

Corentine screamed and swung hard at Siany, knocking her shield from her hands. Siany tucked and rolled, dodging Corentine's strike. Corentine stepped back with her sword pointed at Siany. She started circling her, trying to scope the battle behind them. Her men were losing. She saw King Father

Ryker in the battle, rallying his soldiers to defeat her. How could this be? She saw another dragon fall dead because of a phoenix. Those birds she had not been prepared for.

Corentine glared at Siany. She remembered her backup plan. If she couldn't take the castle, then she'd give Sealyn grief. Corentine gathered the black mist to form a dragon again under her. She flew above Siany.

"Come down here and fight, you coward!"

"No. No. No, little princess. This was not what I wanted in the first place," she lied, trying to save her pride. "Taking the palace would have been great, but my main mission will be much more satisfactory." Corentine called for the Blackclaw. The dragon flew by her, and she shouted, "You know your mission. Execute now!"

With blazing speeds, the Blackclaw flew away from the palace. Siany was confused. What could Corentine be after? Why was Corentine just sitting there in the sky, not attacking? Just staring back at her. Where did that dragon go? Siany's green eyes followed the dragon's direction, then her heart sank. Her face went pale, and she looked up at Corentine.

"Waiting here --*for that*-- was priceless. You should see your face. Give my best to Sealyn." Corentine flew back toward the

Tor and called her men to retreat. The Elysian soldiers cheered as they watched the Stoltlanders run away.

"Stop! No! It's not over!" The soldiers turned to Siany. "Everyone, hurry. We must make haste to the NexGen field. Dun! Dun! Hurry!"

Two other phoenixes joined Dun in the fight with the final Org. One clawed its eyes out; then the other ripped its wing off with its beak. Dun delivered the killing blow with his claws to its neck. The dragon fell to its death, and then green flames engulfed the phoenixes. They sped to the NexGen field.

When the out-of-breath Elysians made it to the field, they saw the dead dragon, but the field was on fire. Siany ran behind the large dragon so she could see. The sight was forever burned into her heart and mind. All the beautiful Emangaton flowers were burned along with every Nicht baby in them. Siany dropped to her knees and wailed. Lady Novely ran to Siany and knelt with her. They both hated the sight of the burning field. There were children in there, but there was nothing they could do now. Queen Mother Graelynd fell into her husband and sobbed. Dun limped to Siany and nudged her. She looked up and saw he had tears in his yellow eyes, and then he nodded his head toward the dead dragon.

Siany didn't want to look. She didn't want to know this dragon had taken another life. But whose life? Who would have been here? And then she knew. She turned and saw the lifeless Lady Raquel wrapped in black claws. Lady Raquel who had protected the Heart of Elysium. Lady Raquel who saved her husband's life from a Stoltlander in the Battle of Betrayals. Lady Raquel who was loyal and a friend to Sealyn. Lady Raquel, wife and mother, who will forever be missed.

Lord Aerrick ran to his wife, weeping. Nichts finally made their way to the field after realizing what happened. The sound of hundreds of Nichts crying could only be described as pure, broken innocence. Ice Nichts helped put out the fires, but nothing was found alive. The Nicht babies needed only one more week, and then they would have been born. They would have been the start of a new generation.

Siany was so angry. The Nichts were innocent. They weren't a part of this war. Why did Corentine order this? Why? A small half-burned Emangaton flower petal landed on Siany's shoulder. She gently grabbed it and held it in her hand, and then balled her hand into a fist. An entire generation of Nichts was just wiped out. Siany looked to where the Nichts had gathered and saw

Maekel. Her heart broke even more. Maekel, who was so excited to be a mother, had her dream and joy stolen from her.

She stood and walked over to Lord Aerrick. He was stroking his wife's hair, crying. Raquel's children were also there now. The red-headed boy kicked and punched the dragon's hand, screaming for the dragon to let go of his mom. The little girl was holding onto her dad, trying to comfort him.

King Father Ryker put his arm around Siany. "This is probably the saddest day in Elysium's history."

My most beloved lady,

I have a secret I must share with you. I need to tell someone; you're the only one I trust. First, a carriage will be coming to collect you and your three daughters. You will join me here, and then once you arrive, we will be married without my stepmother's consent.

My love, my secret is that I did not send all the adult dragons like Corentine said to do. I kept several, well, most, of the pregnant ones. Malum screwed everything up, which rushed my plans. I needed many more months to have a true dragon army, but the army sent was mainly uncontrolled juveniles.

Corentine wouldn't accept that for an answer, so all my dragons were slaughtered. I'm afraid if she finds out I kept the dragons, then she will blame me for her battle loss, which is why I'm sending for you. She's been blackmailing me with our love. Please make haste and pack only your necessities. I will see you soon.

All my love,
Prince Haedon

CHAPTER 29

THE MAMMOTH KING AWAKENS

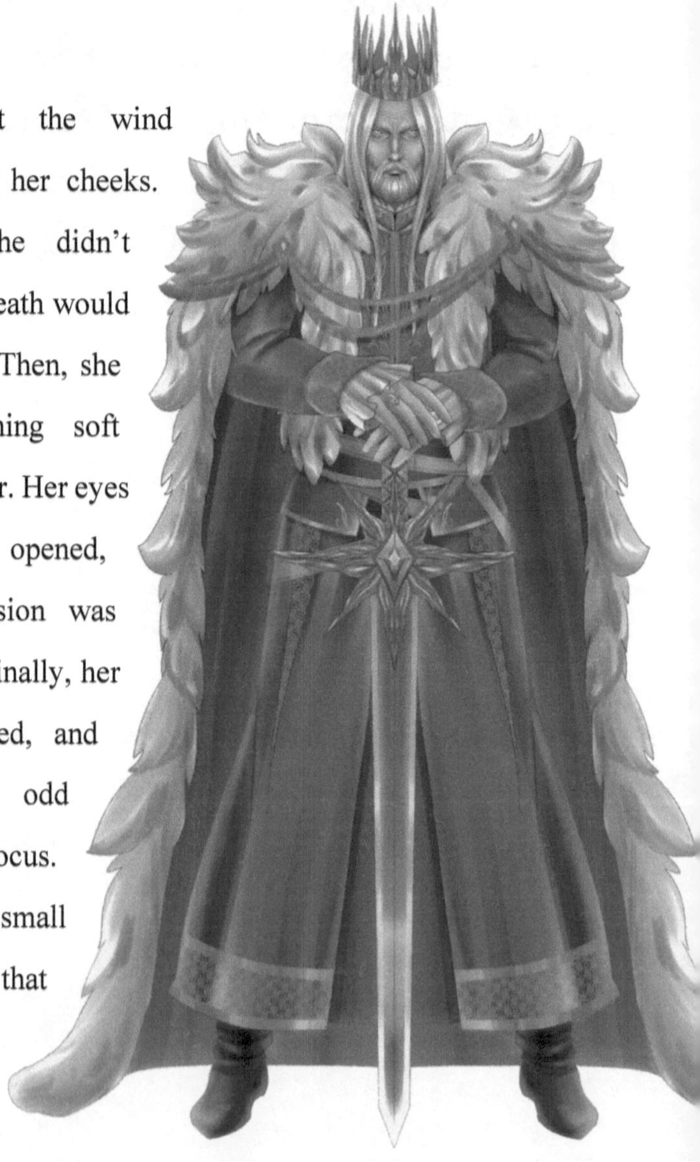

Sealyn felt the wind blowing on her cheeks. Strange. She didn't know that death would have wind. Then, she felt something soft poking at her. Her eyes gradually opened, but her vision was indistinct. Finally, her eyes adjusted, and something odd came into focus. She saw a small tunnel. No, that wasn't right. She shook her head and blinked. It was a trunk, a mammoth trunk!

"You must be Queen Sealyn Araelien, the third-generation bloodline," an ancient voice said.

Sealyn gave a confused expression. Was this mammoth talking to her without moving its mouth? She had to be dead. This was crazy.

"You're not crazy. This is real. You've come to ensure that the curse stays broken, correct?"

Sealyn tilted her head. "Yes." But her lips did not move. This entire conversation was happening in her mind. Her head felt like she had a bad fever. Char saw Sealyn's eyes open and ran to her.

"Sea, are you all right?"

"I think so. Is Sakul…"

"I'm right here. We're both fine, Sealyn, but we're a little nervous about the large mammoth army in front of us. They keep staring like we're supposed to do something."

Sealyn heard the mammoth chuckle. Could mammoths chuckle? She needed a bed and a drink, lots of drinks. She felt the dried blood on her cheeks and lips. Reaching her hand up, Sealyn asked for help. She tried to stand without wavering but was not in her best health right now. She was so feeble.

"Queen Sealyn Araelien, I am Nawrooshall, King of the Mammoths. The humans of Len Nove broke our covenant thousands of years ago. I still feel that betrayal and will not offer that covenant again with them, but I will offer it to you."

"What will happen to the Len Novians?"

"They can live here, but we will not trade with them as before."

"I will accept the covenant, but allow me to take the burden and shame of their mistake on me. We've all made mistakes and need forgiveness. Give the Len Novians the magic of old, and once again, they would be able to communicate with you. I will help appoint a council that will ensure accountability for this covenant. Len Nove can finally flourish, but only if you reunite yourselves with them."

The Mammoth King shifted his stance. Char heard grumbling between the mammoths. He was very uneasy. He was grateful they were alive when the ice dissipated instead of exploding and killing them, but to say he was stressed was putting it modestly. Char needed ale. "Sealyn, what is going on?"

"I'm working on a deal."

"How? Nothing is being said."

"Just trust me, Char."

Char sat in the melting snow. He was wet and tired, not to mention famished. He wanted to go home. How could Sealyn ask him to trust her? Wasn't she the reason they were face-to-face with a mythical mammoth army?

"We agree with your terms, Queen Sealyn." The large mammoth laid down and motioned for Sealyn to climb on him. She followed his instructions, climbed the giant mammoth, and sat on top of his back. His hair was coarse and smelled damp. "Unclasp the necklace. It is yours now. The magic that binds the covenant will make it fit you."

Sealyn undid the beautiful necklace and watched it transform its size to fit around her neck. "But I have nothing to give you."

"You don't, but I know someone who does. Tell your two friends to mount my seconds. We need to get to the palace quickly."

Sitting on top of the ancient creature, Sealyn looked around and saw they were in a valley. It was beautiful. Almost all the snow was gone. They stood next to the river, which was finally flowing after being locked away for thousands of years. The river was clear, and she could see the bright blue stones at the bottom.

"This was where the old magic told us to retreat after the betrayal. The humans could not enter our valley."

Sealyn saw the hesitation of the mammoths. This had been the one place to keep them safe. Now, they had to face their uncertainties and step outside their comfort. Sealyn patted the Mammoth King, hoping to give him reassurance.

Sakul was mesmerized. He was riding a mythical mammoth in Len Nove. In all his wildest thoughts, he could never fathom this story, but it was real. This was really happening. He was the little boy Sealyn found in the woods with *needlebob needles in his foot to a man mounted on a legendary creature in a foreign kingdom. He couldn't wait to tell Sorcha. He looked at Char and laughed. They were safe. They could finally breathe easily.

When they reached the top of the valley, Sealyn gasped. There was a large meadow filled with blue butterfly pea flowers. She remembered being with Jace in her vineyard, tasting her wine infusions with the blue butterfly pea flower. Jace. She needed Jace.

"Say, old-timer, how fast can ancient mammoths run?" Sealyn sparred.

An odd sound of groans and laughter came from the mammoths. Char's eyes opened wide. He did not like what was happening. He felt his mammoth tense, so he clasped the coarse hair even harder and leaned his body low. The mammoths took off. The air brushed against the mammoth army, and they smelled the enchanting scent of the butterfly pea flowers. This was the exact antidote they needed to rid them of their reservations.

Vibrations shook the walls of the ice palace. Everyone braced themselves, preparing for the worst. They heard gasps and praises outside. Fraeya glared at Jace. "I'll deal with you later. Come. Let us see what has arrived."

The Len Novians and Elysians hurried outside and saw Queen Sealyn, Lord Char, and Lord Sakul mounted on giant mammoths. The Len Novians dropped to their knees in homage. Jace saw Sealyn, and he lost his breath. He ran through the crowds of people with the Elysians right behind him. "Sealyn! Sealyn!" Jace shouted.

When Jace stopped beside the Mammoth King, Sealyn swung her leg over and slid down the mammoth, falling straight into Jace's arms. The two held onto each other, never wanting to let go. Jace felt how thin her body was. She needed some kind of care, but at that moment, he felt she needed his embrace more than water, more than food.

Jace pulled back ever so slightly, tilted her chin up, and gently kissed her lips. They were dry, but he didn't care. Her lips would always taste sweet to him.

"I see you made some new friends."

"Oh, Jace. I've missed you so much that it hurt me." Sealyn squeezed Jace again. Jace tried not to squeeze her back. In his arms, she felt like he could break her. Char and Sakul landed not so gracefully and joined their friends. Sakul frantically looked for Sorcha. The royals of Len Nove stood behind the Elysians.

The king nodded his head. "Queen Sealyn, I'm glad you're back safely. Allow me to introduce my wife, Queen Fraeya."

Sealyn felt Jace stiffen. "What is it, Jace? Is something wrong?" Jace whispered in Sealyn's ear what happened right before they arrived. Sealyn felt her ears grow hot. How dare she say such wicked things about Jace. "Queen Fraeya, from one queen to another, it's an honor. Now, allow me to introduce my king and Elysum's king, King Jace." Sealyn looked up into Jace's silver eyes, the very eyes Fraeya wanted to condemn him for having. What the world called inadequate, Sealyn called perfection.

Jace smiled. Her passion to protect him was possibly his favorite characteristic about Sealyn, or, at least, today it was. Now tomorrow? He guessed he would just have to wait to find out because they had a tomorrow. Finally, he looked forward to the next day.

Sealyn walked to King Egil and extended her hand. He took it, and his eyes dilated. After thousands of years, a Len Novian heard a mammoth's voice. Zuri suddenly realized what was happening and wept tears of excitement and joy. Jace saw Finn tearing up, so he wrapped his arm around his shoulders. He didn't understand what was happening but felt this must be a big moment for the Len Novians.

"King Egil, I am Nawrooshall, King of the Mammoths. I'm here because Queen Sealyn and I have reached an agreement. Mammoths will make the old covenant through her and her bloodline." Egil's eyes narrowed. He felt betrayed by the Elysians. "However, Queen Sealyn added an amendment. She requested the fault of the past be laid on her shoulders and to give the Len Novians access to the old magic to communicate once again with us." Egil's eyes softened. His expression was filled with shame.

"This is a good deal, Egil," Sealyn said. "Len Nove can thrive, and we can become strong allies like never before."

Egil's eyes filled with tears. "I accept these terms. It would be an honor to live in peace and have a utopian society with the mammoths."

Queen Fraeya stood beside her husband. She reached into the side satchel strapped around her. Gasps echoed around the palace square when Fraeya revealed the lost crown of Len Nove. This was the crown the mammoths gave to King Atticos, and the necklace was what King Atticos had given the mammoth king at the beginning of the beginning. Now, they were exchanging them back.

"Fraeya, King Nawrooshall says there should be a strip of cloth that has the words to say to bind the spell. It should be in the bag." Fraeya dug in the bag and found a worn strip of cloth, but the words were faded.

Nawrooshall growled. "Queen Sealyn, you must speak these words for the magic to bind."

Sealyn took the cloth from Fraeya and examined it. A faded pattern bordered the cloth, and words were too far gone. She squinted hard. It was obviously the old magic tongue. Suddenly, Sealyn's mind wandered back to when they were leaving Fort

Kippen, and Quinley and Revalyn handed her a scroll. It couldn't be. Sealyn dug into one of her side pockets, hoping the scroll was still there. She opened it and saw the letters looked like the cloth. Perhaps the young ladies discovered she would have to accept this covenant to finish the curse.

She spoke with confidence and swayed slightly. "I accipere onus."

Blue sparks that looked like tiny fireworks exploded around Sealyn and the Mammoth King. It was glorious to watch. The crowds cheered and began celebrating with their lost loved ones. The mammoths and the Len Novians spoke with one another like they were old friends, finally reconnecting after a long separation.

Sealyn caught her hands on her knees. She felt different. Something was happening to her. Jace held her, fearing the worst. This magic kept taking from Sealyn. Sealyn felt her muscles burning, then throbbing. She inhaled deeply and felt her lungs expand further than they ever had. Her body transformed before everyone. She had been frail and thin from the excessive use of magic, but now, her muscles were defined, and she looked healthy. The olive color returned to her face. She felt strong, and she looked it, too.

"You have the mammoth strength now, Queen Sealyn. Use with wisdom and caution." King Nawrooshall bowed his head. Jace swept Sealyn into his arms now, not fearing her frail state.

Musicians entered the courtyard, and while the mammoths and people danced, Jace leaned in and whispered into Sealyn's ear again. "How'd you do it? How'd you break the curse?"

Sealyn grabbed Jace's hand. "Someone else would like to tell you." Sealyn looked at King Nawrooshall and grinned.

"She figured out what would break Len Nove's curse: accountability. You see, King Jace, the bond between mammoth and human keeps us accountable to prosperity and goodness, but when there is no answerability, the Len Novians will fall to the spell of the curse: lethargy."

"Really? That's Len Nove's curse? Slothfulness."

"Yes, it seems small, but if left unmonitored, it can grow and fester. Eventually, the Len Novians chose to do literally nothing. Some fell asleep and never woke up because they didn't want to. They would have rather slept than be productive, which is how Queen Fraeya ended up in the ice catacombs like so many others."

"You said Sealyn figured it out, but how or what did she do?"

Nawrooshall gave a weird mammoth smile. "It was already in her mind, but she spoke her ideas. She had a plan for Len Nove. She wants to keep an Elysian council here to ensure Len Nove remains faithful and loyal to its oath to us. The old magic judges a person's heart, so when Sealyn spoke the words needed to free us, the curse was broken because her heart was pure, and discerned culpability would cure the land."

Jace felt so proud of Sealyn. She was, without a doubt, the most remarkable person he had ever known. Suddenly, ten Blue Horn unicorn riders came into the crowd. Because of the unicorns' speed, the riders made a four-day journey within half a day. The unicorns sparkled from sweat, and the riders looked tired. They were in shock at the mammoth army but quickly dismounted and knelt before their king and queen.

"Majesties, we bring Elysian news." The Elysians in the crowd gathered closer. They had to be speaking of Doebromir's group. The king nodded for them to continue. "They were taken prisoner on the Stoltlander trader ship. The ship called Abbadon."

"No. Please say it isn't true," Sealyn said. "Did you see the Elysians being taken on board?" The rider nodded. "Describe them, please."

"There were five in total, majesty. Four men and one female."

Sakul shouted. "What did the woman look like?"

"She was average height. Very beautiful. Black curly hair and dark skin."

Sakul sighed in relief and then also began to panic. Sorcha was a prisoner on a Stoltland ship. Pinx and Norella looked at each other. Pinx whispered. "Rivers. What happened to Lady Rivers?"

Norella shook her head. "I don't know. You know those boys would never leave her behind unless…"

"No. Don't say it. Don't. Please." Pinx began to cry.

Sealyn tried not to look at her friends. The rider didn't realize he had just given confirmation that they lost a great friend. "Anything else you can tell us, sir?"

"Pirates."

"Pirates? What about them?"

"They've also been at port. They sailed not long after the Abbadon ship left. I don't believe they are working with the Stoltlanders because the pirate captain led them, majesty."

"Don't all pirate ships have a captain?"

"Well, yes, majesty, but this one is from Korpam and wears this title like a crown."

Sealyn cocked her head to the side. "Crown, you say. Does this man think of himself as a Pirate King?"

"He does not use those words, but everyone treats him as such. You will know him by the tiger helmet."

"And why would he not work with Stoltland?"

"He lets it be known his distaste for Stoltland and well, all kingdoms, really."

Sealyn huffed. "Pirate." Sealyn placed her hand on the man's shoulder. "Thank you for this information. It's been most helpful."

Sakul stood next to Sealyn, barely able to breathe. "Sealyn. I mean Queen Sealyn. What are we to do? We must go after them."

"We will, but we have no ships with us. We must return to Avondelle, gather the army, then make haste to form a plan. For now, we will feed our hungry bellies and sleep here for the night, then leave in the morning. I'm sure the journey back will be much easier without the snow."

"But.."

"Sakul, don't forget you're not the only one with loved ones on that ship. Ezen is my blood, and Sorcha is like my own sister, not to mention that the other three are my childhood friends. This is painful for all of us."

Sakul backed away and bowed. He hated the thought of Sorcha being in chains on a boat heading for their enemy, but Sealyn had a compelling plan, and this time, he would volunteer to go on the queen's quest.

CHAPTER 30

AND WHILE WE'RE THERE

The next day was a bittersweet goodbye to the Len Novians and the mammoths. The city hung blue ribbons all along the streets, bidding farewell to them. As they were almost in the forest, Madilina looked back one more time and saw a dream come true. There grazing in another blue butterfly pea flower meadow was a white Diamond Horn unicorn. Its tail, also made of tiny diamonds, swooshed back and forth, looking unburdened by the world. Madilina smiled. One day, she would come back, but for now, she had a lot of training and learning about her new powers to accomplish.

After a much shorter journey to Fort Kippen, the caravan saw the mourning flag flying at the fort. Their hearts dropped. What had happened while they were away? Once inside, they sat at the table in the great dining hall while Lady Lizz filled them in on what destruction awaited them in Avondelle. Cries and wailing went around the room.

Sealyn ran from the room and continued running until she reached the high tower. She told the guards to leave, then screamed as loud as she could. Corentine would pay. She wanted to rip her from limb to limb. How could she kill such innocence? Why? Why would baby Nichts be her target?

She tried channeling Dun and felt pain. Was he hurt? Was he helping others who were injured? She channeled her message to Dun about where they were, hoping to comfort him and everyone else. Her anger was still boiling. She dropped her fist down on the stone wall and cracked the top stone. To her surprise, she didn't break any bones. This must be the mammoth strength Nawrooshall talked about. She had to gain control of her anger.

After a few hours of sitting alone on top of the tower, Sealyn stood, startled because she saw green streaks of flames in the sky.

They were moving at lightning speeds, coming toward the fort. What was this magic? She thought she should be afraid, but she felt oddly calm. Once the flames grew closer, she recognized them. These were like Dun's green flames, but it wasn't Dun.

She moved to the edge and watched thirty giant green phoenixes land. She had no idea there were green phoenixes other than Dun. Running as fast as she could, Sealyn ran through the dining hall, calling for everyone to follow. Her breath caught when she saw the magnificent creatures. The leader of the group walked to Sealyn and bowed his head. Dun had instructed them to take the caravan home. Sealyn was relieved and nervous to return home.

In flight, the mood of the Elysians was both somber and grateful. They were ready to be home but dreaded what they would see. Dragon destruction would take a long time to rebuild. Would Avondelle ever feel safe? Can Tors be destroyed? Who survived? So many questions plagued their hearts and minds.

When the phoenixes landed at the front steps of the palace, Siany tackled Sealyn in a hug. The two sisters clung to each other in grief and in love. They both had feared this day would never come. Darkness was starting to set in. Sealyn would not be able to see the true destruction until the morning.

"Where is she?"

"Where is who, Sealyn?"

"My sweet Maekel."

"I'll take you to her. She stays in your chambers, never leaving."

The royal family and Vinurs greeted everyone. Ryker and Graelynd hugged their daughter, Sealyn, and cried joyfully. There was a hesitation to greet Jace, but Queen Mother Graelynd ran and embraced him as if he had always been a part of their family. "Welcome home, my son. My king." She curtsied, and others followed her lead.

Sealyn burst through her chamber's doors and startled Maekel and Trit, who had been sitting on the coffee table in front of the candle-lit fireplace. Sealyn ran to Maekel, who flew into Sealyn's arms. Her tiny tears had the biggest effect on Sealyn. Sitting in front of the fireplace, they both sobbed without saying a word because they already knew. This was a mother's grief.

Jace stood in the doorway and watched the brokenness before him. He couldn't go in. It was his mother who had done this, after all. Instead, Jace sat in the hallway beside the door and wept.

The next night, Sealyn tossed and turned. She kept replaying the day in her head. She had visited the Tor's forest, the NexGen field, Lady Raquel's house, Lord Stawyer's house, Lady Rivers's family home, and finally, the Crystal Fort hospital. She was tired of having a broken heart. She rolled over and looked at her Jace sleeping. She was happy he was finally getting rest. Hunger and grief kept her awake.

She slipped out of the green covers, not waking Jace. She wanted him to sleep as long as he could. Tiptoeing to her tall bookshelf near her bed, she pushed back the book *Avondelle's Famous Recipes* until she heard the soft click, then she pulled the bookshelf open like a door and walked through, quietly closing it behind her. She stomped her feet, and the fire flowers awoke with their lustrous lights.

Sealyn ran down the stone-walled, secret tunnel, which led to the kitchens. She pushed open the wooden door at the end, with its hooks that hung the chef's cloaks and aprons. To Sealyn's surprise, she was met by familiar faces. Sitting on top of the countertops were Char, Sakul, Favien, Pinx, and Norella. They were all in their nightsleeps, eating treats and cheeses just like they would do when they were children.

"Of course you would have a secret passageway to the kitchens," Char said incredulously.

Sealyn grinned. "You know me well. I'm guessing you all couldn't sleep either?"

"I think it's going to be a while before we get a full night's sleep," Norella responded. Pinx nodded and laid her head on Norella's shoulder. Pinx's nightmares were filled with cages and wolves. She hated closing her eyes.

"How is Jace? I know this can't be easy for him," Favien said. He took another sip of ale. He had trimmed his brown beard, but his hair remained long and wavy.

"You're right. This isn't easy for him. He feels like this is all his fault, but it's not. Corentine made her decisions, and she must pay for them, not Jace."

"I agree!" Sakul said affirmatively with a mouth full of pastry. "She has to pay."

Norella took a sip of her wine. "Sealyn, how are you feeling about Lady Pyry being in the dungeons? We all heard about it from Adalina."

"Hmm. How do I feel about the person who orchestrated the separation of my army from us, which then ultimately led to Stawyer's and Rivers's deaths?" Sealyn shook her head. "I'm fuming but cannot pass judgment because of my anger. I need to be clear-minded for her trial."

Favien was scared to ask his question but felt weary about what he had heard, so he had no choice. "Is it true that there was a pregnant dragon, and Lord Prince Brandle performed surgery to save the babies, and now we have dragons here?"

"Yes. My cousin saved the dragon babies, but please don't fear. Madilina will oversee raising the babies. The interesting thing about a Noxhorn dragon is that because its flame is so destructive, nature demands balance. When a Noxhorn gives birth, she gives birth to two dragons. One will have the blue flame, and one will breathe innocence."

"Which innocent dragon did she carry?" Favien asked.

"The *Bellus dragon or, as most call it, the bubble dragon."

Norella chuckled. "How cute. Those dragons stay miniature and spew bubbles, right?"

"Correct."

Pinx lifted her head and remembered the scroll she and Norella kept from Sealyn. The conversation brought the memory back. She had to keep quiet. Sealyn could not handle hearing another heartbreaking story. She would keep the secret until the right moment. Instead, she sighed and changed the subject. "So what happens next, Sealyn?"

"We go after the Abbadon ship, right?" Sakul suggested passionately.

"Well, I have news on that very topic. It appears that the pirate captain made port at Pebble Beach. The same port where Lord Prince William has been stationed, testing our new fishing ships."

Char gasped. "Is he ok?"

"Of course," Sealyn chuckled. "You know my cousin, Will. He can charm a tiger of any stripes. Will sent me a scroll detailing his encounter with the pirate captain and what he advises we do."

"The suspense is killing us, Sealyn," Favien said.

"The Abbadon ship can't handle shallow waters. It will have to go out deep around our coastline, then up our western coast. The ship will continue north until it reaches the cargo trade routes."

Char jumped off the counter and poured another glass of wine. "Sealyn, you can't be suggesting what I think you're suggesting."

Sealyn noticed Char had shaved his beard but kept his longer hair and pulled it half back. "I am. We will leave from one of our western ports and wait on the Abbadon ship to arrive, then take back our people."

"So where exactly are we going? Because I'm volunteering this time!" Sakul raised his glass.

"We leave for Shunal in three months. This will give us enough time to help mend our kingdom and prepare our deep-water ships for the quest," Sealyn smirked. "And while we're in Shunal, let's break another curse."

My Dear Sweet Cousin and Queen,

I write to you urgently and know this news will be hard to hear, but please trust me.

At Pebble Beach Port, I met not just any pirate captain today, but the Pirate Captain, the one with the tiger helmet. He told me that there are five Elysian prisoners on board Stoltland's Abbadon ship. Three other ships accompany it. Their route will be to Shunal for the cargo route since their ships can't handle the shallow waters.

The Pirate Captain said he would help you on your quest—for a "small fee," of course. He also said that part of his cooperation is meeting you and King Jace at your western port. I know pirates of any sort are not to be trusted, but once you meet him, you will understand why I'm telling you to do this. Just look in his face, Sealyn—trust me.

He said his ship is faster than the Abbadon fleet, so he will pass the ships within another day's sailing, so make haste, my dear cousin.

The fate of your people rests in your hands, and now, the hands of this pirate.

I hope to see you soon.

All my love,
Lord Prince William "Will" Dovinus

LIBRARY OF CREATURES

•<u>EXIGUUMS</u>: First mentioned in Book 1 and Book 2, Chapter 1. Exiguums have a genetic code that prevents them from growing beyond their newborn size. They still mature just like normal elephants but remain small for their whole lives. Exiguums have special colors. Mainly purple and blue, but sometimes

grey. Exiguums are fuzzy instead of rough. Their eye colors vary from green to blue.

•<u>LENETTE</u>: First mentioned in Chapter 1. A lenette is a creature from the old magic with black eyes that look too big for its tiny head. Smaller than a butterfly--they have bodies of golden caterpillars with two sets of wings: pink outer wings and orange inner wings. During the day, they soak in the sun's rays and then illuminate the darkness at night.

•<u>NICHT</u>: First mentioned in Book 1 and Book 2, Chapter 1. Nichts have heads that look too large for their arms and legs, with beautiful wings, and are known to make words plural when not necessary. Nichts vary in size by their classification. Earth Nichts are the largest, growing to the size of a human toddler. Others are as small as a human's hand.

•<u>CAELIDON:</u> First mentioned in Book 1 and Book 2, Chapter 1. A Caelidon is a winged horse with its mane and tail composed of feathers. Fastest of the winged horses, very dangerous to ride.

•<u>NIGHTSWEEPS:</u> First mentioned in Chapter 3. Nightsweeps look like eagles, but their wings are that of a bat and have razor-sharp claws with a black beak and body. The eyes have perfect night vision. They can glide at great speeds with no sound.

•<u>GLATOMONT:</u> A glatomont is a large predatory bird. It has long, skinny legs with fish-like scales to help it swim and run through water fast. A full-gown glatomont stands around seven feet tall, but its wings are small. It cannot fly but does use its wings to excel forward at quicker speeds. Their beaks are long, almost as long as swords, and just as sharp.

•<u>MISPS:</u> First mentioned in Chapter 9. Misps have terrifying claws and teeth that tear through rock easily to create tunnels and nests. Their eyes are large and yellow, and they have long tentacles that are the length of their small bodies. They can only fly for seconds because their wings are oddly crystalized, which makes them too heavy to fly.

•<u>LORKIN</u>: First mentioned in Chapter 12. Lorkins are pure white (even claws and teeth) with blue eyes. These reptiles are like crocodiles but have more blubber to handle cold temperatures. They are also twice the normal size of crocodiles and have an extra row of teeth. They move at rapid speeds to catch the river trout. Males have blue tips on their tails, but females do not.

•<u>SURZEE</u>: First mentioned in Chapter 13. They have giant ears, small round heads, and big blue eyes that glow. They have light blue tails that are skinny with fuzzy white tips. Their bones are light, making them almost weightless. They bounce from place to place like tiny mice. They have razor-sharp teeth that are strong like metal.

•<u>ARKOOTHA BEAR</u>: First mentioned in Chapter 15. These bears are larger than most bears and solid white with blue underbellies and blazing blue eyes. The outside of their front paws have long, sharp hooks that are curved like a mammoth's tusk. Arkootha bears have a high-pitched growl. They're also very fast, even in snow. They resemble polar bears but have heads more shaped like grizzly bears.

•<u>ICE HORN UNICORN</u>: First mentioned in Chapter 16. The Ice Horn unicorn has a horn made of solid ice; the horn looks like an icicle. Its hooves are clear and look like ice but are not ice. Its coat, tail, and eyes are white.

•<u>DIAMOND HORN UNICORN</u>: First mentioned in Chapter 16. The Diamond Horn has a horn and hooves made solidly of diamonds. It's very valuable, which makes this unicorn a target. Its tail is also made of strands of tiny diamonds. The coat looks silver, shines in the sunlight, and glows under the moonlight.

•<u>BLUE HORN UNICORN</u>: First mentioned in Chapter 16. The Blue Horn unicorn has a blue horn and hooves. Its eyes, mane, and tail are also blue, but it has a white coat.

•<u>ORG DRAGON</u>: First mentioned in Chapter 26. Org dragons' top halves are black, while their lower halves look like they were dipped in white paint. Orgs spit balls of fire that explode upon impact. Some of the larger Orgs can create craters after their fireballs explode on land.

•<u>TOXICON</u>: First mentioned in Chapter 26. The Toxicon dragon spits acid instead of flames, very lethal. These dragons range in purple hues and black claws. They also have spikes also their back and tail.

•<u>NOXHORN DRAGON</u>: First mentioned in Chapter 26. Noxhorns breathe blue flames, the hottest of flames, for the longest period of time. They're also the smallest of the fire-breathing dragons. Their electric blue scales aren't as hard as other dragon scales, but they fight like nothing can kill them.

•<u>RANA FROG</u>: First mentioned in Chapter 26. Rana frogs usually grow to the size of a large dog. They have jagged mouths and red eyes. Some have smooth skin, and others have warts covering their backs. Rana frogs love foul foods and, well, anything that smells horrible.

•<u>NEEDLEBOB</u>: First mentioned in Book 1 and Book 2, Chapter 29. They are in the spiny rodent classification. Most needlebobs are shimmering gold, but those found in Stoltland have black tips. Needlebobs love thick forests and spend their days under ferns' shade, hunting beetles. Needlebobs may look cute, but beware—their needles contain powerful hallucinogenic poison. Once a needle pierces its victim's skin, the poison takes thirty seconds to release its effect. Hallucinations can last for hours and, in some worst cases, days.

Needlebobs prefer to roll from one place to the next instead of walk. Their needles tuck and form around its body, allowing it to form a shell for easy rolling.

451

ACKNOWLEDGMENTS

Completing a second novel is still a shock, but great accomplishments always come with an extraordinary support team, so I need to recognize certain people who may or may not have realized their spark in making this book come to life.

My incredible husband, Kyle Massie: thank you for giving me grace and time to write and read aloud. I appreciate all the encouragement and motivation you give every day. I love you as much as Sealyn loves Jace.

My supportive parents, Rhett & Gwen Salley: thank you for showing up. Just being there for book signings and lunches is more than most can dream of, yet you continue to be there. Thank you for demonstrating dedication.

Mindy Salley, my sister: thank you for allowing me to ramble on about my ideas for the book. I know how little spare time you have, so it means the world that you would take time to read my work and discuss it.

C.A. Meadows, author of Lost in a Nightmare: thank you for connecting. Authors need other authors to keep each other accountable and to have those conversations that only authors understand. I'm glad I'm not alone in my writing.

My friends: thank you for understanding my declines. Having to say "no" to events or hang-outs is not easy, but in order to finish writing, I needed to decline many times. I'm very grateful for your understanding, patience, and participation.

To my Beta Readers: Mandy Farr, Jessica Lanning, Michelle Blair, Graham Goggins, Theresa Shaw, Jeanne Degatano, and Avery Griffin—Thank you for taking the time to read each chapter in its raw state. Your feedback truly made a huge difference in editing and content for the book. I really appreciate you all so much.

My editor, Kristyn Winch: thank you for an excellent job editing the book. I loved your pace and feedback. I hope to work with you on every book moving forward.

Miblart: thank you for another excellent book cover.. Thank you for your patience in working with me and for all the edits.

YukKami Art, digital artist: thank you for the beautiful character and creature art you've done. Each piece is loved and adored. I appreciate your talent and time.

And above all, the entire credit and glory goes to the good Lord. Thank you for giving me a creative mind and the many blessings you have given me. All praise to you.

ABOUT THE AUTHOR

MAEGWEN SALLEY-MASSIE is the author of *The Emerald Queen Rises* and *The Mammoth Awakens*. She will be writing five other books to complete this series. She grew up in the Pee Dee Low Country of South Carolina with her loving parents and sister. Her childhood was spent mainly outdoors building forts, riding horses, playing capture the flag, riding ATVs, and playing volleyball. She began writing *The Emerald Queen Rises* during the Pandemic as therapy and since then fell in love with writing her high fantasy series. She is a woven polypropylene specialist by day and a fantasy fiction author by night. Her favorite food is sushi, and loves to travel the world. Maegwen currently lives in Myrtle Beach, SC with her husband, Kyle, their cat, Khaleesi, and new Australian Shepherd, Pogue

Book 1 in The Emerald Queen series

For more information about Maegwen and her books,
please visit:

www.greenfernspublishinghouse.com
www.theemeraldqueenrisesbook.com
www.maegwensalleymassie.com

Or follow her on Instagram @MaegwenAuthor

www.ingramcontent.com/pod-product-compliance
Lightning Source LLC
Chambersburg PA
CBHW031239310726
48971CB00004B/1085